JAN 2 8 1989	DATE DUE		
MAR 3 1989			
MAR 1 0 1989			
APR 3 1989			
APR 1 1989			
JUN 2 1989			
JUL 2 8 1989			
OCT 2 1989			
NOV 7 1989			

Smart
Moves

Other Toby Peters mysteries not to be missed

Also by the author

Smart Moves

A TOBY PETERS MYSTERY

Stuart M. Kaminsky

A THOMAS · DUNNE BOOK

ST. MARTIN'S PRESS • NEW YORK

Library of Congress Cataloging in Publication Data

Kaminsky, Stuart M.
  Smart moves.

  1. Einstein, Albert, 1879–1955—Fiction.
2. Robeson, Paul, 1898–1976—Fiction. I. Title.
PS3561.A43S6 1987   813′.54   86-26156
ISBN 0-312-00190-8

First Edition

10 9 8 7 6 5 4 3 2 1

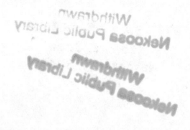

This one is for Peter and Toby together.

In matters concerning truth and justice there can be no distinction between big problems and small; for the general principles which determine the conduct of men are indivisible. Whoever is careless with the truth in small matters cannot be trusted in important affairs.

—Albert Einstein, *Einstein on Peace*

Smart
Moves

1

I was leaning out of the window of a room on the twelfth floor of the Waldorf-Astoria Hotel in New York City, but I wasn't enjoying the view. My right hand was trying to hold on to the tearing sleeve of the frightened dentist who dangled and swayed in the April breeze. My left hand gripped the windowsill in spite of the arm behind it, which ached from a very fresh gunshot wound. The blood from that wound was staining my rented tuxedo and my hand, making it hard to hold on to the sill and my sanity. I wasn't worried about losing my dignity; I'd lost that half a lifetime earlier. My knees were propped on either side of the open window as I tugged, grunted, and pleaded with the tearing sleeve to hold till I got a grip on Shelly Minck's sweating, outstretched, and very pudgy right hand.

My back ached. I have a bad back. I earned it a lifetime earlier after a bear hug from a large Negro gentleman who wanted to get a close look at Mickey Rooney at a premiere. My job had been to keep people from getting too close a look at MGM's hottest star. That's how I got my bad back. All this would have been enough to give a normal private detective cause for concern, and I was concerned—more than concerned, I was on the thin edge of panic. What turned the panic to near hysteria was the loud and determined kicking at the hotel room door by a killer who had planted knives in two people within a week and had a bullet ready for me when the last splinter of wood came off the door. I turned my head quickly toward the door to see how well it was holding up. It wasn't. But the sight of a corpse on the bed with a knife sticking straight up out of its chest urged me on to greater effort.

Another stitch came loose on the sleeve and I could see Shelly's glasses slip down his perspiring nose as he turned his mutton neck and looked down.

"Toby, for God's sake, for my sake, for Mildred's sake. Toby, get me up. Get me up, up, up, up."

He tried to find a foothold in empty space, but all he did was tear a few more stitches, add a little pain to my back and arm, and make me realize that it was more likely he would pull me with him than that I would perform a miracle and wrestle his doughy 220 pounds through that window. Behind me I could hear the wooden door moan with each kick.

"Shelly, stop jumping around," I shouted.

A horn blared far below us on Park Avenue, followed by a crash of fenders and more horns followed by shouts of anger. A church bell rang somewhere far away, reminding me that it was Easter Sunday. I could smell some sweet food drifting up from a restaurant far below. I wasn't hungry.

"What's going on down there?" Shelly demanded.

"What the hell's the difference? Stop kicking."

"Then pull me up. I'm losing my glasses. I can't see without my glasses."

The door behind me was definitely giving way. I could hear it splintering. Then something behind me cracked. It might have been my back or my aching knees. Blood trickled down my sleeve from my gunshot wound and I felt dizzy. This was not the ideal way for a nearly fifty-year-old private detective to spend an evening. Or maybe it was.

The whole thing had started about a week before when a tall kid scientist from Princeton found me at a Los Angeles restaurant waiting for rice pudding. The kid scientist was named Mark Walker. He had a job for me back in New Jersey. I'd never been in New Jersey. I said sure, went home, and packed my .38 and my one clean change of clothes in the small battered 'gator suitcase I had earned as part of a fee from Hymie of Hy's For Him on Melrose in Los Angeles. I'd found Hy's missing grandmother for him. He'd given me five bucks and the suitcase. The next job I did for Hy I was smarter. I found his wife and get ten bucks and a shoulder holster. The Princeton kid, tall and gangly and looking more like a basketball center than a math genius, waited patiently while I checked out my room in Mrs. Plaut's boardinghouse and left a note for my next-door neighbor and best friend Gunther Wherthman, who stood no more than a yard high and made his living translating almost any language into or out of English. Gunther was off seeing a publisher.

In my note I told Gunther I'd be in touch and that he could have anything he wanted in my refrigerator. I was sure there was nothing he would want. There probably wasn't anything he'd be willing to eat without washing it with Rinso.

Princeton waited while I checked myself in the small mirror underneath my Beech-Nut gum clock. The face was dark, battered; the nose was flat, without meaning, shape, or bone. The dark hair was short and turning grey at the temples. It was the face of an over-the-hill boxer, a middleweight who had taken two many prelims with up-and-comers. I was pleased. It was a face that went well with a private detective's card. That face had seen a lot, been through a lot. I smiled at me. It was a goofy smile. I turned to Princeton and announced that I was all set.

On the way downstairs we met my landlady, Mrs. Plaut. She came up to Princeton's waist, tilted her white-haired head upward and gave him a careful examination. "You look to be a clean-cut American," she shouted. "It is not safe to associate with Mr. Peelers."

"Mrs. Plaut," I shouted. "If you tell that to all my clients, I won't have enough money to pay my rent."

This gave her pause. She adjusted the hearing aid she had recently purchased and looked at me. Then she looked at Princeton.

"Mr. Peelers has been known to shoot and otherwise do damage to people. However, he did arrange for me to meet Marie Dressler. Would you like to see her photograph? I took it right on our porch."

Walker looked to me for help. I had none.

"It isn't Marie Dressler. It's Eleanor Roosevelt," I explained.

This did not seem to take care of his problem.

"Mrs. Plaut," I shouted.

"You no longer need shout," she shouted. "I am capable of perfectly normal hearing now. Not like Uncle Eustace Varney, who lost the sense of both sound and touch after spending a week in a hollowed-out redwood near Fresno in eighteen and sixty-four. Uncle Eustace and the Sutcliffes had been hacking and hewing at that tree for a week when it fell and they were trapped in the hollow until passing lumberjacks hearkened to their faint calls."

"I don't . . ." Walker began.

"Mrs. Plaut, we have to be going. I've left my sugar and gas ration stamps on the table in my room. Mr. Wherthman will take care of my Crosley. Please, I beg you, do not drive it."

"I am a careful driver," she replied indignantly, taking two steps back and almost tumbling down the flight of stairs. I grabbed her arm and she shook me off. "You are insulting the widow of a veteran of both wars and a great many years behind the wheel of his Ford."

As I eased Walker past Mrs. Plaut and down the stairs, she remained above, righteously looking down. Her dark green dress and billow of white hair made her look like a thin, wilted dandelion in late summer.

"I'll be in New Jersey, Mrs. Plaut," I shouted. "I'll probably be back in a week or two."

"Be cautious, Mr. Peelers. Remember what Cousin Chaney said and be prepared for new chapters," she called as we went out the door into the March afternoon.

"What did Cousin Chaney say?" Walker asked as we

moved to the waiting Yellow Cab at the curb. He had called it from the pay phone on the landing outside my door, while I wrote my note to Gunther.

"Who knows?" I said with a shrug, opening the door of the cab.

"Should I bother to ask about 'the chapters'?" he asked as he got in next to me.

"Airport," I told the cabbie, who nodded and went about his business. "Mrs. Plaut thinks I'm a book editor who moonlights as an exterminator. She's writing a book about her family history. I'm editing."

He shook his head in understanding, pulled up his knees, and faced forward. I think he was beginning to wonder if Albert Einstein had made a reasoned decision in sending him all the way to Los Angeles to retrieve a busted-up private detective who lived in Olsen and Johnson land.

I picked up a copy of *American Magazine* at the airport, let Walker arrange for the tickets, and hummed "Tuxedo Junction," trying to give the impression that I flew around the country three or four times a week.

Anyone who flew in an airplane was insane. The damned things could just stop up there and fall down, killing everyone in them and whatever cows happened to be moaning away in the field below, but I pretended that flying was like taking the bus to Santa Monica. Princeton sat there calmly, tickets in hand, watching the crowds flow by. He was looking for movie stars. There weren't any. He should have been worrying about Japanese zeroes that might be lurking anywhere, ready to shoot down passenger flights. It was 1942. We were at war. Even if we weren't, those damn planes were always dropping out of the sky. I was getting angry with him and everyone else in the airport, except the guys in soldier and sailor uniforms. They had no choice.

I looked at my magazine. A girl on the cover smiled at me. She had a ribbon in her hair. She was playing with four dogs, one black, the others brown. I read a story about Australia, another one about arms for MacArthur, and then one about smoking out Jap spies. I read the whole damn magazine before we were anywhere near the Midwest.

We were on TWA, five flights daily to New York. I sweated my way through the flight, the stop in Denver, the stop in Chicago, the stop in Toledo, and stepped out of the plane in New York City sometime on the night of March 31, seventeen hours and fifty-four minutes after we had boarded in Los Angeles. Courage returned and I stopped hating Princeton while we picked up his car in the parking lot, a blue 1940 De Soto with four doors. I had worked my way down to mild annoyance when we stopped in Teaneck for coffee and a sandwich. I was on speaking terms with him when we hit Princeton about an hour later and I gave him a less than sullen "good night" when he dropped me at the Collegiate Hotel and promised to pick me up at seven the next morning to meet Einstein.

The room was small, but it had a radio. I listened to Mr. Dithers shout at Dagwood, Blondie shout at Mr. Dithers, Daisy bark at Blondie, and Baby Dumpling cry at Daisy. When Dagwood apologized to Baby Dumpling the tale had gone full circle. I closed my eyes and fell asleep on the floor of my room where I had moved my blankets to protect my cardboard back.

When I woke up the next morning, some birds were going mad outside my window. They were perched in the branches of a tree I could see from where I lay, wondering if I should try to move. I watched them for a few minutes till they flew away and then tried my back by rolling on my left side. I felt something, but it wasn't acute pain so I sat up and tasted the morning tin in my mouth, rubbed my hand over the greying stubble on my chin and touched the scar on my stomach to be sure it was still there. It was really two scars, both from bullet wounds, joined like bleached white twins. One was given to me by a former movie starlet who didn't like my thinking she had killed her husband. The other scar came from a bullet

fired by a Chicago cop who didn't like my knowing that he
had murdered a handful of people. The twin scars itched
pleasantly in the morning and reminded me that I was alive.

The knock at my door was polite, not too loud but definitely a knock. I grunted "Come in," and got up as the door
opened. Mark Walker, the kid scientist, was standing there,
suit and tie, freshly shaved, holding a newspaper in one hand
and a bottle of orange juice in the other. He looked at the
scarred wreck of a detective in front of him, surveyed my
drooping undershorts, and did his best to hide his lack of confidence.

"It's almost nine," he said, throwing me the newspaper. I
caught it. "You can shave, dress, pack, glance through the
paper, and have a glass of orange juice before we meet Professor Einstein at ten."

"Thanks," I said, stepping forward and tripping over the
blankets on the floor. I didn't fall down. I righted myself and
reached out for the orange juice.

"There's a hotel glass in the bathroom," he said, pulling the
bottle out of my reach. "You can have a glass. The rest is for
Professor Einstein. He has a cold."

"Have a seat while you guard the juice," I said. "I'll hurry
up."

I grabbed my pants from the night before, along with a shirt
from my open suitcase and a pair of socks, which I knew had
the fewest holes of the three pairs I had brought. With the
New York *Times* under my right arm, I moved into the
bathroom and kicked the door shut. The tile felt cool under
my feet. I threw the clothes on the floor, started the water in
the bathtub, and brushed my teeth with the new can of Dr.
Lyon's tooth powder I had picked up for the trip. The tub was
full of hot water by the time I finished shaving. The mirror
and I had a truce. I tried not to criticize the battered face it
held up to me every morning and the mirror, in turn, didn't
laugh at me. Once the stubble was shaved off with a not too-
dull Marlin blade and my hair was combed, the face in the

mirror didn't look too bad. The face tried to smile. It tried that most mornings and looked like a Halloween mask of Lon Chaney.

I checked my watch and put it on the edge of the sink. The watch, which I had inherited from my father, told me it was one o'clock, which was about as close as it usually came. Once in the tub, however, the *Times* told me that it was April Fools' Day, that the British Forces in West Burma were cut off, that the Chinese were trying to hold the line near some place called Toungoo and that General Wainwright had reported a Japanese bombing of a plainly marked American base hospital on Bataan. I let the hot water rub my back and wilt the pages.

"Mr. Peters," Walker called from the other room.

"Coming," I called back, folding the newspaper, throwing it in the corner, and climbing out of the tub to mess up the floor. "You know what it says in the paper? According to the War Production Board, empty toothpaste tubes have to be turned in every time you want a new tube of toothpaste. Same with shaving cream. No tube, no new toothpaste."

Walker seemed at a loss for words as I dried myself and pulled on my underwear and pants so I went on. "What happens if you lose your tube? Christ, everyone loses a tube of something if you give them enough time. And people'll start stealing them from each other's bathroom. Given a long enough war, nobody will be able to buy refills on toothpaste. Everyone's breath will smell like Asta's."

"You use tooth powder," Walker countered as I buttoned my shirt with relief that there were no buttons missing. "I watched you pack."

"You're missing the goddamn mystery of the thing," I shouted. "You've got to let your imagination play games in times like these. Shortages, rationing. You play what-if, part of the national pastime. You complain, worry. It's patriotic."

I came out of the steaming bathroom to a blast of cool air.

Walker was sitting in the not-too-stuffed chair with the orange juice bottle in his lap.

"I'm a scientist," he explained as I looked for my shoes.

"Even scientists can worry about toothpaste," I said, finding my shoes under the blanket I had kicked away when I got up.

"You are not a logical person," Walker said, watching me struggle into my shoes.

"If I were a logical person I wouldn't be in a New Jersey hotel room looking for a pair of worn shoes and looking forward to a glass of warm orange juice and a job that probably won't even pay my expenses."

"If you—" Walker began. But I cut him off.

"I'm not holding you up for a bigger fee," I explained, throwing the blankets back onto the bed to save the maid from one more assault. "I'm explaining behavior."

"I wouldn't know anything about that," he said, rising and reaching for the glass I handed him and pouring me orange juice. It was warm and made me a little queasy, but that passed. I threw my things into my alligator suitcase, nestling my .38 under a faded shirt, and turned to Walker.

"Ready," I said.

Walker drove. He glanced over at me every three seconds to be sure I hadn't spilled any of the juice from the bottle he had entrusted to me. It sloshed around but nothing escaped. I'd put on a semi-matching jacket and tie and looked reasonably respectable. I would have turned on the radio but Walker didn't have one, so I looked out the window and watched the students walk down tree-lined streets. On what looked like a main street, Walker nodded his head and said, "The Institute for Advanced Study is straight down there. That's where I work."

"And Einstein?"

"Professor Einstein is a member of the Institute," Walker said. "But he works in his home. He doesn't need a laboratory, just paper, a blackboard, and books. His laboratory is in his head."

"Must get pretty crowded in there," I tried.

"He keeps it straight."

We turned off the main street onto one called Mercer. The houses were old, neat lawns, nothing fancy. We pulled up in front of 112 and parked. The two-story house was painted white, just like the other ones on the block, with a small veranda and green shutters. We got out. I looked up and down the street and followed Walker up the small walk past two big trees and the five steps to the porch, holding the juice away from me just in case. Walker knocked. We waited. He knocked again and we could hear the sound of steps inside. Then the door opened and I recognized Albert Einstein. He was a little taller than I had expected, about my height. His long hair was almost completely white and not as wild as it usually was in newspaper photographs. His mustache was dark with a few strands of grey. His shoulders were stooped slightly. He wore a limp grey sweater buttoned over a wrinkled shirt that had once been white. His pants were baggy and badly in need of pressing. He wore floppy brown leather slippers with clear cracks in the leather.

"Professor Einstein," Walker said, "this is Toby Peters."

Einstein's droopy face smiled and he held out a hand. I put my suitcase down next to the door and reached out to shake his hand, but he grabbed the orange juice.

"I half a colt," Einstein said, which struck me as gibberish. I must have looked puzzled. "A colt," he repeated. "In my het." He pointed to his head and I figured out that he had a cold in his head. The combination of German accent and stuffed nose kept me alert through the rest of the conversation till I got used to both.

"Come in please," he said, clutching the juice bottle and stepping back to let me in. "Mark, you can go to the Institute. I call you there later."

"I don't have to . . ." he began.

Einstein touched his arm and nodded his head. "You did fine," he said. "Fine, perfect. Mr. Peters and I must talk, and there are things I might have to say that it would be better for you if you didn't hear and didn't have to tell people later or lie about. You understand?"

"Yes, of course," said Walker, reluctant to leave and giving me a last look of suspicion. Einstein ushered him gently out the front door and closed it.

"A good boy," he said, "but . . ."

". . . no imagination," I finished for him.

Einstein nodded in agreement and shuffled down the small hallway, his slippers clopping as he went. We passed a broad set of stairs and turned into a room in the back of the house.

"Theoretical science is all imagination," Einstein said, closing the door to his study. "All in the mind, not in the laboratory. I work on pieces of paper, in my head, and others look through microscopes and telescopes to see if there is anything to see that will prove or disprove what I imagine. But the proof is in the elimination of alternatives. If a thing must be, then it is. If there is order in the universe, then its actions can be discovered, though the meaning may never be."

"I wouldn't know," I said, looking around. "I've been a detective most of my life."

"So have I," he said with a horselaugh. "You'd like some orange juice? Some coffee? I can have one cup of real coffee each morning. I have waited for you."

"Coffee is fine. No orange juice. I already had some."

He nodded again and clopped out of the room. There was one big window covering most of the back wall. Outside I could see a good-sized garden and some big trees. The room itself was cluttered. The side walls had floor-to-ceiling bookshelves. The books looked as if most of them were in German or French. I was standing in front of a big, solid dark wood table covered with pencils, pads, notes, letters, pipes, and books. A desk by the window looked a little neater, but not much.

On the open wall behind me where the door was, I saw some photographs and went over to take a look. I recognized Gandhi but the other two greying guys in suits were a mystery. Einstein solved the mystery while I was trying to read a framed diploma next to one of the pictures.

"That," he said, handing me a white porcelain mug of coffee, "is my honorary membership in Berner Naturforschenden Gesellschaft."

"Right," I said. "And these guys?"

"The one with the collar is James Maxwell, a Scottish mathematician and physicist. And next to him," Einstein said, pausing for a sip of coffee, "is Michael Faraday. You know, of course, who he is."

"No," I admitted. "But I know who you are."

"Maybe," he said, motioning me to a chair and taking a seat himself in a wooden chair with arms. We faced each other, politely drinking coffee.

"Did Dr. Walker explain to you anything?"

"Someone says you're passing scientific secrets to the Russians," I said, finishing my coffee and putting down the mug.

"Small pleasures," sighed Einstein, looking into his now empty cup. "We are tied to our fragile bodies. A simple cold takes away the sense of taste, the pleasure in a cup of coffee, a single morning cigar and with that pleasure gone one becomes irritable, thought is interrupted. I have a housekeeper every morning for an hour. My wife died six, seven years ago. Little things, needed things, are a sign of time. Food, which I enjoy, cleaning clothes, but that you understand. You are almost as indifferent to clothing as I am."

I nodded and said nothing. The great man was stalling. He looked up from his cup and smiled.

"Yes," he said. "You are right. We must get to the point. You were recommended to me by a friend who said you were reliable, determined, and discreet. This friend had a problem with a missing animal. You understand?"

I understood. About a year earlier I had done a small job

for Eleanor Roosevelt when the president's dog looked like it might be dognapped.

"There are things I can tell you," he said softly. "Things I cannot tell. I am involved with a secret project for the United States Navy, that I can tell you. There are other things, things which have to do with winning this war, things perhaps too terrible to consider. I can see by your face that you do not understand."

"I don't have to understand," I said. "I'm here. You know my fee."

"The Federal Bureau of Investigation is, I understand, conducting this investigation of . . ." He raised his arms, groping for the English word.

"Allegations, charges," I supplied.

"Yes. I cannot supply the Federal Bureau of Investigation with complete information. My citizenship might be affected by things in my past and present, my connection to the cause of Zionism is not always popular and my German birth, in spite of my opposition since childhood to Nazism, is suspect."

"Nobody's going to accuse Albert Einstein of . . ."

"Ah, but they will, and they do," he said sadly. "In these times one's reputation loses importance. And I am considered by many to be a relic. Relativity has been questioned, attacked, refuted by those who would believe that the universe is a madhouse, but God's universe is not a madhouse, only this planet. I've made great mistakes in my life. I've assumed that the order of the universe can be seen also in human politics but it cannot. There is no order or logic to politics and so I have committed to causes which alter, change, betray. Now I would like to be left alone to work. I will be sixty-three years old next week. My heart is weak. My fingers do not always obey my commands on the violin and my legs and arms too often betray me when I sail my small boat. I think I can help this country against the horror of Nazism and someone is trying to destroy my reputation to keep me from doing this. I would like you to find these people, expose them, stop them."

"If I can," I said confidently.

"There is more," he added, watching me closely. "Fahre."

I thought he was saying something in English but his accent was getting in the way again so I repeated, "Fahre."

"A radical Nazi group which has put a price on my head," Einstein explained. "I am a Jew. I am a Zionist. I am anti-Nazi and have some reputation. There are madmen who would like to collect the five thousand dollars my head would bring."

"The guys across the street are keeping an eye on you," I said.

Einstein rose and clasped his hands. He gave me a pleased smile.

"I usually wait till after lunch for my single cigar, but . . ." he said and reached for a cigar box, which he opened. He removed a cigar, offered me one which I refused, and lit up, obviously enjoying it. "They named a cigar for me several years ago, a terrible cigar. I'm glad you noticed the men across the street. Dr. Walker has never noticed them."

"At least two there right now," I said. "One was looking through the window. Light hit his binoculars. Another guy behind. Both well dressed."

"Unlike us," Einstein said, pacing as he smoked, clopping as he paced.

"If they were these Fahre people, they wouldn't set up camp," I said, "they'd come in firing. How long have they been there?"

"Since Professor May suddenly had to accept a visiting professorship in North Carolina," Einstein said. "That was a few weeks ago. However, they may be protecting me, or gathering evidence against me, or possibly both."

"So, you just stay around here while I try to find out who . . ."

I stopped because he was nodding his head as he puffed

away. "I have accepted an engagement in New York City, a charity event to raise money for refugees. This will be at the Waldorf Hotel on Sunday. I will play the violin and Mr. Paul Robeson will sing. It is, I understand, Easter Sunday."

"And someone might be around to stop you," I said.

He shrugged, stopped pacing, and looked at me. "The event has been publicized," he said. "I cannot back out of it and do not want to. I do not want those Nazis to think they can make me a prisoner in my house."

"OK," I sighed, standing up, "it's easy enough. I find an assassination squad of lunatic Nazis, put them out of commission while I also figure out who is trying to set you up as a traitor and stop them. All of this without telling the FBI. Is that it?"

Einstein was standing still now. He looked out the window, seemed to have forgotten I was there, and then turned. "Yes," he said. "That is accurate."

"I'd better get started then," I said, not knowing where to.

Einstein, cigar still in hand, went to the desk, opened the middle drawer, found some papers, and brought them to me. "These," he said, "are letters threatening me with exposure for aiding the Russians. The letters are postmarked New York City. The stationery is from the Taft Hotel."

It wasn't much of a lead. I took the small stack of letters and noticed that there was a check on top of the pile made out to Toby Peters. I considered not cashing it and keeping it for the autograph but I had bills to pay and places to go.

"I'll be back," I said.

"And I," he said, looking out the window, his back to me, "will be here."

The breeze played the early spring leaves like glass chimes. The street smelled clean and the check felt good in my pocket. I crossed the sidewalk, suitcase in hand, and waited for a Chevy coupe to pass before I strode across the street and went up to the porch where I had seen the guy with binoculars. He wasn't there now, but someone was behind the curtain to the right of the front door as I climbed the stairs.

2

Before I could knock, the door opened. The guy in front of me didn't look like the FBI. He looked like a grey stork wearing a dark, pressed suit. He was too skinny for FBI, too old. He was almost bald, but the hair that was there was rapidly going grey. There were dark sacks under his eyes.

"Come in, Peters," he said, pushing the door all the way and making a shoveling motion with his hand to hurry me along. The element of surprise was certainly not with me.

"You want a cup of coffee, a beer? We've got Rheingold," he said, leading me into the living room. He stopped and turned to me with a smile that crept up the right side of his face. "Pepsi, you like Pepsi, right?"

"Right out of the bottle," came a deep voice from a high-backed stuffed chair of faded yellow with big pink flowers embroidered on it. The guy in the chair stood up. He was about two inches shorter than I was and about the same age as the guy who opened the door. This one had more hair, all black, probably dyed.

"You don't look like FBI," I said.

"The gravy's in the navy," said the one who had answered the door. "We're retreads, retirees brought back to do our duty. There's a war on, Peters. The Japanese and Germans are trying to kill us and we're trying to stop them. Simple enough?"

"Pretty clear to me," I said. "Can I sit?"

"You may sit," said the short one. "Whether you can or

not depends on whether you have a sore ass or that bad back of yours is acting up."

I put down my suitcase and sat on the sofa, which was just as yellow and pink and flowered as the chair. The whole room was a washed-out vase of flower patterns and faded yellows.

"Place belongs to an English professor named May," said the stork who had let me in. "His wife went on vacation with him."

"At your request," I said, smiling.

"We politely asked him to leave or be considered a Nazi spy," said the shorter one, turning his chair and sitting in it so he could face me. "It's remarkable what you can accomplish during wartime by appealing to people's sense of patriotism . . ."

". . . and fear," his partner added.

"You two had this act going quite a while," I said.

"Hey," said the skinny one, "we go back to Alvin Karpis. Remember Alvin Karpis?"

I was about to answer when I realized the question was part of the act.

"G-men," said the shorter guy. "He called us G-men, gave us the name. Better than a million dollars' worth of publicity."

"Only Karpis never said it," chirped the big guy. "Hoover made it up. A little bit of party chatter for you, Tobias. You'll never get us to confirm it for you publicly though."

"Never," agreed the shorter one with a shake of his head. "You want that Pepsi?"

"Sure. Do you guys have names? Moran and Mack? Gallagher and Shean, Abbott and Costello?"

"Just call us Spade and Archer," said the shorter one. "I'll be Spade. He's Archer."

"He looks more like an arrow," I said.

"I'm on a diet," said Archer. "Spade, you want coffee?"

"I'll have a Pepsi with Mr. Pevsner here," answered Spade, folding his hands in his lap.

"What . . ." I started, but Spade put a finger to his lips.

"We wait for Mr. Archer before we begin," he said. "We're partners. A man honors his partner."

So we waited. I hummed a few bars of "Bess, You Is My Woman" while we waited.

"Gershwin," Spade said. "Can't make up his mind whether he's opera or Tin Pan Alley. Schizophrenic."

"Who is?" asked Archer suspiciously as he returned to the room with two twelve-ounce Pepsi bottles. He handed one to me and one to Spade.

"George Gershwin," said Spade.

"Don't talk about anything, not even George Gershwin, till I get back," Archer warned as he left.

Spade and I sat drinking Pepsi with only a slight belch from me to break the silence. Back with a cup of coffee in about thirty seconds, Archer found himself a seat to my right on a dark wooden chair with a padded flower-patterned seat and looked at me.

"Are we ready now?" I asked.

Spade took a deep gulp, examined the bottle, blew lightly on top to create a low hooting sound, and nodded. "Yes."

"You came to us," Archer reminded me.

"It didn't seem to surprise you," I said, wondering if it would be polite to ask the FBI for a second Pepsi.

"Well within your profile," Archer said. "Impetuous."

"Immature actions," added Spade.

". . . unwilling or unable to always examine the consequences of your actions."

"Reckless."

"Flattery will get you nowhere," I got in before Archer could take his turn.

"Why are you watching Einstein?" I asked.

"He's a national treasure," said Spade.

"A national treasure," agreed Archer after a sip of coffee.

"A national treasure that someone is saying nasty things

about," I tried. "A national treasure that someone might be
planning to eliminate."

"Kill," said Archer. "You can say 'kill.' We aren't sensitive. Our job is to keep Professor Einstein alive and out of
trouble, to protect him from outside threats and from himself.
He has been known to say indiscreet things."

"Like me," I volunteered.

"Big indiscreet things," said Spade. "About pacifism, and
the need for a Palestinian homeland for Jews."

"Not wrong things," Archer added, finishing off his Pepsi.
"But indiscreet."

"You want another Pepsi?" Archer asked.

I said yes and Spade said no at the same time.

"You know about the letters to Einstein."

"Is that a question? If it's a question, the answer is, what
letters? If it's a statement, I sit back and examine you emo-
tionlessly," said Spade, sitting back. "You want me to get the
drinks this time?"

"I'll get them," said Archer.

"So," Spade continued. "We, the Federal Bureau of Investigation, will sit back, watch, and, if necessary, lend a
helping hand."

We waited for refills all around and for Archer to get back
in his chair before we resumed. There was a small chip of
glass missing from the rim of the Pepsi bottle. The FBI wasn't
the perfect host it pretended to be. I didn't give a damn. I was
living dangerously. I drank deeply and realized I needed a
bathroom, but I wasn't about to delay the answers any longer.

"Einstein wants to hire a private detective, fly him in from
Los Angeles, that's fine with us," said Archer. "Spade and I
aren't much for legwork. We'll stay here and keep an eye on
the Professor."

"You want to know where I'm going from here?" I asked.

"We have a pretty good idea," Spade said. "Don't tell us.
It makes us feel as if we're doing our job."

I finished my second Pepsi and looked around for some place to put the empty. Seeing my dilemma, Archer got up with a grunt and took it from me.

"Thanks," I said. "Maybe I'll be seeing you."

"Maybe," said Spade. "Maybe."

There were no handshakes. I picked up my suitcase, and Archer, Pepsi bottle in hand, led me to the door.

I stopped before he opened it.

"You had a tail on Walker," I said. "Either you followed him or had someone pick him up in Los Angeles. He led you to me. Someone called you with my bio before I got off the plane."

"Tape," whispered Archer. "We've got tape machines, the latest equipment. Have a good trip. There's a cab stand two blocks right. Bus station's about ten minutes away."

"Thanks," I said and went back out on the street.

A blond guy with a little blond mustache and an English accent sat next to me on the bus, complaining about synthetic rubber. "The military," he whispered confidentially, "is using synthetic rubber tires now. In a matter of weeks—weeks, mind you, not months—we'll all be riding on synthetic rubber tires. The government may tell me they are as good as rubber. B. F. Goodrich may tell me they are as good as rubber. My local garageman may tell me they are as good as rubber . . ."

"They're as good as rubber," I said, my battered face a fist away from his.

"Right," he said. "There you have it then. They are as good as rubber."

We didn't converse any more on the rest of the ride to Manhattan.

3

In the bus station, I put on my tan windbreaker and got rid of a long-coated guy with a stringy beard who told me the end of the world was coming. I told him that any harebrain who could read the newspaper or listen to the radio knew that. I asked him what to do about the situation and he suggested that I repent. I told him the things I was sorry for were too small to make a difference. Was God up there worrying because I had overcharged a woman in Pasadena three bucks for finding her lost Muffin? The stringy guy was now confused. I explained that Muffin was a black poodle that looked a bit like stringy beard.

"Why did you overcharge the lady from Pasadena?" the stringy guy asked, now getting into the tale.

"Muffin bit me," I explained. "This was back in 'thirty-eight or 'thirty-nine. Muffin bit me and I hadn't had a case in almost a month and I didn't much like the woman."

"So you overcharged her?"

"Five bucks over. She was happy to pay. I felt guilty later and tried to repay three bucks . . ."

"Why just three?" asked Stringy, plunging his gnarled hands deeply into his pockets.

"It cost two bucks to get the hospital to sew up my leg from where Muffin bit me."

"I see," he said. "What were we talking about?"

"Repentance," I said, handing him a quarter.

"God bless you," he said, taking the quarter.

"Not till I repent."

"Perhaps he'll grant you special dispensation for your kindness," said the confused saint, looking around for someplace to spend his quarter.

"Dispensation comes cheaper here than in Los Angeles," I said, grabbing my suitcase before an anemic character in a zoot suit, who had been listening to us, could get his hand on it. Zoot Suit pulled his hand back as if the handle of the case were hot, flashing me an ivory grin not of apology but of embarrassment. He had almost been caught.

"I'll bet you've got a lot to repent," I said to Zoot Suit.

"Not me, mister," he said pointing to himself. "I'm from Philadelphia."

I left them and went out into the street. I knew vaguely where Seventh Avenue and Fiftieth was. I had been in New York a few times. The last time I had been there I had left two teenagers who had run away. I had gone back to Los Angeles and told their parents I couldn't find the pair. The two kids had seemed a hell of a lot more adult than their parents, and I'd decided that they had a better chance together than back home with their battling clan. I had turned back part of the fee for that one. One less to repent in the few days before the world went under.

I walked up past Forty-fourth Street, where Todd Duncan and Anne Brown were playing in *Porgy and Bess* at the Majestic. I started to hum "Bess, You Is My Woman" again. A trio of well-dressed women ignored me as I went humming past. Down Forty-sixth I could see that *Arsenic and Old Lace* was playing at the Fulton. Boris Karloff's name was on the marquee. I had done a job for Karloff a few years earlier but I doubted if he would remember it or me and I didn't have time to look up L.A. people. I had science to save.

A sign in a Marine recruiting station on Broadway and Forty-eighth said I could come in and get a Japanese Hunting License. "Free Ammunition and Equipment—With Pay!" It was almost lunchtime. I stopped at a stand-up corner hot dog stand, put my suitcase on the ground between my legs, and had a root beer and two dogs for a quarter. The root beer was just like home. The hot dogs were great. I had a third with extra onions and went the last block through the crowds of boys in uniform, women shoppers with sharp New York accents, and people I'd rather not touch along the highway of life.

A sign outside the Taft told me I could get COCKTAILS FOR 25 CENTS while I listened to amusing songs by Charlie Drew in the Tap Room. The doorman looked at me and my alligator suitcase and then went on talking to a hack waiting for a fare. I went up the stairs into the Taft and headed across the busy lobby to the main desk on the right. Somewhere behind me in the Tap Room or some other interior saloon a piano played "Let's Face the Music and Dance." I didn't want Kern, I wanted Gershwin, and it made me uneasy.

A couple from the Midwest beat me to registration. Their accents said Iowa. The desk clerk said, "Reservations?"

The clerk wore a blue suit and blue tie. He didn't need a shave. He didn't need a haircut. His fingernails were trim and clean and he owned the world, at least this carpeted corner of it.

"Darrel Davidson and wife, Davenport," the man said. He was short, missing a neck, and sweating. She was short with a vestigial neck, and very dry. The clerk found their reservation, signed them in on the register, and accepted a check from Darrel. Then the clerk rang a bell and an ancient bellhop arrived to take their bags, but not before Mrs. Davidson could ask, "What room is Hildegarde singing in?"

"I believe," said the desk clerk, "that Hildegarde is at the Savoy-Plaza. That is on 58th and 5th."

"I thought she was here," said Mrs. Davidson, disappointed, as the old bellboy started for the elevator.

"We can go down to the Savoy-Plaza," said Mr. Davidson. "Don't let's embarrass Ellie."

Darrel looked to me for sympathy and understanding. I gave him all I could muster as he waddled after the Mrs.

The guy behind the desk looked at me, then at my mottled alligator bag from Hy's, and asked the most sympathetic question he could come up with. "Are you in the Armed Services? There is a twenty-five percent discount to our men in uniform."

At my age I would normally be flattered to be mistaken for a soldier, but I had seen some pretty old privates in the last two years. I had a feeling that if I wanted to go out and get a license to kill Japanese, the Marines might overlook my greying hairs, and wink when I lied about my age. My bad back might give me away somewhere down the line but male bodies were in short supply for this war. "No uniform, no reservation," I said. "I'm here on business."

"I'm afraid if you have no reservation . . ." he began.

"Maybe you should be," I said with a grin, leaning forward. Two women were now lined up behind me, paying no attention to our conversation. Theirs was going strong.

"A client of mine wants me to stay in this hotel," I said. "He and I are going to be working here. He'll be very disappointed if I don't get a room."

I pulled Einstein's check out of my pocket and handed it to the clerk, who was, I'm sure, considering a call for help in getting rid of me.

"I don't . . ." he began, without looking at the check in front of him.

"I do and it hasn't stunted my growth," I said. "Just look at the signature on that check."

He looked. Then he looked again. "I'll have to have this authenticated," he said, looking up with new respect.

"Authenticate, validate, send someone over to the bank. I'll wait right here while you do," I said as pleasantly as I could, turning to smile politely at the three women. They were all well-dressed, hair piled neatly up off their ears, dangling earrings, white billowy blouses with frilly collars. One of the women was a little pudgy. A second was tall, stylish, and formless. The third was about forty and just right. I fell in love with her and would have been content to spend the next hour or so watching her and listening to the three women discuss where they were going to have lunch.

"Are you going to be long?" asked the tall one, the obvious leader. Something about me fixed a polite, masked smile of distaste on her regal face, maybe the air of lunchtime onions on my breath.

"I don't know," I said, looking at the cute one, who looked away. She reminded me of my ex-wife, Anne. "Are we going to be long?" I asked the clerk.

He looked at Einstein's check, made a decision, and said, "No. I'll just check you in."

"Peters, Toby Peters," I supplied and then added, to hear how it sounded to me and the waiting ladies, "Professor Peters."

"Professor Peters," he said. "I'll check on this . . . check while you make yourself comfortable."

"I'm sure Professor Einstein will appreciate it," I said, loud enough for the three women to hear. "Please cash the check for me after you make your calls, and have a bellboy bring the money up to my room."

New respect was in the eyes of the three women when I turned to hand my suitcase to another ancient bellhop.

"You know Albert Einstein?" asked the tall one.

"Albert? Yes, we're working together on supportive energy dysfunctions," I said, waving at the bellboy to lead the way.

The pretty one who reminded me of Anne touched her right ear. I'd remember that forever.

"Is it secret?" she asked, her shrill voice breaking the spell.

"Science stuff," I whispered, putting my face close to hers. She was wearing perfume that smelled like a flower I couldn't place but knew I had smelled as a child.

I followed the bellhop and behind me heard,

". . . always a bit eccentric . . ."

". . . but he didn't look like . . ."

". . . you can't tell by how they . . ."

And then the old guy and I were in the elevator. We were alone with the elevator operator, a woman with a uniform like the old guy's. He told her to take us to five and up we went.

"You really a scientist?" the old guy asked, shifting my suitcase from his left to his right hand and then resting it on the floor.

"What do you think?"

"I don't think," he said. "I make my living on tips. You think too much and you say something that can get you in trouble. I just want the day to go by fast and the tips to be respectable."

"I've got one for you," I said, looking at the elevator operator, who appeared to be deaf as we shot by two and three. "War will be over in a year."

"That kind of tip won't buy me Bull Durham," he said with a sigh. "World is full of comedians. Everyone thinks he's Jack Benny. I live in the Bronx. We've got blackout drills now. Blackout drills. So war jokes don't tickle me. I'm not complaining. You want to tell jokes, I'm a good listener, but not for the war jokes. Aside from that, the guest is always right."

"Except when he's wrong," mumbled the elevator operator as the elevator snapped to a stop. "Five."

The doors slid open but we were about a foot shy of level. She inched the elevator up and missed by almost six inches. That was good enough for me but not for her. She motioned me back when I tried to step off. About two minutes later we were reasonably within target for her to let the bellhop and me debark. Lights were flashing on the elevator board next to her.

"Good help is hard to find," the bellhop commented, nodding at the closing doors of the elevator as he headed down the corridor. "They're lucky guys like me are willing to go back to work."

"You and the FBI," I said.

He walked ahead, shaking his head. He wasn't about to try to figure out an insane guest, especially one who made war jokes and nutty comments about the FBI. The corridor was quiet and dark, the carpet a deep brown with grey vases, wearing away from a generation of shod feet. In front of 514 the bellhop put down the suitcase and opened the door.

The room was small, clean, with a view of another hotel from the window. The bellhop put the suitcase down and said, "Have a good stay in New York."

I handed him two quarters, which he pocketed without looking, handing me the room key.

A hot bath and a toothbrushing later and I was in my shorts, lying on the bed and considering my next move when a knock came. The guy at the door tried not to look at my scarred body as he handed me an envelope with TAFT HOTEL printed in the corner. Behind him a maid stepped forward to hand me a bowl of fruit covered by green cellophane. "The management would like to apologize for any inconvenience," the man said with a fixed smile, touching his Wildrooted hair to be sure it wasn't inconvenient.

"No trouble," I said, resisting the urge to scratch my stomach.

"If there is anything you need to make your stay more comfortable, Professor Peters, just call the desk and ask for Calvin or Alexander."

"I'll do that," I said, taking note and fruit. "I'll really do that, Calvin."

"Alexander," he corrected.

"Alexander, yes," I said, pushing the door closed.

The envelope contained cash from my Einstein check and a note welcoming me to the Taft. I put the cash in my wallet after picking my pants up off the floor and spent the next few hours coming up with no good plan while I ate Florida oranges.

Just before three I took my suit into the bathroom, turned on the hot water, and went back into the room, closing the bathroom door behind me. By four, when I checked, the bathroom was at the level of a zero-visibility fog, but my suit was wrinkle-free. It was also damp, but I was the only one who would know that. After checking to see that I didn't need a shave, I dressed in the soppy suit and went down to the lobby. There was a new clerk at the desk and the woman who reminded me of Anne was nowhere in sight. I hadn't really expected her. I went up to the new clerk, who was as neatly dressed as the morning clerk and a decade older, his hair nearly white. I hung around the lobby, watching him and the passing parade until the desk was patron-free, then strode up, looking as respectable as my body allowed.

"My name is Peters," I said. "Professor Peters. I'm in five-fourteen."

"Yes, Professor Peters," the man said with a false-toothed smile. "I was informed that you were here."

"I was wondering," I said confidentially, "if you could do me a small favor."

"Anything at all," he beamed.

"I'd like to examine the registration books for the past three weeks," I said.

"No," he said.

"Mr. . . ."

"Sudsburry," he replied.

"Sudsburry," I said, as if savoring the name. "This is a delicate matter which I'd rather not explain. You understand, I hope."

"No," grinned Sudsburry. "I can't say that I do, Professor Peters, but it really doesn't matter if I understand or not. I simply can't let you examine the hotel register. I hope you understand."

I understood. I've filled in for enough house dicks to know that you didn't let jealous husbands or process servers kick up cow pies in your corridors, at least not in reasonably respectable hotels.

"If you'll just tell me who you are looking for," he said

amiably, "perhaps I can tell you if they are registered and what room they might be in."

Applause broke out behind us. I assumed it wasn't because of his performance but the end of a piano roll in the Tap Room across the lobby.

"It's a signature," I explained.

"And this has some scientific importance?"

"Yes," I said emphatically.

"What?" he asked reasonably.

"Professor Einstein's son is missing," I explained. "Breakdown. We think he might be hiding in the hotel under an assumed name. The pressure on him has been enormous what with the war and . . . you know. Professor Einstein and I have been very concerned about him."

Sudsburry's smile was fixed and tolerant.

"Hans Albert Einstein is in Zurich," Sudsburry said.

"Zurich?"

"Zurich, Switzerland," said Sudsburry. "Pardon me, Professor, but are you sure it's Einstein's son who is under pressure?"

"We're all under great pressure," I said. "How do you know that . . ."

". . . Hans Albert is in Zurich? The radio."

"Thank you. Professor Einstein will be very relieved, very relieved. Zurich, you say?"

"Zurich, I say," said Sudsburry. "Now if you will excuse me, I've got to get back to work."

He went back to work and I went into the Tap Room to see what all the applause was about and to plot a new strategy.

I considered stealing Sudsburry's false teeth for simple revenge and trying my luck with the night clerk for possible results, but I had the feeling that a Taft rule was a Taft rule. I ordered a Rheingold beer in a big glass at the bar and looked around for Charlie Drew to amuse me, but it was too early for professional entertainment. Some sailors were at the piano. One was playing, the other two singing. They were all young, all awful. The handful of people in the Tap Room loved them. The gallant gobs messed up a medley of show tunes and forgot the words to "After You've Gone," but the afternoon drinkers went wild and asked for more. If there weren't a war on, they would have been ordered to leave by the management, but they were having fun. I tried not to feel like Baby Snooks' Daddy, but I had gone through some rough nights in a few hotels with kids like this who wanted trouble, and something to remember before they sailed out to be shot at and maybe killed.

"Not bad," said a woman, sitting next to me. With a quick glance, she looked all right. A second glance, even in the dark, put her near my age and carrying a lot of memories.

"Not bad," I agreed, finishing off the beer and wiping my mouth.

"Alone?" she asked.

"But not lonely," I said. "How about I buy what you're drinking, I have another beer, and we listen to the aquatic Mills Brothers before I take off for work?"

"I'll settle for that," she said with a grin that made it clear she had been this route too. "Make it Scotch on the rocks, but not too many rocks. We don't want a shipwreck. I've got to get to work myself."

The bartender indicated that he had heard the conversation and showed up with the drinks, as the trio did to "I Guess I'll Have to Dream the Rest," what we'd all like to see them do to the Nazi fleet. We all clapped our hands and I launched into my second beer, feeling better about them and our chances of coming out of the war a winner.

"You got a problem?" the woman said, the slight tinge of a South-of-the-Border accent in her question.

"I'm working on one," I admitted as one of the people in the darkness called for "Old Rocking Chair's Got Me." The sailors obliged with a heavy dose of dah-de-days in place of Hoagy Carmichael's words.

"Maybe I could help," she said, looking into her glass at a melting ice cube.

"Don't think so," I said, considering a third beer.

As she turned to face me on her stool, the light from the bar hit her face, and either two beers or a new perspective said she wasn't as old as I had thought. She looked as if she really wanted to help. There are people like that in the world. They sit around in bars, waiting to hear sad stories and give their sympathy and understanding. Most of them are women. I don't know why.

"I'm a good listener," she said. "I'm a professional listener. I'm on the switchboard of this hotel five nights a week, eight hours a night, listening to people, helping people. Makes me feel like . . ."

". . . you're helping people," I supplied.

"Something like that," she agreed.

"Maybe you can help me," I said, moving my stool closer to hers. She smelled like Scotch and poppies. I motioned for another round and we talked. Three beers is my limit. I switched to Pepsi, punctuated by two trips to the men's room.

Her name was Pauline Santiago. She lived in Brooklyn with a man named Paul, who may or may not have been her husband. Pauline and Paul seemed to have nothing in common but their first names. He was Polish. She was half Mexican and half Italian. He was a Republican. She was a Democrat. He grunted a lot. She talked too much.

"It's an old story," she said.

"But a true one," I toasted with my Pepsi.

"True one," she agreed, finishing off her third Scotch on the rocks.

"You're going to walk out of here and go to work?" I said.

"Why not?" she asked, turning to see what was going on at the piano. A man in a tuxedo, who I guessed might be Charlie Drew come to amuse us, wanted to get to the keyboard. The three sailors were reluctant to give up their conquest. They might not be able to take Midway, but by God they were going to hold onto this enemy Steinway. Charlie protested, joked, pleaded, appealed to the crowd with no success and finally, in a fair but unconvincing display of support for our men in uniform, agreed to let them keep up their concert for a few more minutes.

"I've got a living to make too, boys," he said, looking at the crowd and not the boys. The crowd didn't seem to give a damn about Charlie's living. A drunk called for "Sleepy Lagoon." Charlie Drew volunteered to help. The concert went on.

"Let me get this straight." Pauline Santiago tried turning from the show to my smiling face. "You want to get a look at the hotel register for the last three weeks."

Since I had said this at least four times in the last five minutes, I had nothing to add. I just nodded.

"And you say it's because you're looking for the handwriting of someone trying to scare Albert Einstein?" she asked with a twisted smirk. "Who are you trying to kid? I wasn't born yesterday, you know."

"It's the truth," I said, crossing my heart.

"Truth," she sighed, looking into her now empty glass. "I could tell you some truths that would curl your fingernails. You wouldn't believe the things people say on the telephone."

"I don't listen in on that many phone calls."

"I do," she said, looking around for someone to dispute her claim. No one did. The sailors sang and sounded a little better with Charlie Drew's help, but not a lot better.

"It's almost five," I pointed out. "You said you had to be at work at five."

"Be right back." Holding up a finger, she eased her way off the bar stool, showing a not uncomely pair of legs under her short skirt. In spite of two-inch heels, she made her way with near dignity into the darkness near the rest rooms. The bartender offered me another Pepsi. I turned it down and listened with the growing audience to "Stardust." All we needed was Bogart and a bunch of Nazis and we could have half the room sing the French national anthem while the Nazis belted out "Sonny Boy." When Pauline returned, I had trouble recognizing her. Gone were the heels and the tight dress. Gone was her tightness. Her hair was pinned up and ready for business.

"All set," she said. "I went back to my locker, changed, and soaked my face in icewater."

"Miracle."

"All on the surface," she confided, taking my arm with a grin. She had a nice grin and a large mouth. "You're my husband," she said.

I pulled away. We were almost at the door.

"No," she explained. "I'm going to tell them you're my husband. They've never seen him. I'd never bring Paul around here. I don't want anyone to see the Abominable Snowman of Brooklyn. Just follow me."

We went into the lobby, which was full of people coming in to register, going out for dinner, or waiting for a good time that would probably never show up. I followed Pauline through a door, looking at her in good light for the first time. A little overweight, but not much. Good skin. Nice teeth. Fine legs. Her dark hair was piled high to show her small ears. The face had seen a bit too much but it was a nice face. I didn't think I could hold up as well to her inspection, but I guess I did. At the door she turned to look at me and grinned.

"Ready?"

"Ready," I answered and we went in. I was a little worried about running into Sudsburry, who might take some time from the desk to have a smoke or a Coke with the behind-the-scenes staff, but it was soon clear that the phone room was far from the lair of the keeper of the registration book.

"A minute." Sitting me on a folding chair outside of a door marked PHONE CENTER, Pauline came out in about ten seconds. "Adella will cover for me. I'll be right back."

Beyond the closed door I could hear Adella's voice from time to time, a pleasant tinkle of a voice over the buzz-buzz of the phone lines. Pauline was back in no more than five minutes with three ledger-sized books in her hands. She dropped them in my lap. "Couldn't get the current one," she apologized.

"Probably won't need it," I said. "I'll take them up to my room, five-fourteen, and bring them down as soon as I can."

"I'm off at midnight," she whispered. "I'll come up and get them."

She kissed me, Scotch and poppies and something else knowing and warm and sweet. I couldn't kiss back. My arms were filled with ledgers.

"I can do better," I said.

"See you at midnight." She laughed and went into the phone room. Her laugh was raw, deep, wading right through the troughs of time. She had to be drunk, but she held it better than the kids at the bar.

I skulked back to my room, turned on the light, threw my jacket on the bed, and dropped the ledgers on the desk in the corner. Pulling the letters to Einstein out of my suitcase, I commenced comparing handwriting. I took a break to call Gunther back in Los Angeles. Luck was with me. Mrs. Plaut didn't answer the phone. Joseph P. Hill, the mailman, picked it up and told me that Gunther was out. Hill took down the name of the Taft Hotel and promised to pass it along to Gunther. I hung up and made myself comfortable.

While I worked, I listened to the standard white hotel radio, an Arvin. Fred Allen was the guest on the "Quiz Kids." The kids were a little surprised when the baggy-eyed comic with the thin reedy voice beat them to a couple of answers. Their respect and mine increased even further when Allen identified Lorenzo Da Ponte as the librettist of *Don Giovanni*. I didn't even know what a librettist was. I was almost at the end of the first ledger, with no match to the handwriting, when "Junior Miss" came on at nine on WABC. I'm a sucker for Shirley Temple. It took me almost an hour to finish that first volume.

I was midway through the second volume, MARCH 15–30, when I spotted the name Alex Albanese. I turned off the radio and realized for the first time that I needed glasses. It was a depressing thought. I squinted at the signature, checked and triple-checked it against the letters. It was possible. I checked again and decided it was likely. I checked a twelfth time and decided it was certain. Alex Albanese in Room 1324 had written the threatening letters to Albert Einstein. I was buttoning my shirt when a knock came at the door.

"Toby?" It was Pauline's raspy voice. "You in there?"

I opened the door and she stood, grinning. Her grin dropped when she saw my face.

"You sobered up," she said. "I understand. Happens."

"I was never drunk," I said, holding the door open for her to come in. "I just didn't realize it was midnight."

She pushed the door closed behind her with her rear. "Counting the hours and minutes," she said. "I came for the registration books. Did you get what you want?"

"Not everything," I said, taking a step toward her.

"You've got a way with words," she said, showing big white teeth. They were great teeth, and with Alex Albanese almost in my pocket a little delay wouldn't cost me anything.

"There's a war on. Paul is maybe waiting at home and I've got to get these books back," she said, throwing the big black purse she had been wearing over her shoulder onto the bed. "Let's get in bed and talk later. What do you say?"

I took off the shirt I had just finished buttoning and made a mental note to see an optometrist when I got back to Los Angeles.

An hour later someone knocked on the door. It was a little after one in the morning. I asked who it was and three bullets came through the polished walnut door and cracked the window.

4

"A braham Lincoln," Pauline screamed, looking at the broken window. I figured shock had conjured up the image of Honest Abe hovering over Seventh Avenue. I tried to move her off of me, expecting the guy with the gun to come through the door and improve his aim. Pauline was not easy to roll but I managed, and dived over the foot of the bed, glancing at the door. The lights were out in the room and thin rods of brightness jabbed through the bullet holes. There didn't seem to be anyone on the other side of the door, but I still fumbled for the .38 in my suitcase and came up with it and some underwear. Throwing the underwear and caution to the wind, I went across the room, unlocked the door, and stepped back against the wall. No one shot at me. I stepped into the hall, looked right and saw nothing, and then looked left and saw a bulky male figure with short white hair about to go through the exit door near the elevator.

"Hold it," I yelled, leveling my pistol, not sure if he was the shooter or an innocent resident running from the madness that had broken out. He settled my dilemma by wheeling and taking a shot in my general direction that thudded into the already punctured door about a foot over my head. That was better shooting than I could do. I didn't bother to fire.

The white-haired guy went through the exit door and down or up the stairs. I thought about going after him but two things changed my mind: the broom-thin woman in a night-gown and hair curlers, who stepped out of the room across from mine and screamed, and the realization that she was probably not screaming at the destruction and gunshots but at the fact that she was facing a somewhat scared naked man, carrying a gun. I ducked back in my room, closed the door, and flipped on the light.

Pauline was staring at the broken window. The bullets from Whitey had created what looked like a jagged silhouette of Abraham Lincoln. It was worth calling in to Ripley's "Believe It Or Not." I could even imagine a little cartoon drawing of me and Pauline in bed, with the outline of Lincoln over our heads and the words below us reading: "This amazing outline of Abraham Lincoln was formed in the window by bullets fired into the hotel room of Private Detective Toby Peters, as he lay in bed with a hotel switchboard operator." Since we were in the Taft, it would have been more amazing if the outline had been of William Howard Taft, but who the hell would recognize Taft's profile? While I pondered these questions, I put on the underpants I had thrown on the floor.

"What does Paul look like?" I asked.

"Paul?" she said blankly, finally turning from the window.

"Your husband. Is he big, white hair?"

"No, he's . . . There isn't any Paul. I just made that up," she said.

"You made him up?"

"I live with my mother in Queens," she said, sitting heavily on the bed. Her hair tumbled over her face and down to her over-ample but nicely freckled breasts. "I just go from Queens to Manhattan, Manhattan to Queens, and Louise has dinner ready."

"Louise is your mother?" I asked, slipping my pants on, with my .38 tucked under my chin.

She nodded.

"Nobody shoots at us in Queens," she said sadly.

I couldn't tell whether she was excited or disappointed by the events of the last few hours, but I didn't have time to find out.

"Time to get dressed, Pauline," I said gently but urgently as I shifted the pistol to my pocket and put on a shirt. "We're going to have company in a few minutes and you have to get out of here and get those registration books back."

"My name isn't Pauline," she sighed without moving. "And it's not Santiago. My name is Mary Louise Caldoni. I made up the name Pauline Santiago."

"It's a beautiful name," I said, buttoning my shirt, "but I haven't got time for any more confessions. You've got to get dressed and out of here or you're going to lose your job."

"The police," she said and then stood up to scream. "The police. Oh my God. The police will be coming here."

I handed her her dress and urged her into it without a word. Hotels don't send out for the police until they have to and until they've checked to be sure it is absolutely one hundred percent necessary. Having a squad of cops tracking through your hotel is not top-notch promotion. Hotels like to keep things as quiet as possible. I'd worked enough of them to know.

"I've got to get out of here," Pauline or Mary Louise finally realized, throwing her hair back and looking around for her stockings and shoes.

I found the stockings but didn't hand them to her. I shoved them in her purse and grabbed the registers.

"My . . . Someone shot at us," she said, standing. "My hair. I have to brush my hair."

Her hand went up to her hair. I took it down and put the registers under her arm. She was dazed. No one had ever shot at her before. I had no time to explain things to her, explain that the fear would never really go away, the memory would always be ready to come back. But that was only the bad part. There was also the part I was feeling now. The jumpy, crazy realization that I was still alive, that maybe I had come a cold breath from being dead. It was like being reborn and suddenly appreciating things you hadn't noticed before—the smell of the cool air through the outline of Honest Abe in the

window, the feel of the rough carpet under bare feet—which
reminded me to put on my shoes.

"You're going to be fine, Pauline," I said, ushering her to
the door. "Get these books back and get home to Louise. I'll
talk to you tomorrow."

"I told you my name isn't really Pauline," she said, stopping, wiping away her falling hair, and looking into my eyes
as if great importance were attached to my accepting her sin.
"It's Mary Louise Caldoni."

"To me you'll always be Pauline," I said, opening the bul-
let-pocked door. No one was in the hall, not the guy with the
white hair, not the woman in the curlers, no one.

"But," Pauline pleaded, standing in the hall with her black
purse dangling over one shoulder, the registers under her
other arm and her hair a dark bundled mess, "I'm a Catholic."

"I figured that out," I whispered. "Better get going. We
don't want anyone to know you were here."

"It does look like Abraham Lincoln," she said. "I'm not
crazy or something."

"Just like Lincoln, right off a new penny. Amazing like-
ness," I sighed. "Take the elevator. Get those books back.
Go home."

I stepped out of the doorway, still holding my pistol, gave
her a hug, and led her to the elevator. I pressed the button,
gave her a kiss on the cheek, and padded back to the door to
my room. She looked at me, a damp dishcloth of a confused
woman, and then turned as the elevator arrived. The night
operator, a pencil of a woman, gave us both a look that made
it clear she had seen everything and we were nothing special.
Pauline staggered into the elevator and I waited till the door
closed before I hopped back into my room and reached for
the telephone. It had been a few minutes, maybe two or
three, since the white-haired guy had decorated the window.

"Hello," I said indignantly. "Send someone up to five-fourteen. Get the police. Someone just shot at me through my door."

I hung up before the person on the other end could ask any questions and then I sat down to wait. I was sure that the hotel already had someone on the way up to see what was going on. The call would simply cover me, in case someone asked. Someone knocked at the door no more than half a minute after I hung up the phone.

"You all right in there?" came a man's voice, even, calm, not too loud, with a distinct Irish accent.

I crossed the room and opened the door. The man who faced me looked as if he were on the way to a costume party, dressed as the police sergeant from a cheap gangster movie. He was about five foot ten, slightly overweight, face like a bulldog, grey hair, and a shaggy brown suit. Two cigars protruded from his vest pocket. Hotels liked to let con men and women and pickpockets know that they had a visible pro on duty. The really sharp hotels had a backup pro who didn't look like a cop. The backup's job was to catch the ones that didn't scare away.

"What happened here?" he said, his Irish accent rattling his slightly high voice.

"Who are you?" I asked.

"See-cure-ity," he answered.

"Someone shot some holes through my door, Mr. See-cure-ity," I said with feigned indignation. "I just called your desk and asked for the police, not the house detective."

"Well, maybe we can handle this without calling in the po-leese," he said amiably, looking over my shoulder. "Shall we discuss this in your room instead of the hall, where we might be disturbing the other residents who are trying to sleep? Some of them are our boys in uniform on leave, who deserve a few hours of peace and quiet."

I grunted and pushed open the door so he could get in. My experience with our boys in uniform on leave was that they were not looking for peace and quiet, but I had a role to play.

Security stepped into the room and looked around. I think he even sniffed, though I don't know what he thought he might smell. It was all part of the act. He looked at the broken window and apparently didn't notice the striking resemblance to Abe Lincoln.

"Look like anyone to you?" I asked.

"Does what look like anyone to me?" he said, turning his eyes to me with suspicion.

"Forget it," I sighed and sat on the bed. He stood.

"What happened here?" he said, taking out a notebook and pencil.

"Someone shot holes in the door and almost killed me. That's what happened. Why don't you call the police? Seal off the hotel? I got a glimpse of the guy. About six-two, two hundred pounds, white hair cut short, real short. He had a small pistol, probably a Walther PP."

"A Walther PP, was it?" Security said, looking over the notebook at me. "You got maybe a glimpse of this fella and you could tell what kind of weapon he had? What kind of business you in that makes you an expert on small arms?"

"I'm involved with physics," I said. "I'm on a secret project right now with Albert Einstein. Very secret."

He nodded his head knowingly, though I didn't see how my answer explained how I could recognize a Walther PP in someone's hand fifty feet down a hallway.

"I don't know," Irish Security said, rubbing his recently shaved and talcumed chin. "I just don't know what to make of this. Might have been a drunk at the wrong room, or a mistake."

He looked at the disheveled bed and around the floor. "You were in here alone, were you?"

"Of course," I said, angrily rising from the bed and looking around for any trace of Pauline. "What are you going to do about this?"

"Remain calm," he said, going over to the hole in the window to examine it. "Remain calm." The window told him nothing. He sighed deeply before moving close to me to whisper, though no one else was with us.

"I can't see that the po-leese would be much help here now. We'll find another room for you and I'll send my men out to go over every room, every nook and cranny in the hotel, looking for this white-haired fellow with the Walther. We'll find him. If you're uneasy, why, I'll have one of my men keep an eye on your door all night. And I'm sure I can get the hotel to forget about your bill."

He had no men and no intention of spending five minutes looking for Whitey. He'd probably give the description to the desk clerk and the doorman, and go back to listening to the radio and reading a novel in some corner of the lobby.

"Someone will watch my door?" I said, somewhat calmed.

"Every moment of the night. You have my promise," said Security.

"Then I'll just stay in this room and lock the door. I'm too tired to start moving things around now, it's been a very difficult night. You sure you'll find him?"

"Positive," Security beamed, showing yellow false teeth. "Guaranteed. They can't get away with that kind of thing in this hotel."

Two minutes later he was gone. I propped a chair under the door handle and moved the bed next to the bathroom out of the line of fire. Then I got undressed, looked at my watch, which told me it was eleven, though I knew that was at least five hours from the truth, turned out the light, and got into bed. A lesser or saner man might have been worried, but I was feeling great. I had the name of the guy who had probably sent the threatening letters to Einstein, and I had someone worried enough to take shots at me. I figured the shooting had been to scare me off. Of course Security might have been right. It might have been a random drunk or lunatic or someone who had some other reason for wanting to shoot me. Or Pauline might be Pauline after all and there might be a white-haired Paul who had come looking for her. I wasn't going to cross these possibilities off the list, but I wasn't going to give up on my gut feeling either.

A cool draft came through the hole in the window. I looked at it before I fell asleep. It didn't look like Abe Lincoln anymore. The magical moment had passed. A voice inside my head said, "Cowardly Pianos." I wondered what impish game the voice was playing with me.

"Cowardly Pianos," the voice repeated, and kept it up till I fell asleep and dreamed I was ten years old and holding my father's hand while we stood at the edge of the desert and looked out at an endless line of yucca trees. The arms of the yucca trees trembled and I sensed they were going to reach for me. I squeezed my father's hand and he chuckled.

"Cowardly Pianos," he said. "They're just Cowardly Pianos."

5

A sour, angry screech of a note on the mad piano in my mind opened my eyes and had me grabbing my .38 on the night table and rolling onto the floor even before I knew why I was reacting. I found myself on my knees, facing the door to the room. The chair I had propped under the knob was flat on its back. The door itself had been transformed. I got off my knees and opened the unlocked door in time to see a carpenter whistle his way down the hall.

I closed the door, picked up the chair, and realized that I not only needed glasses to read with but that my animal alarm system was beginning to fail me. It was a depressing thought. The hotel had changed the door first thing in the morning, so waking guests would not be puzzled by the strangely punctuated sight as they groped their way down to breakfast. And I, every sense alert, had heard only the last hinge being clobbered in place.

I reexamined the damned hole in the window. It didn't look like anything but a hole in the window. I put the cool handle of the .38 against my forehead and felt my stubbly face. I had things to do, but before I did them I had to answer the knock at the door behind me. "Who is it?"

"Security," came the answer.

Before I could open the door or say "Come in," he used his passkey and came in.

"Come in," I said.

The talc had worn off his face. He looked tired and a lot

older, but the lightweight jacket and derby hat gave him a kind of Pat O'Brien look. Or maybe Oliver Hardy would be more appropriate. "I'm going off duty now," he said, looking at my soiled underwear and the pistol in my hand. "When I get back at midnight, I expect you to be gone, Peters."

"I thought we were pals," I said, reaching for my pants. "And what happened to your Irish accent? You lost it."

"I put it back in my pocket," he said, backing me up so I had to dance to get my second leg in my pants. "I'll get it out the next time I want to impress a tourist. Now the reason we are not friends, Mr. Detective from Los Angeles, is that you did some lying to me in the early hours of this morning. Maybe it was your final April Fools' Day joke of the night, but this is the day after and I'm feeling tired. This ship does not rock while I'm at the helm. I've got a police department pension and a modest income from this job. I've got a married daughter and three grandchildren. I'll show you their picture."

He pushed back his coat, pulled his wallet out of his back pocket, and opened it. I had my pants on so I could stand up and take a look at the photograph he held out for me. The kids were two girls and a boy. The boy looked like "Security."

"Nice-looking kids," I said, handing back the wallet and reaching for my shirt.

"Damn right," he said, shoving the wallet deep into his rear pocket.

"Look, Security . . ." I started.

"Name's Carmichael, but you don't have to bother remembering it, because you won't have to use it again. Just before you checked in yesterday, you tried to get our desk clerk Sudsburry to let you look at the guest register for the last month or two. Then you tell some tale about Albert Einstein being a relative."

"I didn't say he was a relative," I countered, starting to button my shirt and remembering my stubbly face. "I said I was working with him, which I am, or *for* him on a case. I don't know where Sudsburry got the relative bit."

"Maybe it had something to do with relativity," said Carmichael. "I don't know, but this A.M. one of the cleaning crew found the guest registers for the past three months on the floor of the ladies' room. Beginning to sound like a coincidence to you, Peters?"

I pushed the bed out of the way so I could get into the bathroom. He followed me through the door.

"A coincidence," I agreed, squeezing some Burma-Shave out of the tube and into my palm. I was almost out of shaving cream. I'd have to remember to save the tube. Too damn many things to remember.

"Then someone decides to take target practice on your door," Carmichael went on. In the mirror over my shoulder I could see him tilt his derby back. Maybe he was getting ready to ask, "Getting up in the world, ain't ya, Rico?" I had an answer for that.

"Coincidence?" I tried as I shaved.

"A crock." Carmichael's right hand gripped my shoulder. He was a good sixty or sixty-five but had the grip of a beat cop who had killed many an hour doing tricks with his nightstick. "I don't care what's what or who's who or why's why. Be gone when I come back on at midnight."

"Midnight," I said without wincing, as I held my Marlin razor away from my face.

Carmichael let go of my aching shoulder and went out the bathroom door and out of sight. I heard the door to the room open. "Oh, and the room is still on the house," he called. "My word is good."

The door closed and I finished shaving. I put on my blue tie with the white stripes. It was either that or the black one with the pink roses. Neither one went with my brown suit.

I ran my fingers through my hair, stood on the bed, put my .38 in the ceiling fixture, and then got down. I moved the bed back near the window and looked up. The gun didn't show. Then I went out to breakfast.

I picked up a New York *Times* for three cents and took it into the restaurant coffee shop, where I ordered a stack of pancakes for a quarter and a cup of coffee. There was good news and bad news in the paper, and some I couldn't decide on. The good news was that Pee Wee Reese got married in Daytona Beach, and General Grigorenko not only vowed that the Nazis would never take Moscow but that a Russian offensive would soon begin to drive the Germans out of Russia. The bad news was that the Japanese were moving up the Bataan Peninsula.

The bad news was that another ship had been torpedoed by Nazi subs. The good news was that a baby had been born on one of the lifeboats and was doing well.

"Look on page three, right-hand column," came a man's voice behind me. I turned and saw this chunky guy with a false-tooth smile, pointing over my shoulder with his chin. I turned to page three.

"Right there," he said, inching closer. "Australia is drafting married men up to the age of thirty-five and unmarrieds up to forty-five."

"So?"

"So?" he said. "So even if they start that here, people like you and I are safe. Some people fall between the cracks. We fell between the wars."

"I'm forty-three," I said.

"Hell you say," he said, backing off. "You look . . ."

"And I've got two sons in the Pacific right now," I added, putting down the *Times* and turning to face him.

"No offense, no offense," the chunky guy said, backing off, hands up. "Just idle chatter. Got a brother in the navy myself. I got a bad ticker too."

"And flat feet?" I asked menacingly.

"Flat feet, sure," he said. "Four-F even if I wasn't forty-six."

The son-of-a-bitch was two years younger than I was. This was turning into a depressing day and it wasn't even ten o'clock. I turned back to my coffee and paper and made my plans, while the artful dodger slipped away.

Ten minutes later I stood in front of Room 1324 and knocked. No answer. I knocked again. Alex Albanese was out. I pulled the metal band from my wallet, checked the corridor, and then went to work on the lock. Five minutes later I still wasn't in. I was about to find another plan when a cleaning woman came down the corridor, humming "Make Believe." I pulled out the key to my room, fumbled at the door, and dropped the key. When she was about ten feet away, I clumsily kicked the key under the door. "Damn," I yelped, pretending not to see her.

"What you do?" she asked, halting her cart of towels.

"Can you believe it?" I said with a bitter laugh. "I kicked my key under my door."

"I'll let you in," she said.

She was a rotund, tiny woman with her hair back in a bun. Her chubby fingers pulled a passkey out of her apron, and she stepped in front of me to open the door. It popped open and I reached down quickly to retrieve my key.

"Thanks," I said, stepping in.

"Be careful with those," she said, returning to her cart. "People pull 'em right out of your pocket, they do."

"I'll be careful," I said, closing the door. And I meant to be.

6

Albanese was neat. According to the register, he had been at the Taft for almost two months. There was almost nothing in sight to show that Room 1324 was even occupied. I had been in the hotel only one night and my room was a war zone of broken doors, windows, clothes all over the place, tooth powder and shaving cream staining the sink. The one trace of an inhabitant in 1324 was a newspaper article taped to the mirror in the bathroom. The article indicated that Einstein and Paul Robeson would be performing at a benefit at the Waldorf in three days.

I checked the drawers and found out that Albanese didn't have a gun, brass knuckles, or anything more dangerous than hotel stationery. He did have an assortment of clean clothes all neatly laid out in the drawers, most of it purchased in London. I also discovered that he wore size-32 underwear and shirts with a size-14 neck. Unless he was a Dingka tribesman, I outweighed Albanese, which gave me some comfort as I sat down to wait and continued to read my newspaper. There were a lot of plays to see with people like Eddie Cantor, Gertrude Lawrence, Danny Kaye, and Luise Rainer. Serge Koussevitsky even had the Boston Pops at Carnegie Hall a few blocks from the hotel, but what got me was the show at the Paramount in Times Square. The movie was *My Favorite Blonde* with Bob Hope. On stage, Tommy Dorsey, his trombone, Frank Sinatra, Buddy Rich, Ziggy Elman, Jo Stafford, and the Pied Pipers. If I didn't get killed, I'd find time to get to the Paramount. I hummed "Moonlight on the Ganges" through twice before I heard the key in the door.

I shut up, got up, and moved into the washroom out of sight of the door. Albanese wasn't singing when he came in. I reached over and took down the newspaper clipping. Then I quietly stood in the doorway of the bathroom and watched him walk to the window, look outside, and turn to the telephone next to the bed. He was somewhere in his twenties, thin, dark hair combed straight back. He had a thin mustache and not much of a chin. When he picked up the phone I also learned that he had an English accent, not quite Leslie Howard, but not far from it.

"Yes," he said, "I'd like Ardmore six-five-oh-oh, please."

I hoped I could remember the number. I couldn't move enough to write it down and attract his attention.

"Ah," Albanese said when someone came on the line, "Angela, would you be a good girl and cover for me? I'll be a few minutes late for rehearsal. Tell him I had a call from my mother about the Blitz or something. Blame the Jerries. . . . I know . . . Yes, you are right, no more than half an hour. Promise."

He hung up, his back to me, and said, "Did I sound persuasive? I mean, would you have covered for me with that call?"

"Hard to say," I said, stepping into the room and gauging a leap over the single bed in case he turned with a handful of hardware. "Women sometimes go for that helpless, spoiled-little-boy act. The accent helps too. You really English?"

"Absolutely," he said, turning to face me. "Family from Cornwall. Father's an apothecary, mother's a schoolteacher. We go back a hundred years when my great-great-great-grandfather came over from Naples to peddle pornography to the few literate Anglicans." He looked me up and down and I held up the newspaper clipping.

"I'm an actor," he explained, moving to the wooden chair

near the window and sitting to face me. The light caught him from behind. Nice effect.

"You're also a writer," I said, watching his hands and stepping forward. I dropped the clipping on the dresser and pulled the threatening letters to Einstein out of my pocket. No reaction. I handed him one of the letters. "You wrote that."

He glanced at the letter and nodded with an amiable smile.

"Indeed," he said, handing the letter back. "Normally, I don't write with quite so steady a hand, but I wanted to be sure the camera would pick up each letter, each word. I rather saw the letters as I see my performances."

"Why did you write them?" I asked, hovering over him.

He looked up and the smile twitched. He also turned and lost the dramatic effect of the lighting. "Didn't Connie put you up to this? This *is* one of Connie's jokes, isn't it? I mean, you look like a gangster out of . . . Conrad didn't send you, did he?"

He tried to get up but I put my hands on his shoulders and pushed him back. The light had definitely failed him now.

"See here," he said, his cheeks turning red, "if you're from one of those collection agencies, I won't put up with your breaking into my room. Just give me the bill and I'll make partial payment and the rest when the show I'm in . . ."

"Why did you write those letters?" I said, ready to push him back down. He bounced as if to try again and sat back.

"I don't understand." He almost wept.

"Neither do I, but if you answer some questions, one of us may be able to figure things out. The letters?"

"For the movie," he said.

"The movie?"

"Columbia Pictures," he said with mock exasperation. "They hired me."

"Columbia Pictures hired you to threaten Albert Einstein?"

I had dealt with actors before, all kinds, even looney ones who didn't make sense and loonier ones who did, so I was prepared for a long morning, but I didn't want it any longer than it had to be. I tried to look angry and impatient. Maybe I succeeded.

"Yes," Albanese bleated. "I was hired to star in a two-reel short, *Axes to the Axis*. I was a deluded young American who threatens Albert Einstein. After meeting Einstein, I learn the error of my ways and turn in the Fifth Columnists."

"That is a . . . " I began and then changed direction. "They actually shot this movie?"

"Yes, in a loft near the Village," cried Albanese. "I say, I really can do an American accent quite well. I really can. Listen, 'Can one of you guys stop talking and hand me the catchup?'"

"Yeah," I said. The accent stunk. "Why did you actually have to write the letters?"

"Authenticity, verity," he explained. "The camera actually filmed me as I wrote."

I had a feeling Columbia wasn't at the bottom of this, but it was damned hard to believe that Nazis or anyone else had actually gone through with making a movie, just to set up a simple-minded fall guy like Albanese. "How did the movie come out?" I asked.

"I haven't seen it yet," Albanese said, trying to stand up again. This time I didn't stop him. "The editing takes time, but Mr. Povey said that as soon . . ."

"Who is Mr. Povey?"

Albanese walked over to the mirror in the bathroom and his voice echoed back, "The director, Gurko Povey. He came here to escape the Nazis. He's done magnificent films in Europe."

"Name one you've seen," I said, following him to the bathroom. "No, I'll make it easier. Just name one."

Albanese paused in his examination of his hair but didn't look away from his reflection as he threw his hands out and sighed with undisguised contempt for my lack of knowledge of the European cinema. "I don't remember exactly," he said.

"Something to do with Grungecht or Groomlicht or something like that. They're all in German."

"Was someone on Gurko Povey's crew a big guy with close-cropped white hair?" I asked, watching him watch himself.

"That's a reasonable description of Mr. Povey himself. I tried calling him Herr Povey but he preferred the Anglicized form of address."

"Naturally," I said. "So, how many people were involved in making this movie?"

Albanese finished his inspection of himself and turned to me. He thought he had had enough. "Look here, you break into my room, push me around, ask all manner of ridiculous questions about my career and explain nothing. I'm late for a rehearsal and I can't be . . ."

But he could be. As he tried to walk past me on the "be," the fingers of my right hand caught his neck.

"Actor, you are in trouble," I whispered, watching him turn pink. "Those letters were sent to Albert Einstein. They are threatening letters. And you are an idiot. Now I'm going to let you go and you are going to answer my questions. Try to blink your eyes if you understand."

His face was turning white but his eyes fluttered. I took my fingers from his throat and watched him go through the recovery-from-choking routine. He overacted. I felt sorry for him. He had no future in the theater. Movies, maybe.

"My God," he gasped, staggering to the bed and flopping back. "My God, you've damaged my larynx." Then something even worse struck him. He sat up, his mouth dropped open, and out came, "Then I'll probably never see the film. No one will ever see *Axes to the Axis*."

"There probably wasn't any film in the damn camera," I said, walking to the bathroom and filling a spotless glass with tepid water. I let the truth sop in and came back with the water. He took it and drank and then gave me the glass. I put it down and waited for more light to dawn in his feeble brain.

"Then you must be the police or the FBI or something," he said.

"I'm 'or something,'" I told him. "I'm something that wants answers."

As it turned out, he was someone who was now quite willing to give me the answers I wanted. Ten minutes later I knew that he could take me to the loft where the film had supposedly been made, that he had a bone or something missing from his hip, which kept him from being drafted, and that he had a small role in an upcoming version of *Othello*, which was in rehearsal. He gave me rough descriptions of the camera operator and the sound man on *Axes to the Axis* and promised that he could identify them. In return I promised that Einstein wouldn't give him the opportunity to play an extended engagement in prison. Albanese thought that was awfully good of me and agreed that when rehearsal was over at six I could meet him. He gave me the address and I let him go.

I went back to my room and put in a call to Einstein. He answered the phone himself with a "Yes?" and I told him what I had discovered.

"You believe this Albanese?" Einstein asked softly.

"Yes," I said and tried out the description of Povey on him.

"Who knows?" the scientist said. "It sounds like so many people. Dreams, formulas, these I remember with clarity for decades. I can almost not erase them from my mind. They clutter, come back when I call for something else, but people I forget, faces I forget. They change too quickly. I'm sorry."

"That's all right," I said. "I'll keep on this."

"Without getting killed."

"Without getting killed," I agreed. "The name of that neighbor of yours, the one across the street, where the FBI is staying. You know it?"

"His name? No."

"I want to get the phone number over there. Is there any way . . ."

"The number is Essex three-four-six-nine," said Einstein

immediately. "To me he was Essex three-four-six-nine. It was easier to remember than his name."

"Thanks," I said. "Your cold sounds better."

"There is improvement," he said, with a slight sniff.

We hung up and I called Essex 3469 and on the fifth ring got Spade or Archer. I couldn't tell which. The line was bad. "Yes," he said.

"This is Peters," I said.

"His name is Povey," came the voice. "He's not German, he's Hungarian. If he wanted to kill you, he would have."

"First name Gurko," I threw in.

"Not bad," he answered appreciatively. "You've been talking to the actor. We thought it would take you a couple of days to track him down."

The window was still broken and I had till midnight before Carmichael the house detective put up the No Trespassing sign. I needed help.

"It's been nice chatting with you, Peters," the voice crackled.

"Hold it," I shouted. "If you know about Albanese and Povey, why don't you pull them in, lock Povey up? I could have been killed. Einstein could get killed."

"Maybe half a million people or more can get killed in this war," he said gently. "We pull in one Povey and lose a network, a whole bunch of spies. We've got our eyes on him, nearsighted though they may now be. Look, I've got to get back to Archer for lunch. We're watching Einstein for you. Go ahead and chase Povey, maybe nail him. You've got no connection to the Bureau or the police. They'll figure you for what you are, a private detective on a case."

"I could get killed," I repeated.

"Soldiers are dying every day over two oceans," he said without sympathy. "Anything else?"

"What's the name of the guy whose house you're in?"

"May, Stephen P. May. Why?"

"Does Essex three-four-six-nine sound easier to you?"

"Goodbye, Peters," he said and hung up.

I adjusted my shoulder holster, checked my .38, put on my jacket, and looked in the mirror. I looked like an extra in *Little Caesar,* one of Arnie Lorch's boys. I took off the holster, put it back in my suitcase, and hid the pistol in the light fixture again. The hell with it. I had nothing I could think of to do before six, so I went to the Paramount matinee, ate popcorn and watched Bob Hope get chased by spies. I didn't like the part where the big blonde in the movie gets killed with a knife hidden in a fake snowball while she sings, "Palsy-Walsy." It wasn't funny. Maybe it wasn't supposed to be. A lot of the jokes were lost. The Paramount was filled with girls in short skirts, who should have been in high school on a Thursday afternoon. The girls weren't interested in Bob Hope. They were interested in talking.

When the movie ended, the girls, hundreds of girls, let out a scream. With the lights on I looked around. I was the only male in the theater. Hell, I was the only adult in the theater except for Gurko Povey, who sat absolutely still about ten rows behind me. He was wearing a white suit. He didn't want to be missed. Our eyes met. It was not love at first sight. His hands were folded on his chest and I wondered if he was hiding a snowball with a knife in it. I smiled at him. He didn't smile back, but the girl behind him, her hair done up in curls and a white ribbon, thought I was leering at her. She curled back her lip in distaste, nudged her sorority sister and they both looked at me. I shrugged and pointed at Povey. They looked at him while music started on the stage and Ziggy Elman trumpeted "My Little Cousin." I kept looking back at Povey over my shoulder. The son-of-a-bitch didn't blink. His hair looked even whiter in the theater light, especially with the white suit he was wearing. I was missing the show and the girls were getting restless. One girl on my right who was probably about thirteen but could have passed for sixteen, if she hadn't been wearing so much makeup, shoved her elbow into my ribs and hyperventilated, "He's coming. Oh, my God.

He's coming." Then she looked at who she had poked and got
a little frightened.

"He's coming," I said.

She pulled away from me into the corner of her seat and
looked at the stage. From the reaction in the crowd one might
have expected the second coming of the Messiah. The girls
stood up, hundreds of them, but Povey didn't. I lost sight of
him in the mob. In the noise he could have shot me with a
machine gun and no one would have noticed or cared. I
turned around, slouching to protect my back but not my head,
and listened to Frank Sinatra sing "You'll Never Know." The
kid next to me was crying. It was a religious experience.
When a group in front of me parted for a second like the Red
Sea, I caught a glimpse of Sinatra. He was wearing a grey suit
with big shoulders. He looked skinny and the big bow tie on
his neck made him look even skinnier. He held on to the mi-
crophone and sang, his eyes darting around at the wave of
fluffy-sweatered response to each line. He looked as puzzled
by the crowd as I was. Then the sea closed. I crouched and
made my way down to the aisle, excusing myself as I went,
catching knees in the face, clunks on the head, and comments
like "Dirty old . . . ," "Some kind of . . . ," "Masher." The
girl who said "Masher" actually screamed it, but no one could
hear her over the roar of applause and other shrieks as Frankie ended his song and said "Thank you."

When I made it to the aisle, I stayed low. A few girls
glanced at me but they weren't going to miss a second of
Frankie, who launched into "The Continental." I scuttled to
the back of the theater and stood up looking for the seat
where Povey was sitting. In this game, I wanted to be behind
him and I wanted him to know it. The problem was that I
didn't have a gun and I was sure that he did. I spotted his
head of white hair when Sinatra finished his fifth song,
thanked us all, and left the stage. The crowd called for him,
screamed for him, wept for him, but Tommy Dorsey adjusted
his glasses, cradled his trombone, and tried to explain that

they had a schedule and two more shows to do that day. The girls were not sympathetic, but after a while they calmed down to whimpers. When Dorsey began to play, Povey turned and looked directly at me, no hesitation. I would have felt better if he had smiled. I would have felt angry, but he didn't smile. He just stared at me unblinking. It scared hell out of me, but I smiled at him, turned, and went through the exit door as Buddy Rich went mad on the drums and distracted the female teen army.

It was raining on Times Square, raining and dark. Thunder clapped and I went over my choices. I could try to follow Povey, but he would be ready for that, probably even wanted it. I could get away from him if he was going to keep following me, that wouldn't be a problem. Or I could hide in some doorway or alley and jump out at him and have it out in front of two or three thousand people running past in the downpour. None of the possibilities appealed to me. I decided to go get that shoulder holster and then have the meeting with Povey. I turned left instead of right in case Povey was not alone. Left took me away from the direction of the Taft. I ran down a street, I think it was Forty-fourth, and looked back over my shoulder. No one was following me. The rain had cleared the street of most pedestrians, though there were a few with umbrellas. No one was running behind me. I kept running and made another turn. The sky went mad and I ducked, soaking, into a small delicatessen.

The place was packed with people nibbling the minimum and waiting for the rain to let up. I spotted a stool open at the counter and went for it, just beating out a mailman who muttered something under his breath. I pretended not to hear him and straddled a stool that faced the door. There was no wall behind me but I wasn't Wild Bill Hickok either.

"Shoot," came a woman's voice. I looked up at the scrawny waitress, who had her pencil and pad poised as she waited. I grabbed the menu and ordered the chopped liver on rye and a Pepsi.

"Check," she said and shuffled away.

I watched the door, smelled the food and bodies seeping from the rain, and felt sleepy, but I had miles to go before I slept and a promise to keep. Besides, I was starting to get angry, damned angry. I was angry at the FBI for not helping me. I was angry at the Nazis for everything, and I was angry at myself for that moment of fear back at the Paramount. I wrapped it all together in my gut and got it ready as a present for Gurko Povey. When the sandwich came, I bolted it down fast, keeping my elbows in to avoid knocking over an asthmatic woman on my right and a short guy on my left who grunted every time he took a bite. The chopped liver was terrific. I ate it, my pickle, and all the fries, finished my Pepsi, burped appreciatively, and sloshed my way back to the street after paying my bill.

The rain had let up but somewhere over Jersey the thunder roared. The sky was still dark, maybe even darker. I trotted up Fifth Avenue and turned west again on Fiftieth. Thunder had decided on a return visit to Manhattan when I ducked under the Taft's canopy and ran up the steps and into the lobby. I was breathing hard as I looked around for Povey. He wasn't there. I went to the desk to check for messages. Sudsburry was on duty. We acted as if we didn't know each other as he checked my box and handed me an envelope.

"Life gets tedious, don't it," I said.

"I wouldn't know," he said and turned to another customer.

I tore open the envelope and read: TRY TO FORGIVE ME. PAULINE. I stuffed the letter into my damp pocket and went for the elevator. I had a gun to get, an actor to meet, and a scientist to save. I felt like telling somebody but there wasn't anybody to tell except the little woman operating the elevator. What the hell. Maybe this was a lifelong resident of the big city who would be happy to cluck a little sympathy for a visitor. The elevator came to a stop and the doors opened.

"You want to hear something?" I said to the woman as I stepped forward into the corridor.

"Sure," she said, looking up at the flashing lights of her elevator panel, her yellow hair piled high and stiff, her dreams someplace else. "How about a few bars of something from *Die Fledermaus*?"

The doors closed and I was alone in the hall with the last echo of New York sarcasm to keep me company. I left a trail of wet prints on the way to my room. Thunder shook the building as I opened the door and stepped into the darkness. A crack of lightning turned the hotel across the street white for an instant, and I thought I saw or felt something in the room. The room went dark. I was a target against the hall light. I kicked the door shut and tried not to breathe. I thought I heard someone else breathing. It might have been someone in the next room or my own breath echoing from some corner. But it wasn't, and I knew I didn't have a chance in China of getting to the .38 in the ceiling light before Povey took target practice on my bouncing body. I sensed a figure on the bed. I didn't have time to wait for my eyes to adjust. I took a chance—a step forward and a leap onto the bed. I felt flesh and smelled something like a men's locker room.

The guy beneath me let out a yowl of pain and twisted to his right, breathing cigar-stale breath in my face. His elbow caught my jaw and I rolled onto the floor. He gurgled and went off the bed, but didn't get more than a step away toward the door when I scrambled over the bed and caught him from behind. I had my right arm around his neck and a look of pure delight on my face, which I was happy no one could see. A look like that can get you ten years at the coo-coo farm.

"No, no," he cried, and recognition pulsed through me. I let him go and reached for the light switch. It clicked on.

"Shelly," I said, looking at the crumpled, chubby figure on the floor. "What the hell are you doing here?"

"Being assaulted, assaulted," he told the wall as he adjusted his thick glasses, realized he was looking the wrong way, and found me. "Assaulted," he repeated, reaching up with a pudgy right hand to straighten the hair he did not have on top of his head. I'd seen him do that before, which had led me to the conclusion that Shelly had once not been bald. There he sat, panting and patting. He wore a dark suit, properly rumpled, and a tie coming loose at the collar. He waved my hand away and tried to get up by himself. He grunted, failed and reluctantly let me help him. Shelly Minck belonged back in Los Angeles with his dental office in the Farraday Building. I rented a small room off of Shelly's office and maintained a cooperative arrangement. He messed up messages to me and I complained about the unsanitary conditions of his dental practice.

I leaned back against the wall and watched Shelly stagger to the one small upholstered chair in the room. He sat with a thud and pointed to his neck. "You did this."

"Heredity and overeating did that," I said.

"I mean the marks," he cried, pointing furiously. "You tried to strangle me."

"What are you doing here, Shell?"

"I could be marked for life," he rambled on. "Have to wear a scarf like . . . like . . ."

"Captain Midnight?" I asked.

"Captain Midnight's on the radio," Shelly said in exasperation. "Who the hell knows if he wears a scarf?"

"He's a pilot. Pilots like to have a scarf billowing out when they ride in an open-cockpit plane," I said. "What are you doing here, Shell?"

"Water," he gasped. "I need water."

I got him a glass of water, which he took and greedily gulped down.

"More," he said.

I got him another glass.

"More," he said again.

"No more, Shell. What are you doing here?"

"I was taking a nap, an innocent nap. I just flew in. I'm

tired. I came to see a friend, take a nap and what does he do? He assaults me. Isadora Duncan, she was the one with a scarf. It got tangled up in something."

"How did you get in my room? And how did you know I was at this hotel, in New York?"

He reached into his jacket pocket for an answer and came up with one of his cigars and a wooden match instead. He coughed a few times, lit it, and belched out a plume of grey smoke. It made him feel much better. "I called you at home before I left. Gunther told me you were here. I called when I got to the airport," he explained. "Asked what room you were in. When I got here, I went to the desk, said I was you, told the guy the room number and said I lost the key. He gave me a spare. I tried to call you first but you weren't here."

He sucked at the cigar, an overgrown baby with a brown pacifier. The room was beginning to smell like his office.

"What are you doing here? I keep asking the same question in something like English and I get . . ."

"Meeting," he said. "Well, sort of a convention of dentists. New techniques in dental treatment. Over at the Savoy-Plaza on Fifth Avenue."

I kicked off my shoes and climbed on the bed. Shelly smoked and watched and I asked a reasonable question. "And Mildred didn't mind? Just said, 'Sheldon, take two or three hundred bucks, get on a plane, go to New York and have a good time'?"

"It was Mildred's idea," Shelly said pointing his cigar at me. I responded by getting my .38 down and pointing it at him. "That's not funny, Toby."

My detective's experience told me that if Mildred Minck was not only letting her husband go to New York alone, but giving him money for the trip, her motive was not one of good will. I considered that Mildred might be having an affair with the plumber or milkman, but I knew Mildred too well to imagine her approaching or being approached by any man I had ever seen. It would bear further thought, but first I had to deal with my chubby and unwelcome guest.

"The war," Shelly said, "is great, marvelous."

"We're all enjoying it," I said, sitting on the bed and checking the pistol.

"I don't mean that. I don't mean that," he said. "The war is terrible, terrible, but war dentists are bringing back new experience, new gadgets are being invented that we can use on the home front."

"War dentists?" I said, putting down my weapon and removing my jacket to strap on my shoulder holster.

"You know, Toby, you know. Damn, my neck still hurts. You should be more careful," he said, searching his pink neck for sore spots.

"Well, Shell," I said, adjusting my holster and inserting my pistol, "it's been great talking to you. Have a nice time at the dental disaster meeting and I'll see you back in L.A."

"What? What?" Shelly got himself out of the chair after three tries. "I've got some time. I can help with whatever you're working on. I've helped before, remember?"

I took the dentist's arm and guided him toward the door. "Remember our agreement," I reminded him. "I don't pull teeth and you don't shoot people."

"You're going to shoot somebody?" he asked around the cigar he had stuck back in his mouth. "I knew it. The holster, the gun. You've got a case here."

"No, I'm on vacation." I shoved him to the door and got it open.

"Not for one minute do I think you're on vacation here," he said. "Not one minute. Not even a second."

"Goodbye, Sheldon," I said, ushering him into the hall.

"Not even a lunch together? A breakfast? A show? We could have great times here, Toby. I know New York, I went to school here once."

He looked pathetic, a round lump in the hall all dressed up

with no place to go but a dental convention. I almost felt
sorry for him, but I remembered the times he had almost got
me killed and my sympathy faded. Then I got an idea.
"Where are you staying, Shell?"

"Me?"

"No," I sighed. "Paul Muni."

He looked around for Paul Muni but there was no one in
the hall but him and me.

"I'm not staying anywhere yet," he bleated. "My suitcase is
in your room."

"How about we share a room right here in the Taft?" I
asked, putting on my best smile and holding the door open for
him to return. Carmichael had given me till midnight, but I
needed more time than that to work on Albanese.

Shelly took a tentative step back toward me, his cigar held
out like a protective sword. "Share?"

"Right. You go down, get a double room in your name,
and we share. I'll even pay for the room."

Shelly adjusted his glasses and stepped forward to squint at
me. "You are not an easy person to understand, Toby. Do
you know that? Are you aware of that?"

"It's part of my attraction," I said. "Let's get your suitcase.
I'll pack. If you have trouble getting a room, tell them you're
FDR's dentist and he's planning to stop by and see you."

"They won't believe that," he said, following me back into
the room. "Hey, there's a hole in your window?"

"You noticed. Another reason to get another room."

"And I can maybe help you with this case you're on," he
said, hurrying over to the far side of the bed to retrieve his
case.

"We'll see, Shell. We'll see."

While Shelly went off, I put on a dry pair of socks and my
last clean shirt, packed, and checked my watch. It still didn't
tell me anything. I called the desk and found out that it was
getting close to six. It was still dark outside but the thunder
had stopped. Maybe it wasn't raining. I didn't know how far it

was to the place where Albanese was rehearsing. I needed an umbrella.

Shelly came back ten minutes later, pink and glowing and dangling a key in front of my nose.

"I got two of them." He tossed the key to me. "I told them I was Roosevelt's polio therapist. See, I can think on my feet too."

"You sure can, Shell. Let's go."

I didn't take Carmichael up on his offer to pay my bill. I wasn't through at the Taft. Carmichael had laid down a challenge. Besides, Povey had taken his shot at me here and Albanese was staying here. I got a receipt and checked out after leaving a message at the desk for Carmichael. It was simple: "Watch your back and your pension. I checked out." I went out the front door. It was drizzling but lightly. I went around the block, went into the side entrance, and took the service elevator up to the twelfth floor. When I went into Room 1234 I could hear Shelly singing off-key and loud. I dropped my suitcase on one of the beds and looked into the bathroom. Shelly was sitting in the tub smoking and scrubbing the top of his head with Ivory soap. He was also singing "When you're in love with New York" to the tune of "Begin the Beguine."

"I've got to go out for a few hours, Shell. When I come back, we can go out for dinner."

"Chinese," he shouted. Suds flowed down his forehead covering his glasses. "The native food of our allies."

His voice was raised in song as I closed the door.

7

The rain had stopped but the sky was dark when I stepped out on Seventh Avenue. The Taft doorman checked my clothes and motioned for a cab. I got in and told the driver where I wanted to go.

"That's near the Village," he said, shooting into traffic.

"Right," I said.

He took the corner on Fiftieth, almost killing a guy who looked like Herbert Hoover. Maybe it was Herbert Hoover.

"I'm not in a hurry," I said.

"Then you're the only one these days who ain't," said the cabbie. "You want to know what's wrong with the world?" he went on, looking over his shoulder at me, instead of at the traffic we were heading for on Fifth Avenue. He had a sagging face, covered with bristly white hairs, to compensate for the lack of hair on his head. He squinted at me painfully as if I were the sun.

"No," I said. "Just drive."

"A philosopher," he sighed with a giant shrug, turning around just as we were about to run a light and collide with a milk truck caught in the intersection on Fifth. He hit the brakes and turned to me again. "What's the matter, Jackson? You think you can't learn anything? You think you're too old? I'm sixty-five. Sixty-five. Can you believe that?"

"I'm seventy," I said.

"I can believe that," he said, giving me a sour stare. "Hey, you wanna talk sense or you wanna talk sense?"

"I don't want to talk at all," I said, pointing over his shoulder at the light that had just turned green. The guy in the car behind us hit his horn, and the guy behind him hit his horn, and the traffic tied up behind us all the way to Detroit hit their horns, but my cabbie didn't move.

"Hold your horses," he shouted over my shoulder through the rear window. There was no way anyone outside could have heard him. Only I was given the chance to go stone deaf. "Can you imagine that, Jackson? The Krauts decide to hit us tonight, they can come in on the noise. Patriotism, where is it? What happened to it?"

"Drive," I said. "Now."

I can be very persuasive when my nose is almost touching someone else's and the scent of breakfast overpowers that of my tooth powder. He drove, making a sharp right, and kept quiet for about ten blocks.

"Kids," he mumbled as he raced through lights, missed elusive pedestrians, and banged the heels of his hands on the steering wheel. I didn't answer him so he repeated, "Kids."

"Kids," I said.

"Yeah, whether you like it or not kids are what's wrong with this world," he bellowed. "Am I right or am I right?"

"You're right," I said, wondering how many more blocks we had to go and trying not to look at the cabbie. I watched the stores roll by, their reflections in the jigsaw puddles of rain on the street, pedestrians leaping over or dashing around the water traps.

"I'll say I'm right," the cabbie whispered to himself. "Kids. They go around saying 'solid' and 'jive' and when they like something, you know what they say?"

"'I like that,'" I tried.

"I like . . . Funny. No, they say 'murder.' Does that make you feel like puking right in the street? I ask you."

"I'm offended," I said.

"Sure you are. Who wouldn't be?"

"What about the kids in the army?" I asked, trying to catch

some addresses so I could figure out where we were. We shot
past 1023.

"Oh, the kids in the army. Well, you're gonna get technical
on me, huh, Jackson? The kids in the army," he told God, his
eyes looking upward through the roof of the cab. God would
understand and support him.

"I'm not talking about them," he spat. "I'm talking . . .
here we are. Two bucks even."

I looked around and didn't see anything, no people on the
street. There was a doorway just opposite where the cab had
stopped, lit by a single bulb. I began to think that Albanese
had given me a fake address. "Hold it," I said, getting out.

"No you don't," the cabbie said, reaching for something in
his glove compartment. I knew what I kept in my glove compartment.

"I may not be staying," I said, grabbing his arm. "Here's
the two bucks. You want a tip? You wait."

He shut up, took the two bucks, and I got out and slammed
the door. He took off without the tip, but—like Santa—as he
drove out of sight he pulled down his window and shouted, "I
hope they cut off your gazingas in this neighborhood is what I
hope."

Above the light bulb's dark metal shade I could make out
the words BERT WILLIAMS THEATRE. There was a single
wooden door under the light. I turned the handle and went in.
A stairway, worn wooden steps. I went up with it toward the
sound of voices. It reminded me of a gym I knew back in Los
Angeles. At the top of the steps of the L.A. gym sat an old
pug who knew how many letters there were in every president's name. After he collected his dime, he'd let you work
out or watch the war rejects waltz a round or two. There was
no pug at the top of these stairs, just a dark open floor, uncar-
peted and smelling a little moldy. A partly open door about
twenty feet ahead let out enough light so I could see a dark-
ened box office to my left and some benches and ash trays to
the right. There were posters on the wall. I could only make

out the one nearest the open door. It read IN DAHOMEY and had two black stick figures dancing. There was something sad about it but I couldn't tell what.

And then, from the dark shadow near the inner door a voice came, deep and a little familiar. It scared hell out of me.

"Arise, black Vengeance, from the hollow hell!
Yield up, O Love, thy crown and hearted throne
To tyrannous Hate! Swell, bosom, with thy fraught,
For 'tis of aspics' tongues."

"Hey," I said, looking for someone in the shadows, "take it easy." I let my hand ease up to my jacket, ready to go for my holster, though I had no reason to expect anything but disaster if I had to go for my pistol. About half the time I've used my gun, I was the one who got shot.

"O, blood, blood, blood!" the deep voice answered as a figure moved forward out of the shadows, a sword in his hand catching the first glint of light.

"Hey," I said, my hand inside my jacket touching the reassuring pebbled steel of my .38, "I'm looking for Alex Albanese, not trouble."

The man with the deep voice stepped into a thin yellow path of light from inside the theater. I could still see only his dark outline and the sword in his right hand.

"What?" he said.

"No trouble," I countered, holding up a hand. "Just tell Albanese I'm here."

He stepped further into the light, and I could see that he was a couple of inches over six feet and wearing dark trousers and a grey turtleneck shirt with long sleeves. He looked as if he could take care of himself even without the sword.

"There's a rehearsal going on here," he said. "This theater is closed to everyone but cast and crew." He took a step to his right and hit a switch. A trio of bulbs tinkled on overhead and I recognized the man with the sword.

"I saw *Sanders of the River,*" I said, letting my hands go back to my sides. "*The Emperor Jones,* too."

"I'm sorry," Paul Robeson said. "I try not to see them whenever possible. I must have startled you. I was rehearsing some lines in the corner when you came in. Who did you ask for?"

"Albanese, Alex Albanese," I said. "He's in your cast."

Robeson looked at me and at his sword before answering. "Oh, the Clown," he said.

"That's him," I agreed.

"No," Robeson corrected with a deep laugh. "He plays the Clown. Are you his agent?"

"No," I said. "It's a little complicated. I'm working for Albert Einstein and . . ."

The door to the theater swung open and a woman stuck her head out and looked at us. Then she said, "Paul, I think we're ready to try again."

"Just a moment," Robeson said, holding his hand up without turning to face the woman. His eyes were fixed on me. She turned and went back into the theater.

Robeson walked over to the small table in the corner, placed his sword on it, and sat on its edge. He was somewhere in his forties, but age hadn't caught up with him as it seemed to be doing with me. I had his attention and I explained the threats to Einstein, the trail to Albanese, the shots through my door, Gurko Povey. I left out Pauline Santiago and Frank Sinatra.

Robeson folded his arms, shook his head, and when I finished looked to his right, where no one was standing, his eyes on the *In Dahomey* poster. "Do you know who Bert Williams was?" he asked, not expecting an answer.

"'Nobody,'" I answered.

He looked at me, his eye movement followed slowly by his head, a gesture I figured he was trying out for Othello. "Nobody," he said sadly.

"'That's Life,'" I said.

A smile touched the corner of Robeson's broad mouth. "You have a sense of humor."

"'I Wasn't Prepared for That,'" I answered, and Robeson laughed, a deep laugh that rolled like a song. "That about exhausts the Williams songs I know."

"More than most, Negro or white," he said. "Should I trust you, Mr. . . ."

"Peters, Toby Peters. I don't know. Why not give Einstein a call and ask him?"

"I will," he said. "Spies, murder attempts. It sounds like Shakespeare."

"I wouldn't know," I said. "I'm more a Bert Williams type."

"No," sighed Robeson, "I'm the Bert Williams type. Did you know that Williams was forced to put on blackface to perform in Broadway shows, a Negro forced to put on black-face? That's what I had to do when I was in those movies. Oh, not literal blackface, but the mask of the noble savage. I'm sorry, I'm a bit weary. You know that Einstein and I are doing a benefit on Sunday to raise money for refugee children?"

"I know," I said. "I don't want to scare you, but I think the Fahre or whoever Povey is with wouldn't mind taking both you and Einstein out with one shot."

"A prominent Jew and a prominent Negro," he said, with a shake of his head.

"Maybe the most prominent Jew and Negro in the world right now."

"And maybe you think I might need some protection too?" he asked, pushing away from the table with a knowing look and taking a step toward me. "And maybe I might retain your services?"

It was my turn to shake my head. "Einstein is picking up the tab. Two for the price of one. I've got my assistant here with me, in case things get a little too spread out." I tried not to conjure up images of "my assistant," the thick-lensed Shelly in a bath full of bubbles, singing war songs.

Robeson looked at me again with something that might have been cautious respect. "What do you know about Othello?"

"A hell of a fellow?" I said. "Shakespeare, a rhyme. A small joke."

The cautious respect faded a bit and I could see him considering a new course of action. He looked a little tired as he rubbed his forehead and glanced toward the door to the theater. Voices came through, echoing, "Then put up your pipes in your bag, for I'll away. Go, vanish into air, away!" It was Albanese.

"He's not very good," I commented.

"No," agreed Robeson, "he is not. We'll probably have to replace him. I find it difficult to do such things, but the show is too important to tolerate even one minor mediocre performance. I've done *Othello* before, a decade ago that felt like a century. It means something different to me now. The Shakespeare scholars tell me about love and obsession. I see a dark-skinned man who is used by his society, honored by his society, treasured by his society for his skills, praised to his face and schemed against behind his back, hated for his love of a fair-skinned woman, driven to madness and despair. A man who can fight and love but who is too naive to understand the hatred his very presence brings. And yet he stands forth, enters the land of the stranger, suffers the hatred, proves himself, and kills himself when the world of hatred overwhelms him." Robeson paused, looked up at me, cocked his head to one side as if it were my turn.

"Remind you of anyone?" I asked.

"Remind you?" he asked back.

"Joe Louis," I said.

Robeson laughed again, louder than before, and a trio of actors, two men and a woman, came running into the alcove to see who the comedian was. They looked at Robeson and looked at me. They didn't see anything funny in me. I shrugged, agreeing with them.

"Mr. Peters is my guest at this rehearsal," he said. "He will sit quietly and wait for his friend Mr. Albanese." And then to me, "Perhaps we'll talk again later."

"Don't forget your sword," I said as he turned to the puzzled trio.

"No," he said. "I'll not forget my sword."

He led the group back into the theater and I followed. The theater was more like a loft where during the week old guys probably set up card tables and played poker for nickels. The folding chairs were all over the place and in bad shape, the stage a raised platform about a foot above the worn wooden floor. There was light on the stage but not much in the audience section. On stage, Albanese was talking to a woman with long hair, who was trying to get him to do something. He was nodding his head in affirmation, but there was no look of understanding on his face.

"Irony," the woman said, pushing up the sweater sleeves that refused to stay there and immediately began to creep back down. "Irony, Alex. Are you familiar with irony?"

"Well, I . . ." Albanese began looking around for someone to supply a definition and saw a sea of unhelpful faces, including mine.

"Try it this way," the woman said, working on her sleeves again as if she had a tub of dishes or a floor to scrub. "You are just delivering a message, but you are a clown, a clown who can't help making little jokes. When you mention wind instruments and say, 'Thereby hangs a tale,' you are making a joke about the word 'tale.' You are suggesting the word 'tail,' *t-a-i-l*. It is a dirty joke about wind instruments, tails, sexual parts. Do you understand?"

"Sexual parts . . ." Albanese mumbled, looking around for help. I didn't know what they were talking about, so I was out of it, but no one else seemed inclined to help either. He brushed back his hair with his right hand and said, "I see,"

but he was such a lousy actor that all assembled knew he
didn't.

"Margaret, may I?" Robeson said, handing me his sword
and striding to the stage.

Margaret held up her hands, pushed up her sleeves, and
said, "Give it a try."

"O," Robeson said, folding his arms and leaning toward
the young man playing the musician, "thereby hangs a tale."
The last four words were whispered, lasciviously, a secret
joke, a private joke. Robeson's eyes had opened widely and
looked around, as if he both wanted no one to hear the line
and wanted to be sure there was an audience to his joke.

"I've got it," Albanese said.

"Right," Margaret said with a sigh. "Then after that when
you are offering the musician money not to play, you're playing with the words. Like . . . like . . ."

"Chico Marx in *Animal Crackers* when he tells Groucho
how much he and his orchestra charge not to play," a voice
called out from the audience. It was mine.

"Right," Margaret said with a smile. "Like that."

Albanese nodded, knowingly touched his mustache, and
did the scene again. He strained to please the star, the director, the audience with a delivery that made no sense to him.
He was even worse than the last time.

Margaret pushed her sleeves up again and said, "Let's call
it a day, Paul?"

"It's a day," said Robeson.

"Thanks everyone," she said aloud. "We'll see you all in
the morning. Usual time. I understand it's raining out there,
so cover up and don't catch colds." She walked to a table at
the back of the platform, and Robeson followed her. They
put their heads together and began whispering. Everyone but
Albanese knew that they were deciding his fate.

Men, women, girls moved past me, talking about where
they were going to eat, who was walking to what subway.
Chairs got moved. People laughed, one woman said, "Jose

wouldn't do that," and they all filed out through the door, down the steps, all except Robeson, the woman with the sleeves that wouldn't stay up, me and Albanese, who hopped from the platform and strode over to me, with a simple smile on his face.

"Went rather well, don't you think?" he asked.

"Sounds like something Custer said just before Sitting Bull's last charge at the Little Big Horn," I answered.

"Sitting Bull? I don't think . . ."

"I know," I said. "Shakespeare can wait. Let's get going."

I didn't know how far this place was where Albanese had made the movie. As it was, it was probably too late to find someone there. I might have to do some illegal entering and I preferred to do it while I was reasonably awake.

"Just a moment," Albanese said, holding up a finger. "Left my jacket backstage. Shan't be more than a tick or two."

He left me there holding my sword, crossed the stage, and exited. Robeson looked away from his conversation and toward the door with a slight shrug. The woman talked furiously. When Albanese came back, he was going to be an out-of-work clown.

"I'll take care of it," Robeson told the woman. "You get a table at Tony's. I'll call Essie and tell her I can't make it back to Connecticut tonight."

The woman nodded, energetically gave another tug at her sleeves, and walked wearily from the stage, grabbing a cloth coat from a chair near me. "There are days like this," she said to me and herself as she strolled past.

"Whole lifetimes sometimes," I said, saluting her with the sword.

"Tell me about it." She chuckled and went through the door.

As she exited, Albanese came back in a light jacket nearly pressed. He was all smiles and looked as if he were seeking a partner for a civilized game of bridge.

"Alex," Robeson said, walking to him.

"Yes," said Alex, smile broadening, the novice expecting to be praised by the star.

"Margaret and I think the role of the clown is not right for you," Robeson said, touching the arm of the younger man.

"Not . . . oh, I see."

"We've got a different part for you," Robeson said. "One we think is more suited to your talents."

"Let me guess," Albanese beamed. "Cassio? Roderigo? Lodovico?"

"A soldier," said Robeson softly.

"Ah," said Albanese, looking over at me to share his promotion. "A soldier. I agree. I'm much more suited to soldier than clown, but I don't recall any . . . What scenes does my character . . ."

"He has no lines," said Robeson. "But he is on stage far more than the clown. At least five scenes."

"No lines?"

"No lines," said Robeson.

"Five scenes?"

"Maybe more," said Robeson. "And you get to carry a lance."

"I can do magnificent things with a lance as prop," Albanese said, rebounding.

"We can discuss them with Margaret tomorrow," said Robeson, and then to me, "Peters, if you'd like to join us at Tony's down the street, two blocks left, you are welcome."

"Thanks, but Alex and I have an appointment. Raincheck."

"It's raining now," said Robeson. He touched Alex's arm and strode past me without looking back, a great exit.

Alex hurried toward me, excited. "Did you hear that? Did you hear?" he said, clapping his hands together. "A bigger role."

"Congratulations," I said. "Let's get going."

His hands went to his hips, and he looked like a kid doing an imitation of Errol Flynn.

"I can't wait to begin anew tomorrow," he said, but he wasn't going to begin anew tomorrow, at least he wasn't going to begin a new role tomorrow. A shot cracked from behind me, followed by two more. The first two hit Albanese. The next one pinged off of the sword I was still holding.

8

My hand was stung by the bullet that hit Robeson's sword, but I didn't drop the weapon. I hit the floor still holding it and rolled over while another shot hit a folding chair and pushed it back, as if it had been kicked by an angry elephant. It toppled another chair, but the domino effect stopped there.

Albanese wasn't screaming. He was either dead or close to it, and my chances for future appearances in the theater didn't look too good either. I rolled to my right behind a clump of chairs, turned, and got to my knees. Another shot went past me. I got up and made a charge at the low stage, swinging the sword over my head as I plunged ahead. I swiped at the glowing light bulb dangling over the stage, caught the electrical cord above it, and brought down an electric sputtering rain that ended in near darkness. The next shot hit something metal. I turned and threw the sword at the light bulb in the socket on the rear wall. I missed. The sword clattered to the floor. It was time to try for my .38. I started to go for it, but an accented voice came out of the darkness.

"No, no, no, Peters. Don't touch it. You'll live a few precious minutes longer if you stand perfectly still."

Povey stepped out of the darkness near the doorway, his Walther held out, an extension of his straight right arm, right out of the manuals for proper small arms firing and maintenance. I let my hand go back to my side.

"If you had heeded my warnings, recognized my sincere

efforts to frighten you off," he said, stepping forward, "we would not now be in this situation. This is very awkward for me."

"Hey, I feel for you."

Povey stepped even closer, the light now catching his white hair, and shook his head. "No, no you do not," he said. "Killing you, killing him solves a problem, yes, but it creates another which impedes . . . Is that the correct word, 'impedes'?"

"Sounds right to me," I said, not about to give a lesson in English to a sensitive killer with a gun in his hand.

"It impedes my real goal and opens the possibility of interference from the police, even federal agents. You are a professional who deals with such things, even though on a miserably low level, but perhaps you can appreciate my situation. My task is to dispose of certain people. I get no great pleasure in eliminating you or the actor there."

"No great pleasure," I said. "Just a small kick or two."

"You wrong me," he said. "I'm not in this for pleasure or hate. Those I work for are obsessed with hate, hate of Jews, Gypsies, Negroes. Whatever satisfaction I get is professional. I'll tell you a secret."

He looked around and put a finger to his lips to indicate silence. He was having a hell of a good time. Albanese let out a low groan. "I think the people I work for," he said, "will not win this war. I think I will have to offer my services to your side eventually, but I can wait till I'm sure how things are going. I must sense that delicate moment when it is time to have a sincere change of heart, to come to the Allies with repentance and a gift of secrets. Now I am afraid I cannot converse any longer."

He smiled, dropped his aim to my chest, and I knew I would take a leap at him, knew I would be shot before I reached him. I shifted my right foot forward, deciding to go in low, trying not to think of the bullet that would hit the back of my head or my neck or my spine.

"Keep up your bright swords, or the dew will rust them," came Robeson's voice from the doorway.

Povey turned to the door, leveling his pistol at shadows. I took two steps to the edge of the platform and leaped toward Povey, who was just bringing his Walther back toward me when I caught him, waist high. We skidded back into chairs, spraying them out as we hit. Povey clubbed me on the neck with the pistol, and I threw an awkward left into his kidney. His gun hand was near my face. I bit his hand and he yelped as we rolled over again. He didn't drop the gun, but I had to let go of the bite when he gave me an open-palmed chop to the head with his left hand.

Povey's foot caught my stomach just above the groin, and I rolled backward, coming up almost to my feet. He panted to a standing position in front of me, a film of blood on his teeth as he smiled and prepared to shoot me in the face. Something caught the light behind him and swooshed over his shoulder. Metal clanked on metal and Povey screamed, dropping his pistol. His fingers were bleeding from the slash of the sword Robeson held in his hand, ready to sweep again.

"If this were sharp," Robeson said deeply, "you'd be a one-handed man. Sit down."

Povey spat blood and I tried to stand up. Povey hissed something in German between his teeth and Robeson answered him in German. They went back and forth that way with Robeson advancing on Povey, who held his bleeding right hand with his left.

I didn't know German, but I did know the word *shvartz* which meant "black" and which came out several times in a snakelike hiss. Robeson reached forward with his free hand for Povey, who lowered his shoulder, came under the sword, and ran into the actor, who staggered back enough for Povey to see a path to the open door. He went for it and I lunged after him. I tripped over the body of Alex Albanese, rolled into a pair of chairs, and landed on my back. I lay there exhausted, listening to Povey's footsteps clack down the steps beyond the door.

"Are you hurt?" Robeson asked, kneeling at my side.

"I'm hurt," I said, "but not as much as Alex. I don't think he's dead yet. He moaned a few minutes ago."

We scuttled to Alex, who had two holes in him, one in his chest, another his neck. His eyes were closed, but he wasn't dead, not yet.

"I'll call for an ambulance." Robeson stood, then said "I've aged. Did you know I was an All-American end in football at Rutgers? I had letters in football, baseball, track and now I can't even handle a creature like that." He nodded toward the door through which Povey had escaped.

"He's a pro too," I said. "You'd better make that call for an ambulance and then get out of here. You don't need this kind of publicity."

"Don't see how I can avoid it."

"Leave that to me," I said. "It's my job."

Robeson went through the doors and left me with Albanese. I checked his pulse, tried to talk to him, got no answer. I hid my gun and holster in a prop vase on the stage and came up with what I thought was a somewhat reasonable tale for the police. It took the ambulance about fifteen minutes to get there.

While they carried Albanese off to Bellevue Hospital, a pair of cops in uniform asked me questions and suggested that I go to the hospital to have my visible bumps and bruises taken care of. They were polite when I told them that Alex and I were old friends, that I had come to pick him up for dinner after a rehearsal, and that we had stayed behind to talk about his new role in the play. A stray robber had come in. We tried to fight him off. Alex took a spray of lead and we scared the bad guy off.

The cops were sympathetic, said it wasn't a good idea to leave doors open in this neighborhood. I acted worried about

Alex after I gave them a more or less accurate description of Povey and they let me go. It's nice to be in a town where you don't have a bad reputation. It's like starting clean. It had taken me almost half a century to make the police departments of Los Angeles and its environs discount everything I uttered. New York was fresh turf.

When the cool, damp night air hit me, I felt sick. I held my face up to catch the rain and let the drizzle run off my nose and eyes. It helped. The ambulance had already gone, its siren blazing. I walked about a block away and stood in a doorway to wait. The cops left ten minutes later. I could hear their voices as they went to their car and got in. They were saying something about plans for a Billy Conn–Joe Louis rematch. The incident behind them hadn't even held their attention till they got back on the street. I waited till they had pulled away and turned the corner before walking slowly back to the theater entrance.

The cops had closed the door behind them. It was locked but with the lock of a cheap theater, a place that doesn't try to keep people out, does its best to invite people in. I opened the door with half of a nail file I kept in my wallet, went in and felt my way up the stairs and across the theater lobby. I bumped into a few things and resisted the urge to turn on lights. My neck throbbed hot as the beat of a tango in my head. I groped my way along the wall and up the slight rise to the stage. It took me about thirty seconds to figure things out, but I made my way to the vase and reached in. No holster. No gun. I fished around some more—nothing. Then I calculated the distance from the door to the back of the stage. My neck hurt, my ribs were bruised from my best out of one with Povey, and my gun was gone. Something told me to get the hell out as fast as my legs could move, but before I could act on my instincts, the lights went on and a weary voice said, "Looking for this?"

I turned and looked into the audience area, where Spade

and Archer sat on folding chairs watching my performance on
stage. Spade held up my holster and pistol, the missing prop.

"Do Duke Mantee," Spade said.

"*Petrified Forest,*" prompted Archer.

"I know," I said, stepping off the platform and reaching for
my holster and pistol. Spade held it out for me.

They both looked as if they had eaten something that dis-
agreed with them. Spade, his dyed hair sleeked back, his false
teeth a little too large even for his age, had a pained grin.
Archer, the constipated stork, seemed to have a cold.

"You know where we want to be right now?" Spade asked
as I took off my jacket and put on my holster.

"Back in Princeton, home, Florida?" I guessed.

"Even Jersey would be nice," said Archer dyspeptically.

"Even Jersey," agreed Spade. "You know where we don't
want to be?"

"Here?"

"Who says he's not smart?" Spade said to Archer.

"Not me," said Archer. "I said he was smart, put it in right
in our report."

Spade got up, ran his hand over his knees to get rid of an
imaginary crease, and looked at me as if I were his eldest son
and a disappointment to the Spade family tree.

"We had a nice assignment," sighed Archer. "Sit in that
house, look out the window, listen to the telephone, have a
sandwich or two, a nice assignment for a couple of ruptured
ducks like us. And what happens?"

"Someone threatens Einstein?" I tried.

"Wrong. You happen," said Spade, pacing back and forth,
pausing to push an upturned chair out of the way. "You flush
Povey. He starts shooting holes in hotels and police get involved. Then we get a quick reassignment because we talked
to you. We have to come here and deal with people who
shoot at each other, while two young . . ."

". . . jerkos," said Archer.

"Too mild," said Spade.

"Assholes," I tried.

"Too strong," said Spade with a wave of his hand, dismissing both the suggestions. "Whatever, two younger guys are back in that house in Princeton drinking tea and listening to 'Major Bowes' Amateur Hour' on the radio. We're now in a position where we can get shot, Peters."

"It's the job, fellas," I said. "The FBI catches bad guys. Sometimes the bad guys shoot back."

"But not at us, not anymore," sighed Archer.

"What's the use?" Spade said, turning to his partner. "It's like talking to a mummy." Then to me, "Peters, what can you tell us?"

"Joe DiMaggio's only hitting two-thirteen but the season is young."

"But we're not," countered Spade. "Tell us a story but no fairy tales. We're too old for fairy tales."

I told them and they listened, asking questions, Archer taking notes. When I was finished, they looked at each other. "I don't know," said Spade.

"Who does?" said Archer standing up. "Who does?"

I just stood waiting.

"Here's how we're going to do it now," Spade said. "We'll pick up on this Albanese story, try to find where that movie was faked, see if it can lead us to a nest of Nazi spies. We'll try to track Povey, keep a closer eye on him. You just stay with Einstein when he comes on Sunday."

"What about Robeson?" I asked.

"Doesn't sound to me like they want him, at least not yet," said Spade. "We can ask the Bureau to put someone on him, but ask is all we can do. Truth is we'd be happy to give you a free ticket home if we thought you'd take it, but we know enough about you to know that you won't, right?"

"We've been through this before," I said.

"Can't hurt to try again," said Archer. "You want a ride back to the hotel?"

I took them up on the offer and we drove back in the drizzle. Archer drove. I sat in back with Spade. Archer hummed
the Halo shampoo jingle two or three times, and then
launched into something I didn't know. It sounded like he
made it up. When we pulled up in front of the Taft, I opened
the door and Spade said, "Why don't you at least send the
dentist back home?"

"I'll try," I said. "But he has a convention in town and I
don't think he'll go before it's over. We're talking about a
dedicated man here."

"We're talking about a threat to human health who's been
on the brink of being declared a major disease," said Archer
without looking at me.

"Send him home," said Spade, showing his store teeth.

"Hey, how do I reach you if something comes up?"

"Leave a message for us at the Princeton house or call the
FBI number in the telephone book. Just give the operator
your name, and tell her to have Craig or Parker get back to
you."

"Craig and Parker?" I asked, holding the door open as I
stepped out onto Seventh Avenue.

"M. S. Craig," Spade said, pointing to his partner, and
then pointing to himself he added, "Percy Parker. But keep
calling us Spade and Archer."

"It adds a touch of romance to our humdrum lives," Archer
said wryly.

I slammed the door and they drove off. The doorman nodded as I walked up the steps. The lobby was Carmichael-free
as I headed for the house phones in the far corner. I weaved
through night traffic, took an open phone, and asked for
Room 1234.

The operator said, "Toby, is that you?"

"It's me, Pauline," I said. "How are you?"

"Distraught."

I looked around the lobby for Carmichael. A soldier who
looked about eleven stood under a painting of peasant women

at a well. The soldier was carrying a bouquet of flowers and looking around for someone. Two men, both overweight, wearing suits, were arguing about "merchandise."

"Distraught," I repeated.

"Can I meet you in the bar?" she asked. "I can get Mona to relieve me."

"I really . . ."

"Toby, please. I've got something to tell you."

"Not the bar," I said. "I'm in the room I was calling, twelve-thirty-four. Come up there."

"Who were you calling up there?" she asked. "You have someone up there, some woman up there?"

"Just Shelly," I said.

"Who is she?" Pauline asked, probably tying up phone calls that could mean the difference between Allied victory and defeat.

"He, Shelly's a he, a dentist," I explained.

"You travel with your own dentist?" she asked.

"Just connect me with the room. You can listen to the conversation if you don't believe me."

She connected me to the room and the phone rang. No answer. It rang again and again and again.

"She doesn't answer," Pauline said cattily.

"He," I corrected, "he doesn't answer, Pauline. Meet me in the room in one hour. One hour. Can I get to Bellevue Hospital and back in an hour?"

"Sure," she said, "but why . . ."

I hung up and headed for the side entrance, resisting the impulse to check my old man's watch. Time was wasting and Einstein would be coming to town in less than two days. I hailed a cab and told him to get to Bellevue Hospital as fast as he could.

"What's the hurry, someone dying or something?" he asked.

"Yeah," I answered, rubbing my tender neck.

"Who?" asked the cabbie.

"Everybody," I answered, sinking back in the seat.

"Ain't that right," the cabbie agreed and hit the gas. In spite of the weather and traffic, he got me to the hospital in less than twenty minutes. I paid him and went in.

The war had created a generation of cynics and unbelievers. Before the war you could wander into any hospital and make your way through the place until you found what or who you wanted, without people in white giving you suspicious looks or calling for uniformed guards to lead you to the emergency room exit. Now there were visiting hours and rules and safeguards and people like me to find ways around them. I came armed with scars and lumps and the look of a dazed refugee. When stopped, I was looking for Dr. Hodgdon, whom I was confident I would not run into, since he was busy at his practice almost three thousand miles away in Los Angeles. I took the professional precaution of calling the hospital switchboard from the lobby and asking what room Alex Albanese was in.

"No visitors," the operator said, phones buzzing behind her.

"No visitors," I agreed. "I want to send flowers."

"Room eight-forty-eight," she said. "But he's just come back from surgery and will not be receiving visitors or flowers until Dr. Sanchez gives his approval."

"I wouldn't think of bothering him," I said and hung up.

Three minutes later I was searching the corridors for 848 and putting on my dumb, pained act.

"Can I help you?" asked a nurse pushing a cart.

"Dr. Hodgdon," I said. "I'm meeting Dr. Hodgdon."

"I don't know . . ." She was built like a can of Campbell's Tomato Soup and no one to mess with.

"He works with Dr. Sanchez," I said. I pulled out my father's watch and ignored its misinformation. "I'm late. God, I'm late."

I showed her my bruised neck.

The nurse's face was pink, matching the little cups of pink pills on her cart. She shook her head and perambulated on.

I found 848 and had a story worked out for the FBI agent or two, or the New York Police Department cop I expected but there was no one at the door. Maybe he or they were inside. Walking toward the room, with my shoulder against the wall to keep from being seen too easily from the nurse's station at the end of the corridor, I stopped in front of 848 and walked in, closing the door behind me. There was a single light in the room, a lamp on a small table near the bed, and a tiny white radio near the lamp. There was also a thermometer in a glass of nothing and a small white towel on the table. The walls were bare, except for a third-rate reproduction of a painting of white flowers. Albanese lay there alone in the room, breathing loudly. A white blanket covered him up to the neck and something stuck out of his nose. His face was whiter than the blanket. I walked to the bed and stood over him, waiting, watching, wondering when someone would come in and find me and whether I had it in me to try to wake him. Waking him might kill him. Not waking him might kill Einstein and Robeson. I had come this far, certain that I had to get information from the third-rate actor who lay on the bed with his eyes closed and his mouth open. His teeth were neat, white, even, and real. He was young. He was stupid. He had no talent and probably wouldn't do anything in his life, if he lived, to make the world a better place, but I found myself looking down at a kid. You could have a kid his age, I told myself. If I had a kid, he wouldn't be as dumb and vulnerable as this one, I told the voice in my imagination, which sounded suspiciously like my older brother Phil, who was a police captain back in Los Angeles.

I could have kept up this conversation the way Donald Duck did with his conscience, but it wouldn't have gotten me anywhere. I'd find Povey and his pals some other way. Or maybe Spade and Archer and the FBI would find them. Maybe. I headed for the door and had my hand on the knob when Albanese said something. I moved back to the bed. His eyes fluttered and opened, but it took them a few seconds to put space and time together and a few more seconds to find me.

"Why on earth are you jutting out of the wall?" he croaked.

"I'm not jutting out of the wall," I said. "You're lying down. You're in bed, in a hospital. You've been shot."

"Shot," he repeated, as if it were a foreign word. "Shot," he said as if the word had no meaning. "With a gun?"

"A gun," I acknowledged.

His eyes closed as if he were satisfied and then opened again and found me. "Why did you shoot me?" he asked. "I'm quite parched. Might I have some water, do you think?"

"Better not till you ask a doctor or nurse," I said. "I didn't shoot you. Povey shot you."

"Directors don't shoot actors for poor performances," Alex said, his voice trailing off toward sleep.

Something moved outside the door. Voices. Someone said, "I'll check this side. You go with the post-ops."

"I'll be late for rehearsal," Alex suddenly said in panic, his eyes open wide. He looked as if he were about to sit up. "I'm a soldier now."

I held out my hands to ease him back. "Rehearsal is tomorrow," I said gently. "Your job is safe. A good soldier is hard to find."

His eyes were closed now and his voice low. I leaned over to hear him.

"Don't suppose I'm going to die or anything like that," he said.

"Not a chance," I assured him. "Doctors say you're going to be fine."

His head shook no and he smiled knowingly. "You don't survive a bullet in the brain," he said wisely.

"You weren't shot in the brain. You were shot in the heart."

"The Tin Man didn't have a heart and he lived," Albanese said knowingly as he started to fade out.

"The Wizard gave him one," I reminded him.

"And then he wept and felt pain. Is that a blessing?"

"I don't know. Alex, where was that warehouse where you did the movie, *Axes to the Axis,* Columbia? Povey directed. It's time. I've got lives to save. Describe the men who worked with him. Give me something."

"Pink gardenias under us," he said, grinning and looking at the painting on the wall across from him. The flowers weren't pink and they weren't gardenias. "We walked on pink gardenias," he muttered on. "Augustus Mutt and Jeff and Povey and I and we made a movie. Not a masterpiece, mind you, but a start. I'd really like to see that movie. But more than that, I'd like a drink of . . ."

And then he fell asleep. The door behind me started to open and I grabbed the towel from the table.

"What are you doing in here?" said a woman behind me.

"Laundry service," I said, pulling my notebook out, looking at the towel, and making a squiggle of gibberish in the spiral-bound ragged-edged notebook that had only a dozen pages left. "Lots of complaints from day shift about the condition of the towels, bedding, you name it." I turned to face the woman. She was a nurse, blonde, hair up, all in white, young, pretty, and disbelieving.

"Laundry," she said. "What laundry?"

"Hospital laundry," I said, holding up the towel. "Look at this. Holes, fringes that look like Christmas scarves. No wonder the day shift complained, but look at it from our side. Materials hard to get with everything going to the military. Good help hard to get. Trucks break down and are there parts, even service personnel?"

The nurse walked past me to Albanese, leaned over him, checked his pulse, felt his head, listened to his heart with a stethoscope, and turned to me. "I don't know how you got in here but this man is very ill. He just came up from surgery," she said, taking my arm and leading me to the door, towel still in my hand.

"I didn't know," I said. "Doctor Hodgdon said it would be all right to do my survey quietly."

We moved into the hall and she looked in both directions for help. She wasn't buying my laundry tale. I tried another one. I dropped my voice and reached into my pocket for my wallet, letting my holster show.

"Nurse, you're drawing attention to us and I'd rather you not do that. I'm Agent Archer of the Federal Bureau of Investigation. The man in there, Mr. Albanese, has been shot, possibly by a representative of the German government. My job is to keep a discreet eye on him." I flashed my Dick Tracy badge, the one my nephew Nate had given me and which I kept pinned inside my limp wallet. I didn't let her get a good look at it before I stuffed it back in my pocket and looked both ways to emphasize the importance of secrecy and my mission.

"Just come with me," she said.

Normally, I would have been happy to. Her skin was clear, her eyes a deep, dark brown, and the scent of something sweet fought to overcome hospital antiseptic and iodine.

"I'd rather not . . ." I began, and then was saved by a quivering voice from a nearby room, the door of which was partly open.

"Bedpan," the voice, male or female, I couldn't tell which, croaked out in urgency. "Quick. Bedpan," the voice repeated.

"Bedpan," I said. "I'll wait here."

The unnamed nurse with the strong grip and smooth skin let me go and hurried toward the open door. As soon as she entered, I tore down the hall to the first door marked EXIT. I was back on the street a few minutes later, massaging my neck, which was getting more sore by the minute, reminding me of Povey. I hailed a cab in front of the hospital and got in. "Taft Hotel," I said, "and I've got two questions."

The cabbie pulled into traffic. But it was late and there wasn't much in the way of traffic.

"Ask away," the cabbie said, tilting his cap back, ready to give out with New York wisdom.

"What time is it?" I asked.

"Ten to ten. Next question."

"What do you think of pink gardenias?"

"They look terrific with burgundy roses. Who're you kidding here, Jack? There ain't any such a thing as pink gardenias. I ought to know, I'm from Brooklyn."

Since the matter was now settled, I sat back and watched as another New York cabbie made a valiant attempt to kill himself and me and failed. When we got to the Taft, I gave him a fifty-cent tip for his noble effort. This time Carmichael was in the lobby, but he didn't see me before I spotted him. Using a convoy of businessmen, a flotilla of retired couples out on the town, and a squad of assorted drunks arguing about who would treat whom to drinks, I made it to the elevator and plastered myself against the rear wall, willing the doors to close. "I'm in a hurry," I told the operator. She turned and looked at me as if I were a modern painting. "Nausea," I said.

She closed the elevator doors just as Carmichael, the house dick, decided to scan the neighborhood. His eyes fell on me as the doors closed. My last glimpse was of him striding toward me with a smile I didn't like.

"Floor?" she asked, looking back at me over her glasses.

"Fourteen," I said.

She sped up to fourteen and I got out. She was closing the doors even before I cleared them. I went for the exit and down the stairs fast to the twelfth floor. If Carmichael checked with the elevator operator, she'd tell him I got off at fourteen. Carmichael might believe I was stupid and somewhere on fourteen. Or he might be stupid and think I was on fourteen. More likely he would think I got off on fourteen and went up or down within three floors. He'd peg me between eleven and sixteen, which would be right but wouldn't help him much in finding me. This was the fun part. I

knocked at the door to 1234 and got no answer. I used my key
and went in. The room was dark. I closed the door behind me
and went for the table lamp. Before I turned it on I knew
someone was in the bed. This time it wasn't Shelly.

"Pauline."

"In the flesh," she said. And she was.

Half an hour later we were lying in bed and she started to
tell me her life story. It was the price I was expected to pay.

"I was born in Queens," she began, propped up on one
elbow and watching my face to be sure I didn't doze off. "My
father worked for the dairy." Twenty minutes later she was at
the point in her tale when Mary Louise was nineteen and got
her first job at a plier factory. I was denied the dramatic conclusion of her tale by the turning of a key in the door and the
sudden appearance of Sheldon Minck, Doctor of Dental Surgery, carrying a huge and apparently heavy paper back.

"Don't explain," he said, putting the bag down on the
dresser and adjusting his glasses. "You couldn't get back for
dinner. It happens. You could have picked up a phone, but
what the hell, you were busy, right? Spies, murders. I've got a
generous heart, Toby. You know that. I can prove it."

He reached into the bag and pulled out a bottle. "Trom-
mer's White Label Malt beer," he said triumphantly. "No deposit bottles. Can you imagine that? Just throw them away.
You'd think shortages of everything, they'd want bottles
back."

Shelly glanced at me, adjusted his glasses, and waddled into
the bathroom in search of glasses. Out of sight he let out a
gurgle and rushed back into the room.

"Toby," he said, pointing at Pauline. "There's a woman in
the bed."

"A woman?" I said, looking around and pulling the blanket
up to cover my hairy chest. "Where?"

"Cut it out," he said. "What's going on here? What are you
two doing?"

"Shell," I said, "I know life is not always intimate between you and Mildred, but you must have some idea of what we're doing."

Pauline let out a nervous giggle next to me and said, "I'm so embarrassed."

"Bare-assed is right," Shelly fumed, adjusting and readjusting his glasses. He put the beer bottle down, picked it up again. "You might have told me."

"I'm sorry, Shell," I said. "This is Pauline, a hotel switchboard operator."

Shelly's mouth fell open. "You mean all you have to do is pick up the phone and you get the operator . . ."

"No," Pauline shrieked, and giggled again. "This is embarrassing."

"I'll tell you what," I said. "We'll all get dressed and have a beer or two and talk, get to be real friends."

"I'm already dressed," Shelly said, looking at himself to be sure, then checking the mirror to be doubly sure. "I'm dressed."

"Good," I said. "Then why don't you take the newspaper into the bathroom till we get dressed?"

He grabbed the newspaper and a beer and went into the bathroom, slamming the door behind him. Pauline and I dressed to the accompaniment of Shelly's grumbling. Her dress was a dark thing with flowers on it.

"Pink gardenias," I said, remembering Alex's words. "You ever heard of pink gardenias?"

"No," Pauline said, checking her hair and makeup in the mirror. "Just one Pink Gardenia."

I had one button done on my shirt when she said it. I stopped. "What Pink Gardenia?"

"Somewhere on Second Avenue," she said. "A nightclub. My mother and I went there when Angela Falzano, one of the operators, got engaged last year."

I took the three steps to her, turned her around, and gave her a big, moist kiss. The bathroom door opened and Shelly emerged, holding the *Times* open to the crossword puzzle. "What's the liquid part of fat? Five letters."

I moved away from Pauline with a grin.

"Let's all have a beer," I said. "No deposit. We can break the bottles in the fireplace when we're done."

"There isn't any fireplace," Shelly said, looking around.

"Then we'll break them in the bathtub," I said.

"Like hell you will," screamed Shelly. "Like hell he will," he told Pauline. "I'm not picking glass slivers out of my . . . Like hell."

We each had a couple of beers and Pauline kept threatening to tell her life story to both of us, but she had not reckoned with Dentist Sheldon Minck, who, when fortified with three beers, waxed eloquent on the joys of reconstructing a ravaged mouth and the possibilities of money to be made in artificial teeth. Fascinated as she was, Pauline glanced at her watch and said she had to get back to work. "Almost forgot," she said, snapping her fingers. "That man you were looking for, the one with the short white hair, foreign accent. He's in nine-oh-nine. I asked around."

I almost said, "I love you," when she threw me a kiss and went through the door, but I didn't love her and she didn't love me. We were good for maybe one or two more times together before we started to know each other, and things turned personal and started going sour. It was me, I knew. It happened every time, though there hadn't been that many times. The worst and longest was with my ex-wife Ann. Then, once, there had been a 21 roller named Merle in Chicago. That had ended before we could get into trouble.

"We've got business, Shell," I said. "Get your coat on."

"Great," he yelped. "Albanese?"

"No, he's in the hospital, shot. Almost killed. We're going after the guy who did it."

"I've had a big day," Shelly said suddenly. "I think I'll just . . ."

"Sheldon, adventure awaits," I said, lifting him from the bed on which he had plopped.

Three minutes later we were going down the service elevator to the ninth floor, in search of Gurko Povey.

9

Sheldon Minck was dancing backward down the ninth-floor corridor, adjusting his glasses, starting to sweat, and whispering louder than most humans shout. He slid in front of me but I kept walking. Shelly groaned and whispered, "Let's call the police, the FBI, the house detective. Toby, this is not reasonable. Its not . . . not safe. We . . . you said this guy's a killer."

"Gun and all," I agreed, looking for 909.

"Do you know what a bullet can do to teeth? I've seen it."

"Maybe he won't shoot you in the face," I pointed out, turning a corner as Shelly almost plopped.

"Teeth are the symbol of life," Shelly hissed urgently, gamboling in reverse like an overripe casaba melon. "Teeth are the symbol of each of our beings, a microcosm, rough and white on the outside, sensitive on the inside. Vulnerable, Toby. If you don't take care of them, they wear away. If you shoot them, they die. I have a fear of someone shooting me in the teeth, you know that?"

"If I didn't know it before, I've got it now," I said. "Don't let Povey know. He might aim for your dentures, just to have a little fun."

A door opened behind Shelly and a couple of women stepped out. Shelly, walking backward, collided with one of them, shrieked, and fell. The woman hopped out of the way. The women looked like ancient twins from Iowa. They were both small, thin, and wore identical black hats. "What are you doing?" scolded the one who hadn't encountered Shelly's rear. "Are you drunk?"

"He's a dentist," I explained softly, looking down the hall toward where I imagined 909 must be.

"That explains nothing," said the woman.

Shelly picked himself up, using the wall for support, and smiled limply. "I'm sorry," he said. "We were discussing survival and I didn't . . ."

The women wanted no more of New York revelers. They strode with dignity down the hall, arm in arm, back to Dubuque or Muscatine or over to the Alvin Theater to see Gertrude Lawrence in *Lady in the Dark*. I pointed over Shelly's shoulder and he turned with a gasp, expecting to see a white-haired Hungarian aiming at his teeth.

"What? What?" he cried.

"Nine-oh-nine," I whispered.

"You're crazy," he bleated.

"No, that's nine-oh-nine," I said.

"I mean you're crazy to do this. I'm leaving. I've got my practice, Mildred . . ."

"Mildred ran away with the milkman," I said.

"Stop that!" Shelly nearly wept. "I . . ."

Before he could say anything more, I had my .38 out and my finger to my lips to signal the trembling dentist to be quiet. He wasn't quite quiet, but the weak whimper was close enough. I knocked at the door to 909. No answer.

"Telegram," I said, raising my voice and trying to sound like Fred Allen.

No answer.

"He's not there," Shelly sighed.

A door opened down the hall. I tucked my pistol in my holster quickly and knocked at 909 loudly.

"Gurko," I shouted. "We're going to be late for the girls."

A couple moved past us, turning their heads away, either not wanting to recognize us or not wanting to be recognized. I knocked again as they turned the corner and repeated, "Gurko."

When they were safely gone, I turned the door handle. It was locked. I took out my wallet and found my small metal nail file. Shelly lumbered over to me, just catching the glasses that were about to slip from his nose. A thumbprint blurred his vision. "What are you doing?" he asked.

I showed him by inserting the file in the crack along the doorjamb.

"We could go to jail for this!"

I kept working on the door.

"What is it? A couple of beers and you lose control? Is that it?" he asked. When I didn't answer, he turned his eyes upward and, squinting through the thick lenses and the thumbprint, told God, "He doesn't answer. What can you do with a man who doesn't answer? I ask you."

But God didn't answer either. The door popped open. I grabbed Shelly and pulled him into the room. Before he could cry or scream, I kicked the door closed and hit the light switch. My .38 was in my hand and aimed toward the bed, though I knew that if Povey were there we had made enough noise to give him time to set us up. He wasn't there. Nothing was there. The bed was made, though the cover was slightly wrinkled and there was an indentation in the pillow. Povey probably slept with his clothes on and a gun in his hand. I couldn't picture him in silk pajamas. I tried and smiled.

"This isn't funny," Shelly said, looking at the door. "You think this is funny, Toby? You're a sick man if you think this is funny."

"It's not funny, Shell," I agreed as I searched the room. The bathroom was clean, empty, though one towel and the soap had been used. The towel was folded neatly on the toilet. Shelly stood, his left hand holding his hairy right wrist while I checked the closet. No suitcase, no clothes. I tried the drawers. They were all empty, except for the bottom one, which held a Gideon Bible with a piece of paper sticking out of it in Isaiah, chapter 30, with underlining on the words:

Behold, the name of the Lord cometh from far, With His anger burning in His thick uplifting of smoke; His lips are full of indignation, And His tongue is as a devouring fire; And His breath is as an overflowing stream, That divideth even unto the neck, To sift the nations with the sieve of destruction.

Then, further on the page, there was more underlining: "Both he that helpeth shall stumble, and he that is helped shall fall, And they all shall perish together."

Shelly, who had been reading over my shoulder, muttered, "Somehow I don't find that comforting."

The piece of paper had writing on it, too, neat, black writing worthy of a penmanship teacher: "Peters, I cannot resist irony. Obviously, I have departed, but I do not forget and I do not forgive."

"I don't like that note," said Shelly. "I don't like threats. I don't like irony. I don't like people with guns who try to kill me."

"You're hard to please," I said, tucking the note into my pocket and returning my gun to the holster. "Quick Minck, the game's afoot." I clicked off the light and went out the door, Shelly shuffling behind me, gurgling, "Wait."

We caught a cab in front of the hotel and I asked the cabbie if he knew the Pink Gardenia on Second Avenue. He knew it but he didn't recommend it. We headed there anyway. Shelly sulked for half a mile and then said, "I wasn't afraid back there, you know."

"I know."

More silence for a few blocks, then Shelly tried, "What I said in the hall back there was true. I've been reading *Men,*

Molars and Mysticism by Lichty. You know anything, any part of the body can . . . even your fingernail . . . or . . . a hair from your nostril . . ."

"Hey, buddy, you mind, I just ate," the cabbie called over his shoulder. "I can do without nose-hair talk, you know what I mean?"

But Shelly was too deeply into mysticism, teeth, and a vain attempt to rescue his self-respect. He plunged on, now glaring at me through thick lenses. "The meaning of life is all tied up like . . ."

"A ball of yarn," I suggested.

"Tin foil," tried the cabbie.

"No," countered Shelly. "Like layers of teeth, gums. The mouth is an entry to the meaning. To understand a tooth is to understand life. Or a fingernail."

"To understand a tooth is to understand a fingernail?" asked the cabbie. "Who the hell wants to understand a fingernail?"

"Just drive," shouted Shelly. "Just turn around and drive." He went on, "A poet understands a poem, a cartographer understands a map, a priest understands the Bible, a bartender understands his beer, and a dentist understands teeth. Each can be a profound key to the meaning of life. Don't you see there's no single right way? Beer, maps, teeth can be the key that unlocks the mystery of the universe."

"You ask me," the cabbie said, pulling to a stop, "you and the guy who wrote the book are off your nuts."

"No one asked you," shouted Shelly. "You know what you get for that? You get no tip. That's what you get."

The cabbie shrugged. "The key to my universe is a hack and the figure on the meter. I can make it without the tip. That'll be a buck ten."

I gave him a buck and a half and got out onto Second Avenue. Shelly followed me and slammed the cab door shut. The cabbie pulled away.

"What happened to sensitivity?" Shelly moaned.

"Drowned in Pearl Harbor," I said, looking around for the Pink Gardenia. Cars, trucks, and cabs clunked down the street. It wasn't crowded, but for ten at night it wasn't empty either. People were walking down both sides of the street and stores were open.

A kid on the corner was hawking a pile of newspapers. The rain had stopped, and a cool wet wind blew down the street. The skinny kid was wearing a light jacket. His hair was long and blowing in the breeze. "What's going on?" I asked him, buying a paper.

"Good news or bad news?" he asked.

"Good news," I said.

Shelly tried to talk, but I held up my hand to keep him quiet. "Army Day Parade tomorrow on Fifth Avenue. Sunday's Easter," the kid said.

"That it?" I asked, looking at the front page.

"Lots of bad news. The *Langley,* the *Pecos,* and a tanker were sunk by the Japs. Maybe seven hundred sailors got killed. My brother's in the navy."

"In the Pacific?" I asked.

The kid shrugged and wiped a patch of blowing hair from his face.

"Who knows? They don't let him tell us. But we didn't get no telegram or a call or nothing. His name's Artie."

"I want some papers," said Shelly, handing the kid a dollar. "A bunch of papers. We're having a party. How many you got?"

"You can have them all for two bucks," the kid said.

Shelly handed over another dollar. "Go home," he said. "It's late."

"The Pink Gardenia," I said, as the kid stuck the two bills in his pocket.

"Around the corner, over there," he said, pointing behind us. "But it's closed, boarded up. Thanks."

And he was gone.

"You've got about forty copies of the *Times* there, Shell. What are you going to do with them?"

"Leave 'em there," he said. "They'll all be stolen in ten minutes."

"You think the key to the mystery of life can be found in a newspaper?" I asked, walking in the direction the kid had pointed.

"Kid should be home with his family," Shelly said, plunging his hands in his pockets and following me.

"Underneath that dirty white smock there beats a heart," I said, turning the corner.

The Pink Gardenia was across the street, boarded up just like the kid had told us. The sign for the place was still there, painted in a nice scroll, a pink gardenia dividing the words PINK and GARDENIA. Posters covered the wooden planks on the windows. Three identical war posters were pasted on next to each other, reading, FOR YEARS THE JAPS WANTED OUR SCRAP . . . SAVE NOW AND LET 'EM HAVE IT.

"I can see the headlines," Shelly said, nodding at the posters, "Japs hit by flying junk. Let's go back to the hotel. It's getting cold and the place is closed."

"Look for an entrance leading up there," I said, pointing above the Pink Gardenia sign. There were windows above the storefront, a loft or offices.

"What's up there?" Shelly asked, squinting.

"Columbia Pictures," I said, moving down the sidewalk.

The doorway wasn't hiding, but it wasn't advertising itself with neon either. There was a nightlight inside, but I couldn't see through the pebble-glass door. There was a bell. I rang it and put my hand to my jacket, just in case Povey opened the door. We could hear the bell ring upstairs, far inside the building, echoing and empty. I rang again. Nothing.

"There's no one there," Shelly said.

"Right," I agreed.

"We're not leaving, are we?" he asked, knowing the answer.

"We're not leaving. You want to go back on the corner and sell your papers?"

"I'll stay with you."

We looked around for cops, pedestrians, or stray bums. There weren't any. We could see Second Avenue half a block down, where lights were on and people walked looking for sounds and other people, but we were on a side street in the East Thirties. There were no stray crowds here at night. The rest of the street looked like small businesses, warehouses. I tried my file. It was fine on the bottom lock, but there was a bolt lock on the bottom. "Laugh, Shelly," I said, taking out my pistol.

"You're going to shoot me if I don't laugh?" he said, shaking his head. "You need serious psychiatric help, Toby. You're beyond tooth therapy, I can tell you."

I reached over and tickled him. He danced back with a wild, high laugh, and I turned and hit the panel of glass as Shelly tried to control a second round of gargling laughter. The panel cracked and broke, but the thick pane didn't crumble. Glass fell inside the hallway. I pulled out a few stray shards, reached in and opened the bolt lock.

"Come on," I whispered. "And shut up."

"You make me laugh and then you tell me to shut up," Shelly cried. "We've got to have a serious . . . You're going in there?"

"We're going in." And in we went.

"Toby, someone will see the broken window, for God's sake," he cried, his voice echoing up the dark stairway. "I'll be caught and disbarred."

"Lawyers get disbarred," I said, starting up the stairs. "Dentists get disbanded or defrocked or something."

We were not being silent. I gave up hope of being silent. If Povey were at the top of the stairs in the dark, all he would have to do was step out and shoot the two of us. He probably wouldn't even get a two-dollar disturbing-the-peace ticket for killing us. We were breaking and entering. But nobody shot us. We just galumphed up the stairs, me trying to see into the darkness, Shelly panting and puffing behind me.

"What's up there? What do you see?" Shelly croaked.

"It's dark," I said, stumbling onto a landing. "Look around for a light switch."

I could make out a door in the darkness, but it wasn't until Shelly found the switch that I could see both it and the two doors beyond. One door was marked TOP NOTCH BROADWAY TALENT, with the name AL SINGER in smaller letters under it. The lettering was in black on the same pebbly glass as the entrance to the building. Next to TOP NOTCH was SIG DIAMOND, MUSIC BROKER.

"What's a music broker?" Shelly asked reasonably, but I was looking at the remaining door, which had a piece of white cardboard on it with the words COLUMBIA FILMS stenciled in black paint.

"Somehow I don't think this is Harry Cohn's office," I said, turning the door handle. It was open. The place was big, stretching the length of the building. To our right were the windows we had looked up at from the street. There was enough light to bounce a grey fog across the floor from the low ceiling, but not enough to penetrate the corners. Shelly came in behind me. I stood still a few seconds and put my hand on Shelly's shoulder to stop him.

"All right," Shelly said. "Let's look around and get out of here."

The center of the floor was clear, except for a desk and some chairs and cabinets. It looked like a crude attempt to create an office in the middle of a musty attic. It was probably the "set" on which Alex had written his notes to Einstein. To our left were a few doors and furniture. I listened to Shelly breathe heavily. Something moved in the darkness. "What's that?" Shelly squealed.

"A cat," I said, leveling my .38 at darkness.

"Yes," came Povey's voice. "A cat. Perfect. A cat who has lured two mice into a trap."

"I've got a gun, Povey," I said.

"I see it," he replied, while I tried to get a fix on him. "And I see you, but you obviously do not see me or you would not be looking over there."

"There," shrieked Shelly, pointing into another corner.

I turned in the direction he was pointing. There was someone there but it wasn't Povey. I couldn't see Povey as I spun around, but in another distant corner I could make out a patch of white, the bandage on his hand where Paul Robeson had slashed him with the blunt sword.

It was time to do something and get the hell out of there.

"I'm going to shoot two trespassers," Povey said.

"They'll check your identification," I said. "The FBI knows about you. You won't get away with it."

"But what difference will that make to you? You'll be dead," he said, quite happily. "Besides, it is not I, but the renter of this loft, who will report the act of criminal trespass. And then I will get your Jew scientist. I've enjoyed this game, but my employers are growing impatient."

"Toby," Shelly whispered at my side. "Damn it, do something."

I took a shot toward Povey's dark corner and shoved Shelly to the left, toward one of the offices in the loft. Shelly staggered into a shadow and I rolled after him, bullets coming at me from two directions.

"Through that door," I shouted.

"Oh, oh, oh, oh!" Shelly sobbed and crawled on his hands and knees through the door. Another shot hit the floor behind me, and I scampered after the puffing dentist and kicked the door closed behind us.

"This isn't fun. It's no fun at all," Shelly said, crawling into a corner of the small room. The door I had pushed closed was thick and heavy. I hadn't gotten a good look at it, but I had the feeling that it could stop a bullet. Footsteps, more than one pair, came across the floor outside and I aimed my .38 at the closed door. There were no windows in the room, nothing they could break to get a shot at us. Even I couldn't miss someone coming through the door at this distance.

"The trap," Povey laughed through the thick door. "We would have preferred to shoot you, but you can remain in there till we dispose of the *Juden* and the *Shvartz*."

"Someone heard the shots," I shouted. "The cops will be here."

"No," said Povey. "This is a film studio, remember? We will simply wait for a few minutes outside the door, and if the police show up we will tell them we shoot a movie and we are sorry to make noise."

"Don't come in here," screamed Shelly.

"That's telling him, Shell," I said, my arms weakening but my gun still pointed at the door. Something clicked.

"This used to be a furrier's shop," Povey said. "You are in a small fur vault. And there you will remain. Two mice. No," he laughed. "A mink and a mouse . . . I don't hear you laughing at my joke."

I shot at the door. The bullet thudded into the steel, ricocheted, and screeched past my face.

"Toby," Shelly groaned.

"I don't like you anymore," said Povey beyond the door. "I don't like you at all, Peters."

Someone else spoke quietly to Povey. I could hear the voice, but not the words. I couldn't tell if it was a man or woman or even if the words were in English, and Shelly's whimpering didn't help. The voice stopped and footsteps moved away from the door. We sat listening. Another door opened, probably the one to the loft.

"Let's get out, out," Shelly yelled, getting up.

"It may be a trick," I said. "One of them may have left. The other one might be out there, waiting for us to step out."

A light went on. Shelly was standing, his pudgy hand on the cord of a single bulb, dangling from the ceiling. The room was small, empty, and musty. Shelly sneezed. He turned and tried the handle of the door, a bar of metal that shook but didn't turn. "We're trapped," he said, turning to me.

"That's what he said," I reminded him. I didn't get up.

"We've got to get out of here." Shelly sat, rattling the door handle. "Out. O-U-T. Help me."

"Nothing to help with," I said. I took off my jacket, put my .38 where I could reach it, and lay down. If I could stay on my back, I might not get a great night's sleep, but I'd be able to walk in the morning. "Get some sleep, Shell. Turn out the light and get some sleep."

"We'll suffocate like . . ."

"Mice or minks," I said. "There's a crack under the door. It's not sealed. Turn off the light, in case they decide to come back and try again. In the morning, when people come to work, we'll start making noise and someone will let us out."

"Nobody will let us . . . Toby, we've got to get out."

"You work on it, Shell," I said. "If you get the door open, let me know. If you don't, turn off the light and try to be quiet."

He jangled the door handle a few more times, gave up, and sat down, sweating. He reached into his pocket.

"No cigars," I said.

He put the cigars away and pouted. "It's all your fault," he said, pointing a finger at me.

Since we both agreed, I had nothing to add.

"Turn off the light, Shell," I said and lay back with my eyes closed. He grumbled, moaned, and about ten minutes later turned off the light.

Douglas MacArthur and Koko the Clown came to save us during the night. Koko oozed in under the door. The general came riding through the wall in a jeep driven by a smiling soldier, wearing only underpants. Shelly thanked the soldier and the clown, and MacArthur offered the use of his jeep and driver to save Einstein and Paul Robeson. Koko handed me an oversize fountain pen with a sharp point to use as a weapon. Shelly and I were about to get in the jeep when Mutt and Jeff suddenly appeared with a gun in each hand. "Oh, oh," said Koko, rolling his eyes. He looked around the room, spotted an inkwell, and dived in.

Rather than be shot by two cartoon characters, I shook my shoulders, ground my teeth, and woke up. Shelly was asleep, his jacket under his head, curled in a ball like an overweight cat. Light crept in under the door. I sat up. Except for the ache in my ribs, head, and groin, where Povey had hit me during our dance after the Albanese shooting, I felt reasonably well. No backache. My face was covered with spikes of beard and my tongue with dried glue. It was time to get back to work. I rolled over and shook Shelly.

"Mildred," he groaned. "It's Sunday."

I shook him again.

"Mildred," he cried. "Not in the middle of the night. You promised you'd wait till . . ."

His eyes opened and he sat up. His glasses were at a crazy angle, and his mouth was open as if he had awakened in Oz. "I don't want to be here," he wailed.

"Let's see what we can do about it." I took out my gun, holding it down to the bottom of the door and shooting out into the loft. I waited ten minutes, while Shelly complained about missing breakfast, his dental meeting, a change of underwear, and his toothbrush. Then I shot again. Something or someone stirred. Voices in doors beyond doors or from the street. About three minutes later I could hear the outer door to Columbia Films open. We put our heads down to the floor and yelled, "Here, we're in here."

A few seconds later the metal door opened, and we looked up at a tiny man in a grey suit and vest. "Who're you?" he asked.

"Actors," I said. "We got trapped in here last night after a shooting."

"Actors?" the little man said, patting back his thin white hair. "I'm Al Singer, the agent. You got representation?"

We got up off the floor and moved past him. "No," I said. "I can get you a booking, maybe two, three weeks in Miami," he said, following us. "I need a gangster type and a fat second banana for Phil Silvers' act. It's an emergency. What do you say? Train fare, twenty bucks a night, may make you a regular part of the show if they don't find the two schlemiels who ran out on Phil."

Shelly limped and I ached to the door.

"Think it over," Singer said behind us as we went down the stairs. "Name's Al Singer. I'm in the book."

I dug into my pocket for my notebook and found it as we walked to Second Avenue. People, cars all over the place.

"I need a toilet," Shelly said, looking around. He spotted a small quick-fix restaurant and headed for it. The place was half full, and the clock on the wall said it was almost eight. Shelly went for the toilet and I went for the phone.

"What'll it be?" the guy behind the counter called.

"Bowl of Wheaties and a coffee for me," I said, pulling out a pocketful of coins and losing some on the floor.

"Eggs, ham, coffee," shouted Shelly, going into the toilet.

I got the operator and had her give me the number in Princeton. No one answered at Einstein's. I tried the number across the street. Archer answered.

"I thought you were in New York," I said, looking at the counterman, who was pointing to the two seats he was holding for Shelly and me.

"We're back here," he sighed. "Orders from headquarters. The kids are in the big city. We're scientist-sitting again. What do you want?"

"I ran into Povey last night. I thought you were going to pull him in?"

"Don't tell anyone, Peters, but sometimes even the FBI doesn't find someone in a city of five million in four or five hours."

"Povey said he was going to get Einstein and Robeson," I

said. "I had the feeling he was on his way to one of them last night."

"We put some people on Robeson last night," Spade said. "Einstein's safe across the street with his numbers. I can see the place from here."

"Then why doesn't he answer his phone?' I asked.

The counterman looked up over a customer and motioned to me that my Wheaties were served. Shelly came out of the toilet and made his way to his eggs. "You need toilet paper in there," he told the counterman.

"I'll go see," said Spade, and he hung up.

I hung up too and hurried to Shelly. "Put that stuff in a sandwich," I said, scooping a few mouthfuls of milk and Wheaties into my mouth. "We're going to Princeton."

"I'm too old to go back to school," Shelly said wearily. "I've already gone to Utah State Dental."

"Let's go, Shell," I said, taking a few more spoons of cereal and gulping down some coffee.

A guy sitting to the right, trying to read his paper, looked at us out of the corner of his eye and decided not to make an issue of our boorish manners.

"Put my friend's stuff in a bun," I told the counterman.

"What's the hurry?' the man said.

"We've got to save Albert Einstein from Nazis," I explained.

"Gotcha," said the counterman, moving Shelly's plate in mid-bite. "That'll be eighty cents for the two of you."

"I'm not going," said Shelly, pulling his plate back. "I've got a dental conference here, remember?"

"Suit yourself, Shell. I'll see you later."

I left him with the check and heard him order another egg as I hit the street. The first cabbie said he wouldn't go to Princeton. The second one gave me a flat fee of fifteen bucks. I told him it was a deal, handed him the cash in advance, and sat back, wondering if Einstein would be alive when I got to New Jersey.

10

By the time we pulled up in front of the Einstein house in Princeton, the expenses for transportation on this case had caught up with my advance. If Einstein were still alive, I'd need more money and a new notebook. The old one was full, and the spiral had just about given up any hope of holding onto the few remaining pages.

"You want I should wait?" the cabbie said as I handed him some change.

"No thanks. I'll catch the bus back."

"You want some advice?" he asked as I closed the door.

"Why not?" I said.

"Shave," he said. "Neighborhood like this they'll think you're some kind of bum."

"Thanks," I said, and ran up the steps to Einstein's house. I rang the bell, knocked at the door, rang again, tried to see through the windows. No dice. I went around the back of the house and looked through the big window of Einstein's study. He wasn't in there. I tried the back door and wasn't surprised when it was locked. I was surprised at how easily I opened it with my penknife. If the FBI was watching this place, how come I was getting into it so easily without even trying to hide?

"Hello," I yelled, pistol out, as I walked through the kitchen, trailing dirt from the garden. No answer. I opened the refrigerator and took out a couple of carrots and a half-empty quart bottle of milk. Alternating chomps on the carrots

and gulps of the milk, I went through the house looking for
Einstein's body. I was coming down the stairs in the front hall
when a key clinked in the door. I sat down, .38 in my lap,
popped the last piece of carrot in my mouth, washed it down
with a gulp of milk, rubbed the stubble on my chin, and
waited while the door opened and Mark Walker walked in.
He was moving quietly as he stepped in. He didn't see me for
maybe ten seconds, which was a little surprising.

"What's up, Doc?" I said, remnants of carrot still fresh in
my teeth.

"Ah," Walker gasped. He didn't look or sound like Elmer
Fudd. "Mr. Peters . . . I . . . what are you . . . where
is. . . ?"

"I am dirty and hungry and he is not here," I said. "What
are you doing here?"

"I'm supposed to pick up . . . some things from Professor
Einstein to take to the Institute," he said nervously. "They're
in the study."

"Hold on, Doc," I said, getting up, milk bottle in one
hand, gun in the other, face a Brillo grey. "No one touches
anything till we see the great man."

"You don't think . . ." Walker began, his hand going to his
chest.

"Usually I don't, but I'm working hard on it right now.
Let's not argue here. I spent the night on the floor of a fur
vault with a snoring dentist and bad dreams. The guy who
locked me in that vault told me he was on his way here to turn
Einstein into a martyr or meat sauce. So, don't touch anything and don't irritate me. I don't have the tolerance or the
intelligence to deal with either one."

"It's Saturday," Walker said, looking at me and adjusting
his jacket and tie. "Professor Einstein is probably out on his
boat."

"Boat?"

"He sails a boat?"

"What else does one sail?" Walker asked reasonably, while

I tried to imagine the fuzzy-haired scientist with a yachtsman's cap on his head and wearing a navy-blue jacket with gold buttons embossed with little anchors. I couldn't do it. There was a phone on a small table at the foot of the stairs. I put the milk bottle down, put my .38 back in my shoulder holster, got out my notebook, riffled through the pages, and found the number I was looking for. The operator connected me with the house across the street, but Spade and Archer didn't answer. No one answered. I hung up.

"Let's go," I said. "Get me to him fast."

"But . . ."

I finished off the milk and motioned him to the door. "Now," I said, and he believed me.

We drove through Princeton and into farmland. Black-and-white cows paused in their chewing to look stupidly at us as we shot up the two-lane road in silence. I passed the time by rubbing my thumb over my chin and not thinking. Thinking had never really worked for me. My plans usually fell through, confused me. Blundering ahead, trying to touch all the bases twice, and sticking my head up every once in a while to draw the bad guys into taking a wild shot or two had been my method in the past. So far I'd survived with it. So I decided that the best thing to do was find Einstein, get him out of the open, watch for Povey, and hope for help from the FBI.

Walker said, "Here," about five seconds before he turned into a side road, and I looked for the lake between the trees. We shot through the thin forest and into a parking lot next to a golf course, beyond which was the lake. Walker had said it was a little lake. It looked about the size of Manhattan to me. Little boats with sails lulled around in the stiff breeze and they all looked the same.

I jumped out of the car as soon as it stopped. "Which one?"

Walker, at last sensing urgency, leaped out and scanned the small fleet.

"I don't . . ." he began, and a golf ball shot past us, missing my head by about two feet. A thin kid carrying a bag of golf clubs slung over his back came across the parking lot toward us, the clubs jangling above his shoulder.

"Sorry," the kid shouted. "Where did it go?"

Walker pointed to a ball that had come to rest against the tire of a black Ford.

"Over here, Dr. Carlisle," the kid shouted, and Dr. Carlisle, six irons in his pudgy little hand, came storming past us. He wore a little white cap, a checkered sweater and white pants. His bottom bounced as he moved seriously toward the Ford.

"Goddamn," Carlisle muttered as he passed us, "I hate this game."

I put my hand out and grabbed his arm. I got a fuzzy handful of sweater but it was enough to stop him. Carlisle, red-faced and angry, looked up at me.

"Let go of me," he said. "Do you know what you've got a grip on?"

"Reality," I said.

"No," he said through clean teeth. "The sweater of A. J. Carlisle. And that is a mistake."

"Zipping a ball past my head and not apologizing is also a mistake," I said, moving my grip from his sleeve to his collar.

"Mr. Peters," Walker said. "We're here for . . ."

"Einstein," I said, without taking my eyes from Carlisle.

The caddy had returned. From the corner of my eye I could see that he held a putter in his hand. "Let Dr. Carlisle go," the caddy said.

"Or what?" I asked.

"Or I'll put your head into that sewer," said the caddy. "And I play a hell of a lot better golf than the Doc."

"Peters," Walker urged. "Professor Einstein."

"That's it," said Carlisle, trying to straighten his sweater when I let him go. "You're friends of that Nazi."

"What Nazi?" I said, reaching out for Carlisle again, but

the golfer had taken refuge behind the skinny caddy, who held up the putter to ward me off.

"White-haired guy," said the caddy. "Dr. Carlisle almost hit him on three."

"Three has a hell of a dog leg," explained Carlisle. "And who knew he'd be wandering around on the course."

"He was on the sidewalk near the hot dog stand," the caddy explained.

"How long ago?" I asked, stepping forward and ignoring the putter.

"Half hour, maybe more," said the caddy.

Walker and I left them standing in the parking lot, and I imagined a sudden rain of wet concrete covering them and leaving a statue for all to drive around for the next decade or so. Behold, the famous Golfer Cowering Behind a Caddy with a Putter. Note the Norman Rockwell touch, the nostalgic realism of the rumpled sweater. And for those who looked carefully, there would be the ball at their feet waiting forever for Carlisle's next assault.

We hurried past the clubhouse and down to a dock, where about fifteen sailboats were moored. "Can you sail one of those things?" I asked Walker.

"No, I'll try to find someone who can." Before I could stop him he was racing back to the clubhouse. I ran down to the dock and onto its grey planks. At the end of the dock I looked out, hoping to see something, Einstein, Povey, a passing water taxi.

"Mr. Peters?" came a voice behind me. I turned and found myself facing Albert Einstein in rumpled white pants and a light-blue sweater over an unstarched white shirt.

"Someone's trying to kill you," I said, looking around for Povey.

"I know," said Einstein, walking past me to a sailboat tied to the dock. "A golfer. I do not understand the game of golf. Too direct. Too much on a line. You hit. You walk. You hit again. And each time you play, you try to hit it fewer times than the time before." He climbed into the boat, holding the edge of the dock for balance. While he talked, he began to untie the sail.

"There must come a point at which the person is no longer able to reduce that number. But that is only in theory, like running against a clock. One would think that a point would come at which one could go no faster. But wait. Perhaps a fraction of a second today, a fraction of a second tomorrow. Or perhaps someone else will be a fraction of a second faster. And perhaps someday there will be a golfer who can put the ball on the tether . . ."

"Tee," I corrected, looking around for Povey, my hand ready to go to my gun, even though I knew I was no match for Povey's shooting.

"Tee, yes," said Einstein, as if he thought the word *tee* was an important discovery. "There will be a day when someone can hit the ball off each tee directly into the hole. What then? What will be the goal? The thrill? To do it faster? With blindfolds?" He started to untie the line that held the boat to the dock.

"I'm casting off," he said. "You may climb in with me and sail, or remain on the dock in a state of puzzlement."

I clambered into the boat, almost tipping it over. No Povey. No Walker in sight.

"Push us away," said Einstein, reaching into his pocket for a pipe, which he placed between his teeth.

I obeyed and looked at him. "You don't believe me," I said.

"Oh, I believe you," replied Einstein, "but I don't see that panic will make the situation less tense. For more than twenty years I have worked and planned, and Nazis have made me run and hide and move and worry. Politics are a waste. You have been paid an agreed-upon fee to both clear my reputation and give protection. Today I sail, Nazis or no Nazis. I sail."

We sailed.

Well, Einstein sailed while I watched the shore, the sky, passing boats, and anything that glittered in the noonday sun. Something did catch the light back beyond the dock. I thought it was a golfer, possibly Carlisle rocketing golf balls at unwary travelers. "Let's talk," I suggested.

"Let us sail," replied Einstein, puffing on his pipe, his wiry curls of white hair billowing in the breeze.

"Povey is around here somewhere," I said calmly.

Einstein nodded his head in calm understanding.

"If something happens, go overboard and swim for the dock," I told him. He shook his head a gentle "no."

"I do not swim," he said. "I sail."

We were heading for something. He kept checking by looking around the flapping sail. I sat low in the small boat and had trouble seeing what we were heading for, but see it I did when we were within a dozen feet of the black rock jutting into the water.

"Watch out for the rock!" I shouted at Einstein, who calmly smiled and nodded as if he were in his study working on some problem.

The wind hit the sail, slapping it back. I ducked before the damn thing hit me and turned as we came within inches of the rock. I could hear the wake of the little sailboat lap against the rock. Einstein was smiling contentedly.

"Anything else you want to play games with?" I asked. "A land mine maybe, or a minesweeper? You're not the only one who can't swim. I mean I can swim . . . a little, but I couldn't make it ten yards if I had to drag you along." I pictured myself laboring through the water, maybe trying to reach the rock, with Einstein floating on his back, his pipe in his mouth, his hands folded peacefully on his chest while he looked up into infinity.

"I got my idea for what people call relativity while on a sailboat," Einstein said with a small shake of his head, as if he remembered the moment well and regretted it at least a little. "I imagined a man on a dock, a bigger dock than the one here, and another approaching him in a boat. I could even imagine two lighthouses. You see the idea came not in the form of a mathematical formula but in the imagination, in pictures. The proof, ah, there are those who say there is no proof. But that," he said with a wave of the pipe he had removed from his mouth, "is the past. It is the present, the future we must talk of."

"We're going to hit that boat," I said, calmly nodding at the larger motor boat moving toward us. "Across the bow."

The use of the word "bow" exhausted my nautical knowledge. It was now up to the sailor-scientist.

With another wave, Einstein dismissed the possibility of collision and went on talking as we shot in front of the bigger boat. "This Povey," he said softly. "He doesn't know why they want me dead. He is a token, a pawn, and I am . . ."

"A knight," I said.

"Maybe a bishop," Einstein corrected. "He thinks they want me dead only because I am a Jew. No, they want me dead because they think I am working on their destruction, working on a weapon so powerful that it would end this war in one day, one morning, one hour. And they are working on the same weapon. Does this frighten you, as it frightens me, Mr. Peters?"

"It has not brought a new ray of sunshine into my already dim and busy day," I said, my eye on a boat about our size heading toward us. Far beyond the boat, on the shore, a tall man looked out at us. I couldn't tell who it was, but he was about the size and shape of Mark Walker. "Watch out for that boat heading our way," I added.

Einstein seemed not to hear. He had a tale to tell and I wasn't going to get in the way. "Ten years ago," he said, as much to himself and the sky as to me, "a young man came to me and said my ideas about energy and mass could be used to create a weapon, a bomb in which almost any material with mass could be converted to energy and start a reaction so that a small bomb might destroy a city."

"A city?" I asked, humoring the old man while I studied the boat approaching us.

"I told him he was mad," Einstein laughed. I didn't see anything funny in the story, but he was a genius. Who the hell knows what geniuses think is funny.

"And now . . ." Einstein went on, "and now I find myself urging this country to make such a weapon and offering my help. But they turn me down. You know why?" He didn't wait for my answer. "Because I was once a German. My fear of German aggression, German hatred, was with me when I was a boy. I ran to Italy, renounced my German citizenship when the United States was giving away secrets to the Germans. But you see, Mr. Peters, your friend Povey and his friends do not know this. They think, not unreasonably, that the man who made popular the idea of converting mass to energy, a man who is the enemy of the German state, must be working on such a weapon. And they are wrong. I am working for the Navy on something of far less importance. Yet they, the Germans, hire fanatics to ruin my name, to kill me, to stop me from doing what I am not doing. Is that irony?"

"It's irony," I agreed, getting worried about the boat that was about a hundred yards away and headed straight for us. "I don't think that's Don Winslow coming to our rescue."

Einstein looked up at the oncoming boat but his mind was still on the bomb. "Perhaps such a bomb is not a good idea. I've considered that too. What if a reaction begins and can't be stopped? Would the world be destroyed? Will the bullet that destroys the termite also bring down the house?"

"I've got a better one," I said, pulling out my .38 and pointing it at the sailboat about thirty yards away. "Will the white-haired guy with the gun over there get us before I get him?"

With this, Einstein decided to look at the boat bearing down on us. No doubt about it. It was Povey. I could see his face, his grin. He didn't look surprised to see me. He should have been. I didn't like that. I liked even less his aiming that Walther at me.

"Get down, get low," I shouted at Einstein, who went on puffing on his pipe and gave a sharp push to the rudder. I don't know how I knew it was a rudder, but I did. My nautical vocabulary had doubled as my chances of survival were cut in half.

The two small boats were now headed straight at each other, which did several things. It made us a bigger target. It also brought us closer to Povey, who looked too damn comfortable steering that little boat with one hand and aiming at us with the other. Using the side of the boat to steady my hand, I aimed. The boat bobbed from side to side. I fired. Nothing. The bullet probably sailed past and plunked harmlessly into the water. Maybe it made it all the way to land and hit Carlisle the golfer in his fat ass. I almost laughed. A professional killer was within twenty yards of me and I was angry at a golfer. I had heard the game could get to you.

"Turn around. Get the hell out of here," I shouted, as Einstein continued to steer right for the killer. Amused, Povey shouted something and laughed. I couldn't tell what he shouted. The Walther came up, his arm straight, both eyes open the way they're supposed to be. A breeze caught a loose strand on his bandaged hand and it fluttered like a small bird.

"Over the side," I yelled at Einstein.

"No," he said. He sounded excited but I didn't have time to look back at him.

It looked like we were going to miss Povey by about five feet, come up right alongside him so he could pick us off. What movie was it where a yodeler saved. . . ? Ah, *Monsieur Verdoux.* Charlie Chaplin's about to crack Martha Raye's head open with an oar when he spots a yodeler on the shore watching him. I didn't think Povey would be bothered by a yodeler and I didn't really expect a yodeler in New Jersey. In Manhattan maybe, but not Jersey.

"Thank you," said Povey, as we were almost even with

him. I could see the Walther level on me, not because I was his primary target but because I had the gun. I shot wildly and saw a hole appear in the sail high above Povey's head. He shook his head, showed teeth, and was about to shoot me when Einstein turned our little boat suddenly and we collided with Povey's. Povey fell backward, his hand pushing the rudder. His boat did a sharp spin away from us and he turned to shoot over his shoulder. The bullet hit the wood about five inches from my face. I dropped my .38, got up, and jumped as Povey tried to steady his boat for another shot. I hit the small deck and stumbled forward into the flipping, flapping sail. Two shots, two holes through the sail, from Povey firing at me from the other side. I ducked low under the mast or whatever the hell the piece of wood was, rolled under it, and kicked out toward where I figured Povey had to be. Either he was there or I was dead. I was wrong on both counts. I missed him by a foot and his next shot went well over my head, probably because he couldn't control the boat and kill me at the same time. He should have said the hell with the boat and concentrated on me, but I wasn't going to give him advice. I kicked again. This time I struck hand and gun. I had been hoping for his groin but I settled for what I could get. The Walther plopped into the water, and Povey finally decided to let the wind take us where it would. He jumped forward, his right knee rising quickly into my stomach. My breath was gone, along with my will to fight. Povey stood up over me, reached into his pocket, and came out with a pocketknife. He calmly opened it while I silently grabbed for air. The blade was bigger than the one Errol Flynn used to put away Basil Rathbone in *The Adventures of Robin Hood*.

Povey said something in a language I didn't understand and shifted the knife for a full-weighted lunge at my belly. He never made it. The thud and roll of the boat came together, as he went tripping over the side and I rolled helplessly to the edge of the boat, which almost turned over. As the boat righted itself, I could see Einstein contentedly watching the success of his second attack on an enemy vessel.

I forced myself up on one elbow and looked for Povey. No sign, not a ripple.

"Get my gun," I shouted at Einstein. He might come up anywhere, try to get at us or back up here.

"I don't shoot guns," Einstein said.

Nothing happened in the water. I couldn't believe that Povey couldn't swim. I couldn't swim, Einstein couldn't swim, but Povey was another story. Still nothing happened in the water. I crawled over to the side of the boat and tried to grab onto Einstein's bow. I wanted my .38 in my hand, even if I couldn't hit anything with it. When my hand was touching the rail, Povey's arm shot out of the water and gripped me. I didn't have time to think, only to imagine myself being pulled under that water. I wrapped my legs around the wooden mast in Povey's boat and felt myself stretch out and my arm pop. Povey's bandaged hand pulled at my sleeve. My arm burned with pain, but my legs hugged the mast as I tried to wriggle free of my jacket. Povey still hadn't come up for air.

"Doesn't the son-of-a-bitch have to breathe?" I screamed as my legs were about to go limp.

My eyes closed in pain and then opened. I was on my back about to be pulled into the water. Upside down I could see the frail figure of Einstein standing unsteadily in his boat, holding something over the side in two hands. He let the thing go and something plunked into the water. My arm was released. I pulled it back in agony.

"What did you hit him with?" I groaned.

"Anchor," said Einstein, pulling the rope back up to retrieve the anchor. "Guns I do not approve of, but murder I approve of less."

Povey didn't come up again. Einstein tied Povey's boat to his and began the slow sail back to the dock, while I scanned the water for Povey, keeping my arms well within the confines of the small boat. As Einstein headed for shore, I almost passed out from the pain. Once he took out a notebook and jotted something down. "Images come at the times most unexpected," he said to me.

At the dock, I kept looking back, even when two men helped us out of the boat. "What was that shooting?" said one leathery old guy.

"What happened to the white-haired guy who stole Al's boat?" asked his equally old but slightly less leathery companion.

Einstein handed me my .38. With one hand it was a little awkward getting it back in the holster but I managed. The two old guys looked at each other, at us, and then out into the lake.

"Never saw anything like this before," said the less leathery one.

"What about Eric on the roof over at the Glenn place?" said the other.

"That was worse," said the first guy, "but not like this."

We left them ranking disasters and I staggered alongside Einstein, who asked, "Did you bring a car? I don't drive and we should get you to a hospital."

"Walker," I gasped. "His car, around here someplace. I think I'm going to pass out. Get out of the way."

Before I could fall, someone caught me. It wasn't Einstein. He was in front of me.

"Thanks," I said to whoever was behind me, as he helped me sit on the edge of the dock. "Could have cracked my head."

"What happened to your arm?" said Carlisle's caddy, who eased me down. "Damn thing looks like it's on by a thread."

Cheered by his observation, I bit my lower lip and watched Carlisle stride over to us from a clump of trees.

"Are you a caddy or the Red Cross?" he shouted at the caddy. Carlisle's little hat bobbed on his head and threatened to slide off.

"Hurt his arm or something," the caddy explained. "Looks like it's hanging by a string or something."

Carlisle looked at me and then at Einstein. Recognition crossed his pudgy face. "You're somebody, aren't you?" he asked Einstein, pointing a wood at him.

"Yes," Einstein admitted.

"You're a doctor . . . Doctor . . . you're Einstein, for Christ's sake," Carlisle said, scanning Einstein while I lay in pain. Carlisle turned to me. "He's the real Einstein."

"I know," I moaned.

Carlisle got on one knee next to me and put down his wood. He looked at me and at my arm and whispered, "Einstein, for God's sake. You know him or something?"

"I taught him everything he knows," I whispered, closing my eyes.

Something grabbed my limp arm and my eyes shot open, thinking that Povey had crawled out of the water, determined to drag me back into the dark lake. Carlisle had a grip on my wrist with one hand and my shoulder with the other.

"This will hurt," he said.

"Wait," I panted, trying to stop him with my free hand. But I was too weak and too late. He pulled and there was a loud pop, and a monster whose teeth looked like a beartrap gobbled the limp cord that had been my right arm. This time I passed out.

11

When I opened my eyes, I saw Carlisle looking down at me. I also saw a ceiling, which meant that I was no longer on that dock next to the golf course.

"What'd you do?" I said around a dry, swollen tongue.

"Put your dislocated shoulder back together," Carlisle said. "I'm a rotten golfer but a hell of a doctor. Try to move it. I've got six more holes to play and at this pace I won't be finished till Labor Day."

I sat up and looked around. Einstein was across the room looking at me. No Walker. No caddy. I tried to move my right arm, expecting agony, but none came.

"It doesn't hurt," I said.

"Of course it doesn't hurts," Carlisle said, standing up. "Everything's where it belongs, instead of where it doesn't belong. That's the scientific explanation. You want some advice?"

"Sure," I said, feeling the cot under me as I put my feet on the floor.

"Take a shave. You look like some killer out of Dick Tracy."

Carlisle took off before I could thank him. There were golf balls to lose, miss, and mangle. He had no time on his free Saturday for murder attempts and dislocated detectives.

"You are better?" said Einstein, stepping toward me.

"I'm better," I said. "You saved my life back there on the high seas."

"And you saved mine," he said. "I've never killed anyone before. I'm finding it very difficult, very difficult."

I stood up without falling, tried my legs and found them working. I took a few steps like the Scarecrow in *The Wizard of Oz,* and pronounced myself ready for duty.

"He was trying to kill you," I reminded Einstein.

"I am aware of that," he said, fishing in his pocket for something.

"He was working for the Nazis," I added.

"That too I know," said Einstein, taking out his pipe and putting it to his mouth.

"And he's probably not dead," I concluded, reaching for the door. "That was a small anchor and Povey is a big man. Besides, I looked back and didn't see the body come up. Anyone report a body floating out there while I was out?"

"I don't . . ." Einstein began, removing the pipe.

"Look, I'm trying to cheer you up by telling you that a paid killer who tried to shoot us isn't dead, that he's probably soaking wet and mad as hell and ready to try for you again. Like 'Wild Bill' Elliot, I'm a peaceable man, but we'd both be happier if Povey were squaring off against Old Nick right now. You want to make big bombs that kill thousands of Germans, but cracking the skull of one Nazi goon is too much for you."

"Your point is well taken," Einstein admitted, following me out the door.

"Sure it is," I agreed. "You handle the violence and leave the philosophy to me."

Einstein chuckled as he followed me out the door and down a small white-painted wooden corridor. We opened the screen door at the end and went out into the afternoon. I patted my gun, tested my arm again, and looked around for Povey. People were playing on the golf course, but Carlisle was nowhere in sight. Neither was Walker, though his car was where we had left it. Einstein watched the golfers and I watched everything. I was about ready to give up, head back to the clubhouse, and call a cab, when Walker came running up from the lake, his jacket flapping, his long legs gangling. He should have been faster.

"What happened? Professor Einstein, are you all . . . is anything . . . ?" he panted.

"Where were you?" I asked.

He stood, trying to catch his breath as he looked around, right to left, back to front, scanning the horizon as if trying to remember where he had been, trying to see it. "Looking for you, around the lake, everywhere," he stammered.

"Did you happen to run into Povey?"

"Povey?"

"Big white-haired guy with fangs, carrying a giant scimitar and a Tommy gun or two, sopping wet with a bandaged hand," I prompted. "You couldn't miss him."

"You're joking," Walker said looking at me and then at Einstein. Einstein shrugged.

"A little, perhaps," Einstein said soberly. "Perhaps a little."

"Let's just get the hell out of here," I said, knocking on the window of the car.

There wasn't much conversation on the way back to Princeton. Walker asked Einstein again how he was, and Einstein said he thought his cold was much better. I sat alone in the back, brooding and watching Einstein's mane bob on his shoulders, in contrast to Walker's neatly shaved neck and short hair nailed down with Wildroot.

With luck, pluck, and little sleep, I was keeping Einstein alive, but I knew luck was the big reason. We hit Einstein's house and he invited us both in, though I had the feeling he didn't want us to take him up on it. We took him up on it. He told me where a razor was when we came through the door. Einstein spotted the empty milk bottle I had left on the table, shrugged, and left it there. I grunted my way up the stairs as they moved to the study.

The bathroom was small, a towel on the floor, the medicine

cabinet partly opened. I opened it all the way and found an old straight razor, with a pearl handle and something written on it in German. I lathered, shaved without cutting my throat, looked at myself in the mirror, wiped the drops of soap from my shirt and grinned a horrible lopsided grin at the pug in the mirror who looked as if he were having a good time. It was then I decided for the two-hundredth time that the guy in the mirror was some kind of looney. My ex-wife Anne had seen it in my face long before I did, that young-old face with dancing brown eyes and a smashed nose, smiling when things were complicated and people with assorted weapons were trying to take him apart for scrap.

"This is what it's all about," I told the grinning fool in the mirror, not knowing what I was talking about but knowing I meant it and it was the truth. I waited for an echo to answer "Fraud," or "Nevermore," but there was no echo and no answer. I dried myself off with the towel from the floor and went back downstairs. Without checking on Einstein, I went outside, looked both ways and into bushes for a white-haired Hungarian assassin, a breed that had recently been spotted in the area, and dashed across the street. A curtain moved in the living room of the house I was heading for, but no face appeared. I went up the steps and knocked. No answer. I knocked again, louder. No answer. I knocked again and shouted loud enough to be heard in Ohio. "Open the damn door or I'm going to send J. Edgar a very nasty letter," I shouted.

The door opened and Spade reached out and pulled me in, closing the door behind me.

"You're supposed to be protecting Einstein," I said, "not dying your hair." His hair was about three shades darker than it had been in the theater. Instead of making him look younger, the darker hair made the contrast with his lined face even more evident.

"Now you're getting cruel," he said, smoothing back his hair.

"I'm sorry," I said and I was. "But where the hell have you guys been?"

"We're not perfect," he said, pointing toward the living room.

"I noticed," I said. "Povey tried to kill me. He tried to kill Einstein. You said you'd be watching him."

Archer was standing tall and stoop-shouldered at the window, looking back at me as if I were a job for Bromo-Seltzer. "We were watching," Archer said. "You want a Pepsi?"

"No, I . . . you got a sandwich with that Pepsi?"

"We got a sandwich," Spade said to me, and then to Archer he said, "It's your turn to make the sandwiches."

"My . . ." Archer began, dyspeptically pointing to himself. "What about breakfast? That doesn't count? It's not a meal? You forgot about breakfast?"

Spade advanced into the room, his false teeth clicking with rage. "I didn't forget breakfast, but someone in this room forgot coffee and rolls at a little after ten. Someone forgot, someone who can check it in the log. Does someone want me to get the log?"

"Forget the sandwiches," I said. "Just forget the damn sandwiches and tell me where the hell you were."

Spade and Archer glared at each other for about ten seconds and turned reluctantly to me.

"First place," said Archer, "don't stand out there on the porch and yell at us. The whole neighborhood knows the FBI is in here now, maybe the entire Fifth Column."

"And the Girl Scouts," added Spade.

"And the Girl Scouts," agreed Archer. "Don't do that. Povey isn't working alone."

"What the hell has that . . ." I started.

"While you were playing Fletcher Christian on the pond, we were piecing the network together," said Spade. "You sure you don't want that sandwich?"

"No sandwich," I said. "What network?"

"We have no legal obligation to tell you," Archer said.

"You sons of . . ."

"But we will," Archer went on. "Povey works for a German born in the United States, a man named Zeltz, Carl Zeltz. Zeltz is the one who helped set up the fake movie business."

"He's got a flair for the dramatic," said Spade, moving to the sofa to plop down and adjust his hair.

"Right," said Archer, pacing as he told his tale. "And Zeltz has an assistant, a young assistant who was assigned to watch Einstein and find out how much Einstein is involved in a project we can't tell you about."

"The bomb," I said.

Archer stopped pacing and Spade froze where he sat. Their faces went even paler than they already were.

"You know about the bomb?" Spade said.

"I know what I know," I said.

"Let's not be childish here," Archer said.

"You two fight about who got the sandwiches last and you tell me I'm childish?" I shouted.

"This is different," said Archer. "A sandwich isn't a bomb and don't you forget it. Who told . . . what did Einstein say?"

"I don't go around telling the FBI what my clients say. It wouldn't be good for my reputation. Let me get this straight. Povey could have killed Einstein any time, but this Zeltz is holding him off because he's trying to find out more about the bomb?"

"Something like that," agreed Spade reluctantly. "But we have reason to believe that Povey isn't listening to Zeltz anymore, that he's gotten angry, that a visitor from California, a private detective who doesn't shave very much and does things without thinking, has riled him up and he's out for Einstein's head now."

It was my turn to sit down. I found an uncomfortable Louis the Somethingth chair and soiled it with the remaining dirt from the bottom of Einstein's boat. "You mean that I'm responsible. . . . You're trying to say that Povey is trying to kill Einstein because of me?"

"Believe it," Spade said with a big, false-toothed grin.

"And you want to know who Zeltz's infiltrator is?" asked Archer with a less-than-pleasant grin of his own as he advanced on me.

"Walker," I guessed.

"Now you get the cigar," said Archer.

"He's over there now with Einstein," I said, jumping up.

"So," cried Spade. "You think he's suddenly going to bash his head in with a poker or throw a hand grenade? His job is to get information, he's not a killer. We watch Walker. He leads us to Povey and to Zeltz. That's the plan, Peters. You are making a disaster of that plan."

"You are interfering with the defense of the United States," added Archer.

"I'll have the sandwich, salami or ham," I said. "I say it's your turn." I pointed at Archer, not because I thought it was his turn, but because he was hovering over me like a D.A. digging for a confession.

"You'll take what we've got," he said, throwing a dirty look at Spade, who smirked. Then Archer stalked out of the room.

"Thanks," said Spade.

"Fair is fair," I said, standing up. "Why don't you warn Einstein about Walker?"

Spade sat back, hands folded in his lap, and shook his head at my amateurishness. "Who knows if he can act? He might get angry, give it away, get himself killed. Or maybe we tell him and he doesn't believe us and tells Walker. The whole thing is over and Zeltz has no reason to keep Einstein alive. Or Zeltz just panics and runs and we lose him. It gets complicated."

Archer came loping back with three sandwiches on a plate and an open bottle of Pepsi. He handed me the Pepsi and I took the sandwich without the thumbhole. Archer offered the plate to Spade, who took his time making his choice. I drank and ate. It tasted like Spam and mayonnaise.

"What now?" I asked.

"Now," said Archer, taking a bite of his sandwich and making a face at it. "Now we keep watching and you stay with Einstein. We try to take out Povey and let Walker lead us to Zeltz."

"The trick," I said, finishing off my sandwich, "is to keep Einstein alive while we do this. Einstein and Robeson."

"Robeson," Spade said scornfully, struggling through his sandwich with false teeth. "Robeson is a decoy, a false scent. If Povey gets them both, it looks like Nazi negro-hating—not that the Nazis will be displeased if Robeson gets killed."

"Not displeased at all," agreed Archer. "But the real goal here is to find out what Einstein knows and to get rid of him. Is all this finally sinking in, Peters?"

"It's sinking," I said.

"Good," said Archer. "Goodbye. Don't come back here. Don't call us unless it is an emergency equal to Pearl Harbor. Just stay with Einstein and let us do our job."

I finished off my Pepsi as Spade walked over to the window, pulled the curtain back, and resumed the vigil. Archer took the empty bottle and the plate. "The visit's over," said Archer over his shoulder, as he exited with the dishes. "You know your way out."

I found the door and went across the street. I wasn't worried about giving anything away to Walker, but I wasn't as sure of the game plan as the FBI seemed to be. What if Zeltz or Walker or Ivan Shark or whoever the hell was trying to kill Einstein decided that things were getting a little too warm, that they might as well cut their losses, cut down Einstein, and head for the border? I had a feeling the FBI was more interested in catching spies than saving scientists and actors. Spade and Archer did not inspire confidence.

Walker was gone when Einstein let me in, and before we could talk the phone rang. With me following, he shuffled back to his study and picked up the phone. It was someone named Rudolf. They went on for about ten minutes about changes in an article, with Einstein repeating the changes over and over till he was sure Rudolf had them right. When he hung up, Einstein looked at me with large moist eyes.

"Rudolf is my son-in-law," he explained, reaching for a cigar on his desk, then changing his mind. "He edits my work. My secretary, Helen, will come in later and retype the manuscript. It is hard to think of abstracts when one has possibly killed a man with an anchor."

"Look . . ."

"Hard," he said, picking up a pencil and checking to see if it was sharp, "but not impossible. Why do you suspect Mark Walker?" He had moved behind his desk, sat down, and fumbled for some papers. He hadn't looked up at me.

"Where did you get the idea . . ." I started, but he was shaking his head sadly and pulling out a pad of paper and making it clear that whatever denial I might make would travel to infinity.

"I saw your irritation with him at the lake," Einstein said, reaching for a glass of orange juice, which had probably been sitting there half a day. "Then you run away for fifteen minutes and come running back. Where did you go? Across the street to see the FBI. Why did you come back and look around with suspicion? Because you were looking for someone you suspected. There was no one here but me and Dr. Walker. I think I would not have noted such things if I myself were not carrying suspicion of my young colleague. But I just talked to him of such things and I am certain that he is not my enemy."

"You're a scientist," I pointed out, "not a detective."

"Yes," he agreed, "I see something miraculous in my mind and then I attempt to prove or disprove it with logic, numbers. I bite at it, shout at it, challenge it, and hope that the questions will not erode the miracle. And you as a detective . . ."

"No miracles," I said. "No big questions. Someone's in trouble. I check everything out I can think of to get them out of trouble. I put my body on the line. You bite, shout, and challenge in your head. I do it on the streets, in alleys, hotel rooms, bars."

"Yes," said Einstein with a sigh, taking a pained gulp of orange juice, "I deal compassionately with people in the abstract. I love humanity but I do not feel greatly for individuals. I'm sure a talk to my first wife, who's in Geneva, will confirm this. And you seem to have no feeling for humanity as a whole, but you touch individual people. The difference between a scientist and a detective?"

"Maybe just the difference between one scientist and one detective," I said. "I hate to bring this up, but I'm out of cash. I've had to take cabs all over . . ."

Einstein held up his hand and I shut up. He opened the desk drawer, retrieved his checkbook, and made out another check.

"I give a full, detailed accounting at the end of the case," I said, taking the check and pushing it into my jacket pocket.

"I do not usually talk this much," Einstein said, looking up at me and then turning his chair to look out of the window at his garden.

"You probably don't have many days like this one either," I said.

"I find my physical powers decreasing," he said, his back to me, his eyes on a pair of robins in a tree. "I require more sleep. I doubt if my mental capacity has diminished. My particular ability lies in visualizing the effects, consequences, possibilities, and bearings on present thought of the discoveries of others. I can no longer even do mathematical calculations easily. I do these rough notes and others, like Walker, do the details later. It is not easy to lose the few friends a person like me has. I hope you are wrong. I hope we are wrong about Walker."

I said goodbye, said I'd be in touch with him when I had

something, or I'd see him the next day in New York for the Waldorf-Astoria benefit. Einstein waved over his shoulder, sipped orange juice, and watched the birds in his yard. I let myself out and met a woman in her forties coming up the steps. She wore round glasses and a black cloth coat and carried a briefcase. She looked at me suspiciously and hurried past me to open the door. I looked across the street at the moving curtain, behind which lurked Spade or Archer. There were still two ways to go. Either I stayed with Einstein and tried to protect him or I went after Povey—one defensive, the other offensive. I remembered something Knute Rockne, the Notre Dame coach, had once said: "You can protect the goal like a gladiator, but if you don't go out there and kill a few Romans the best you can do is tie, and tying isn't winning." At least I think Rockne said it. Maybe it was Connie Mack.

I caught a bus back to Manhattan. I didn't bother to look out of the window; I was getting used to the ride. Besides, I needed time to think. A woman and a two-year-old kid sitting next to me ate cheese sandwiches all the way. The kid's nose was running. I told the woman, who informed me that it was what the noses of little kids tended to do. I suggested that she wipe it. She said she didn't have anything to wipe it with. I suggested a cheese sandwich. She suggested I could have one of her cheese sandwiches and wipe myself with it. We went on like that, passing the time like the two seasoned travelers we obviously were, the troubles of the world forgotten in our sophisticated banter. The kid kept eating his sandwich, which got soggier mile by mile, and the woman kept talking to the kid about me.

"Some people don't know how to mind their business, Ralph," she said. Ralph opened his mouth to reveal an amalgam of cheese and bread. Ralph kept his mouth open most of the time, chewing or not. He remained openmouthed and unanswering through New Jersey.

"Some people who never had kids don't know what it's like

to travel with kids, Ralph," the mother said as we crossed the bridge into Manhattan.

Ralph whimpered or sniffled, his cheese hanging limply toward the floor.

"Want to see my gun, Ralph?" I asked sweetly.

The woman snarled at me in disbelief and scorn, a snarl undoubtedly perfected by decades of living with some man more frightening than the mash-nosed grumbler riding next to her. She was a cloth-coated wreck, her hair a mess, skin papery, her banged-up suitcase scratched and coming apart.

"I was joking about the gun," I said.

"Some people . . ." she began between clenched teeth.

"I apologize," I said. "I'm sorry. I've had a rough century. You look like you've had one too."

"My husband's a soldier," she said, glaring at me as if I had just insulted her. "He's fighting Nazis, Japs, and Jews for people like you."

When I was working at Warner Brothers back in 1935, a wild-eyed old guy spent a week trying to get in to tell Ann Sheridan that Christ had died for her sins. My job was to keep him from bothering her. One day he jumped out at her when she was getting into her car. I was about ten yards back and running.

"Christ died for your sins," he screamed at her.

Sheridan raised an eyebrow, opened the door to her car, and said, "I wish he would have asked me first. I could have saved him a lot of grief."

I saved myself a lot of grief, leaned back, closed my eyes, and wondered what kind of kid Ralphie would grow up to be. I never got around to thinking about spies, murder, and the FBI.

It was almost five when I hit the Taft. I walked from the bus station. I was spending Einstein's money and my own too fast, and I figured I could think on the way. I was wrong. I checked the lobby for house detectives, killers, and telephone operators, spotted none and dashed for the elevator. I paused in front of 1234 and knocked, even though I had a key. There was no answer. I opened the door and went in.

The light was on, and Shelly, fully clothed, lay on his back in the bed, snoring. My bed was piled with pamphlets and brochures. Shelly's glasses were twisted over his forehead, his hands folded on his rising and falling belly. Our landlord, Jeremy Butler back at the Farraday Building in Los Angeles, had once seen Shelly asleep in his dental chair. Jeremy, a former wrestler who had given it up for full-time poetry and acquisition of doubtful real estate, had referred to Shelly's "undulating paunch." We had stood over Shelly as Jeremy described the dozing dentist as a "beached whale, a sleek, somnambulant mammal, capricious, unthinking, perhaps holding an unknown world in his navel, an unknown world in which a fraction of a second is a million times a million years. And when the whale wakes and turns and the roaring snore of the universe he controls stops, that unknown world will roll from his navel and tumble to the unclean floor destroyed, unnoticed."

I didn't remember all that. Jeremy had written it down before he left. He wrote most of his observations in neat notebooks and then turned them into poetry. He gave me a copy, and I remembered it as I looked down at Shelly. Jeremy's "Notes on a Sleeping Dentist" had disturbed me for a while. Later it made me feel pretty good, I don't know why. But philosophy could hold my attention for only brief periods of time.

I locked the door from inside, took off my jacket, removed my holster, and moved my right arm in a circle. Still no pain, though I could feel that the arm had been somewhere it didn't belong. While I was circling my arm, my hand hit the corner of the dresser and knocked over a glass of some flat brown drink Shelly had left there. The glass started to fall and I tried to catch it. I backed into the second bed and a pile of brochures sloshed noisily to the floor. Shelly sat up in panic as I put the now empty glass back.

"It was him," Shelly shouted, his glasses dangling dangerously from one ear. He was squinting blindly in my direction and pointing at me.

"Shell," I said gently. "We're alone. You're safe. You don't have to go Quisling on me."

Shelly groped wildly for his glasses, eventually found them on his ear, and put them in front of his eyes where they might do him some good.

"God *damn,* Toby. God *damn,*" he said, almost focusing on me as I folded my arms and leaned back against the dresser. "I can't forgive you."

"For what?" I asked.

"For . . . he asks me 'For what?'" Shelly said, shaking his head. "You almost got me killed last night. I'm here for a dental meeting. I'm a dentist."

"There are those who would dispute that claim," I said soberly.

"There are, are there?" Shelly said, struggling to roll over. "I've got some evidence here, right here." He scooped up some brochures from my bed and shook them in my direction like legal documents. "I haven't been wasting my time here. I haven't been wasting my money."

"Mildred's money."

"Mildred's and my money," he said, his fingers clutching the pamphlets to his chest. The slick sheet visible to me carried a picture of a giant tooth, a giant blue tooth. "Listen," he went on, searching furiously through the literature for some proof of his professional skill. "Why do teeth have to be white?"

"Most of them aren't," I said. "Most of the people I know have no teeth, yellow teeth, or false teeth."

Shelly wasn't looking at me or even listening. He threw paper around, searching for written support. "Gold teeth, silver teeth," he said. "Dr. McGraw-Osborn of Denver says that teeth can be healthy and any color. Women paint their eyes, their nails, color their hair. Why not their teeth? Do you know what it would mean if people began coloring their teeth with McGraw-Osborn's new process?"

"It would solve most of the world's problems and end the war?" I guessed.

"No, no, no, no," Shelly said, shaking his head. "It would make me rich. I'd have the exclusive rights to the process for California, Oregon, and the state of Washington. I'd even get Guatemala free."

"Shell, Povey tried to shoot me today. He almost tore my arm off and Einstein cracked his skull with an anchor," I said wearily.

"Yourself," Shelly said, throwing down his papers in disgust and adjusting his glasses. 'You only think about yourself. I'm talking about a great new scientific discovery that could make me rich, change the way people look."

"I'll tell Einstein about it," I said. "People with rainbow smiles."

"No," Shelly said in disgust. "This is no joke. It would just be a few teeth here and there, a single color, like beauty marks. You've got to have imagination, Toby."

"And enough bucks to pay Dr. Dan McGraw for the right to peddle green mouths in California," I said.

"Dr. McGraw-Osborn," he corrected me.

"I wish you luck, Shell. Right now I've got to wash up, change clothes, and find Paul Robeson."

"You're going to a play?" Shelly said. "Why didn't you say so? I could use a play. How about that Danny Kaye . . ."

"Robeson," I said. *"Othello."* I pulled a pair of almost clean underwear from my suitcase, selected a shirt I had only worn once and which had enough of a button left on the left sleeve to fake respectability, and moved to the bathroom.

"George Bernard Shaw," Shelly guessed.

"Shakespeare," I corrected.

"Right, Shakespeare," Shelly said with a laugh. "I knew that. Just slipped my mind. You want to see Shakespeare?"

"Right," I said, going into the bathroom and closing the door on him.

"Shakespeare isn't in English," he shouted. "Let's just get a couple of beers and see Danny Kaye or something with girls in it."

"I think there's a dentist in *Othello*," I said, turning on the bath full force. Shelly said something, I don't know what. I thought the words "pastel dentures" were part of it. I didn't care. He'd be there when I got out. We'd get a Pepsi or a beer and have a pastrami sandwich, and then before the night was over I'd arrange another chance to get us killed and we'd find ourselves a dead body. But I didn't know that at the moment. I climbed into the tub and felt the heat, the steam, and the beat. I sang what I though was Glenn Miller's arrangement of "Little Brown Jug" and closed my eyes.

12

Before we left the room I tried out my Lionel Barrymore voice. I thought it was passable. Shelly thought I sounded like Horace Horsecollar in the Disney cartoons. I needed a voice, because I wanted to use the phone and I didn't want Pauline to trap me in conversation if she happened to be on duty. With my Barrymore rejected, I could have gone with Mickey Mouse, but I'm not sure Mickey Mouse would have gotten the information I needed. I let Shelly call Bellevue Hospital and ask: (a) "What is the condition of a patient named Alex Albanese?" and (b) "Could I speak to the man guarding Albanese's door?"

The answer to the first question was "satisfactory." The answer to the second question was, "There's nobody guarding the door. Should there be?"

Shelly hung up and I considered the possibilities. First, there was someone on the door but the nursing station had been told to say there wasn't. Second, there was someone watching the room at the hospital but they were doing it secretly, using Albanese as bait. Third, there wasn't anyone guarding Albanese. I shared my thoughts and concerns with Shelly, who wanted to know where we were eating. I told him we'd see when we got there and led the way out of the room, after checking the telephone book for the address of the nearest costume rental shop.

"Vibration alignment," Shelly said as we rode down the elevator. "When you think of the future of oral health, of a decent appearance for the mouths of millions of slightly deformed Americans, you have to consider the possibility of vibration alignment."

The woman operating the elevator, and the old man who was the only other passenger, looked at the rotund dentist in momentary panic to see if he was talking about some malfunction in the elevator.

"It's a new process," Shelly went on whispering to me, loudly enough to be picked up by German submarines within fifty miles of the Atlantic shoreline. "I saw a demonstration of it this afternoon at the convention. A doctor named Max Collins from Iowa figured it out from the latest experiments in military medicine. You put this kind of thing . . ." Shelly pushed his glasses back and manipulated his hands to give me the general outline of the "thing," which must have looked something like a giant piece of popcorn. "You put this kind of thing on the patient's teeth, attach it to this electric-machine thing, and press the button. The machine vibrates the teeth into proper alignment."

"Isn't it a little dangerous, Shell?" I asked. The old man shook his head in agreement over my concern.

"Sure, a little," agreed Shelly, "but the dentist wears special gloves and gets the hell out of the room when the vibrator is on."

"So the dentist is safe," I said.

"Right," Shelly beamed.

"And you saw this thing straighten someone's teeth?" the elevator operator said, turning to us with disbelief.

"A demonstration," Shelly said. "On a dummy. The teeth were every which way and then the vibrator was turned on and they went straight."

"I'm convinced," I said.

The elevator door opened on the first floor and Shelly followed me out, saying, "Good. You have that space between your teeth that . . ."

Two things stopped the conversation. First, I handed Shelly

the check Einstein had given me, complete with my endorsement, and told him to go cash it at the hotel desk since he was registered and I wasn't. He went, vowing to return to the subject of vibration alignment, which I liked even less than rainbow teeth. Second, Carmichael spotted me and approached on little flat feet.

"We had an agreement, me friend," he said with a big fake smile.

"Your Irish accent is back," I noted.

"People might be listening to us," he said, smile frozen, looking around at the people who passed us and paid no attention.

"Carmichael, you issued an order. I am not registered in the hotel. I'm here to meet a friend who's here for a dental convention. We're going to have dinner, take in a show."

"A friend?" Carmichael asked. "And where might this friend be at the moment?"

At that moment Shelly returned, examined Carmichael through his thick lenses, and handed me a hundred dollars in fives and tens.

"Dr. Minck, this is Mr. Carmichael," I said.

Neither man put out a hand.

"You're really a doctor?" Carmichael asked.

"Are you really from Ireland?" I asked.

"I'll not be grinning from ear to ear in a second if you keep up this banter," whispered Carmichael. Then to Shelly, "Your friend here says you're here for a convention. You mind telling me a bit about the convention?"

"Mind?" I said. "It's what keeps him alive."

Shelly launched into the alignment vibrator, the chocolate teeth, and a few other crackpot gimmicks he had been saving for dinner. It took about three minutes for Carmichael to declare defeat and make an excuse to flee.

"Very interesting, Doc," he said, "but I've got me rounds to make. I'd appreciate it if you kept your friend as far from me hotel as you can. Have a good visit to our fair city." And

Carmichael beat a retreat as Shelly, mouth open, told me that the man was "rude."

"I wasn't finished telling him about the multi-extractor," Shelly said. "Why did he ask if he wasn't interested? And how could anyone help but be interested once they heard about these things? I tell you, Toby, we are on the edge of an oral revolution."

"Let's try not to fall in," I said and hustled him out into the street.

The night was clear and a little cool. No sign of rain. We walked and Shelly talked. The only thing worthwhile he told me was that there had been an announcement at his meeting that the government was changing its mind about requiring people to turn in used toothpaste tubes before they could get new full ones. They were, however, considering putting a two-cent deposit on the tubes.

"I'm glad to hear that, Shell. Now you don't have to stock up on black-market toothpaste for Mildred."

"No," he beamed. "I've already bought some special New York presents for Mildred. She'll love 'em. I got here a set of those new plastic ice cube trays. A buck ninety-five each."

"Sounds like the perfect gift," I said, stopping to look in the window of a tie store. Shelly came to my side and looked at the red piece of cloth in the window.

"What're you looking at?" he said. "That tie?"

"No," I said calmly. "I'm looking at the reflection in the window of the guy who's been following us since we left the hotel."

Shelly started to turn his head, as I knew he would, but I was ready for him. I reached out, found his neck with my fingers, and directed his gaze into the window.

"There, next to the tie, to the left," I said.

The follower wore a hat that covered his eyes and a coat much too heavy for the weather.

"Toby, I just want dinner and a show," Shelly said as I

steered him into a nearby store. "No more guns, no more shooting, no more crazy people."

Leone's Costume Rentals was a long, lean, unimpressive store from the outside. Just a door, a small window, and chipped gold lettering on the window. We were the only customers, at least the only ones I could see. The shop stretched back into darkness. I looked out the window for the guy in the coat and hat but didn't spot him.

"What're we doing here?" Shelly asked. "I thought we were getting something to eat and going to a show."

"How'd you like to meet Albert Einstein?" I asked. "How'd you like to see him give a concert?"

"Concert? He does science stuff," said Shelly, shaking his head and curling his lower lip up as he bent to examine the assortment of fake mustaches in a glass case in front of him.

"He plays a violin, too," I said. "You want to meet him or not?"

"Sure," Shelly said, touching his upper lip where a mustache that would make him look like a cartoon walrus could go. "If it doesn't get me killed."

"Then we need tuxedos. The concert's tomorrow. Einstein's paying."

Shelly shrugged and reached over the counter to find some way of getting at the mustaches.

"You want to get your wrist wrung?" came a voice from the darkness at the rear of the store.

Shelly's hand shot back as we watched a woman step out into the shade. The only light inside the shop came from the single murky window and a pair of low-watt bulbs high above us. From twenty feet away the woman looked like Barbara Stanwyck. Up close, her grey-black hair and sagging dress suggested Florence Bates.

"Nice costume," Shelly said, nervous about being caught with his hand almost in the mustache jar.

"Which one?" she asked.

"Which one? The one you're . . ." he began.

"We need tuxedos," I cut in. "One for him, one for me. Both by tomorrow morning. Can you do it?"

The woman brushed back her mop of hair, which flopped forward again, and looked out the window for some source of energy to sustain her against the out-of-town likes of someone like me. "Barrymore once gave me three hours to find an alligator suit," she said, turning back to me.

"John or Lionel?" I asked.

"Ethel," the woman said. "Two hours to come up with six cyclops masks for Belasco. And Helen Hayes one time had less than twenty minutes to replace a Civil War nurse's uniform that had been stolen. I satisfied Barrymore, Belasco, and Hayes. I can certainly come up with two tuxes in twenty-four hours, even if one is odd size."

The "odd size" comment was for Shelly. He adjusted his glasses and said nothing.

"It won't be cheap," she said, trying again to keep her hair from blinding her. "Twenty bucks for the two of you. All of it in advance."

I took out my wallet, handed her two tens, and waited while she scrawled a receipt.

"You want to get our measurements?" I asked, pocketing the receipt.

She laughed and shook her head at my foolishness. "You know how long I've been doing this kind of work?" she asked. "Do you know who my first customer was?"

"King Arthur," Shelly mumbled under his breath.

"William Gillette," she said triumphantly. "I suggested his Sherlock Holmes costume. You," she went on pointing at me. "Neck fifteen-half, jacket forty, waist thirty-six, inseam thirty-two. Sleeves thirty-six."

"Right."

"And you," she said, turning her finger to Shelly, "neck sixteen-half, jacket forty-six, waist forty-four, inseam twenty-nine, sleeves thirty-two."

Shelly started to applaud grimly. The woman folded her arms in triumph across her chest.

"Perfect, Mrs. Leone," I said. "And you can just deliver them to room twelve-thirty-four at the Taft Hotel."

"I'm not Mrs. Leone," she said, backing into the darkness with a sly smile. "My name is . . . of no consequence." And then she was gone.

"I suppose we should applaud," Shelly proposed.

"The performance was fine," I said. "Let's hope she can deliver the tuxedos on time."

Back outside we found ourselves on Forty-fourth Street near Times Square. We strolled toward a restaurant sign and went into Streifer's Restaurant, where we were shown to a table not far from the door. I sat facing the street and Shelly, seeing the menu, temporarily lost interest in the guy with the hat.

"It was just your imagination," he said after ordering the seven-course Jewish dinner for seventy-five cents.

"You're right," I said, seeing the figure stop outside the window and look toward us. I couldn't make out a face but there was something familiar about the guy.

We ate and Shelly talked. The guy with the hat disappeared but I didn't think he was far away. I think I had a chopped liver sandwich with a slice of raw onion. I know Shelly ate anything that dared come within five feet of our table.

"Great pickles," he said.

"Great pickles," I agreed, and paid the bill.

I didn't see our tail on the subway platform and I didn't see him get on the subway car with us. He had either given up or was better than he had seemed. Shelly tried to talk, but I pointed to my ears and shouted that the train was too noisy. He crossed his arms and sulked for the seven or eight stops before we got off.

I didn't have much trouble finding the little theater where I had met Robeson and where Albanese had been shot the night before. I wasn't prepared for the small crowd of people in the upstairs lobby when we got there. We headed for the theater entrance and were stopped by two men who asked us for our letters.

"Letters?" asked Shelly. "I'm a dentist."

"I'm sorry," said one of the young men, "but this is an invitation-only dress rehearsal of *Othello*."

"We'll buy a ticket," I said.

"No tickets. Only potential backers have been invited," said the second young man.

"Tell Mr. Robeson that Toby Peters is here," I said.

The young men looked at each other, at me, at Shelly. Then one of them repeated my name and disappeared. Shelly and I watched the crowd of rich people waiting, talking, drinking coffee. They didn't look rich. The men wore sports jackets or suits. The women wore dresses with frilly shoulders. Most of the women had their hair up off the neck. There were some nice necks in the crowd and some that had been around. The young man who had left returned and motioned for us to follow him. Shelly and I entered the theater, which was set up for a performance. The stage was bare. Our guide led us past the stage, beyond a curtain, and into a dark, narrow corridor that smelled like Chinese food. He stopped in front of a door, knocked, and when Paul Robeson's deep voice said, "Come in," he opened it and stepped back.

We went in and the young man took off, closing the door behind him. The dressing room was small, more like a closet. Robeson was seated on a white painted metal chair facing us. He wore a silky shirt with white trim and a shiny coat with a row of big gold lion-head buttons running down each side. This time he looked older than he had the day before. I could see flecks of grey in his sideburns. He looked at me and at Shelly.

"This is Dr. Minck," I said. "Shelly Minck. He's a friend."

"Pleased to meet you, Doctor," Robeson said, but he had something more important on his mind than polite introductions. Robeson reached across his dressing table for a piece of paper and handed it to me. The writing was neat, in large inked letters, but it wasn't in English. It made no sense to Shelly either.

"It's German," Robeson explained. "It says that I will be killed onstage tonight if I dare do a love scene with Uta."

"It's probably Povey and his people," I said, handing the note back to Robeson, who seemed neither frightened nor angry. If I had to describe his mood, I'd call it "depressed," but it wasn't quite that either. "They're trying to make it look as if you're the primary target, trying to stir up publicity."

"About what?" Shelly asked.

"Desdemona is white," explained Robeson. "There are many people, not only Nazis, who don't want this production to be mounted. If the backers believe that they are in danger or that a major racial controversy will arise, they will run for the exits with polite excuses."

He looked up at me for a response and saw something he didn't like. "'Nay,'" he said deeply, "'yet there's more in this. I prithee, speak to me as to thy thinkings, As thou dost ruminate; and give thy worst of thoughts the worst of words.' Othello says that to Iago in Act Three. Simply put, it means what's on your mind? Tell me the worst."

"I think it's more than just a scare," I said. "I think they're likely to really try to kill you."

"Toby," Shelly bleated, mouth open. "You told me we were just going to see a play, have dinner, see a play. Then spies are following and someone's trying to kill people again. I don't want any part of this."

"Your friend is right," said Robeson, standing and straightening his jacket, checking it in the mirror. "I'll alert the crew, the ushers. This is a very small theater. Everyone here has an invitation. An intruder will be easy to identify."

"Then what?" I said.

"Then the police grab him," said Shelly. "It's a good plan."

"The police won't come here. And if they do and something happens, it will be in all the papers tomorrow. That'll probably kill any chances of raising money for the production," I said to Shelly. Then to Robeson, "Am I right?"

He shrugged and said, "Probably. Who knows? A racial attack might bring out a new source of liberal money. Then I'd probably be accused of staging the attack."

"You worry too much about the maybes," Shelly said, anxious to get out of this.

"I have a law degree," Robeson explained. "It taught me to think too much of too many options. Options can freeze a man into inactivity."

"We'll be in the audience, keeping an eye out for Povey or anyone else who might not belong," I said.

Robeson, arms folded on his chest, shook his head no and then explained, "There's a fire marshal out there. All seats are taken. The audience is at the maximum. You could stand in the lobby, but if something happened you'd probably be too late."

"You wouldn't think of putting this dress rehearsal off for a day or two, would you?" I asked, knowing the answer.

"Great idea," said Shelly, rubbing his hands together. "Put it off and . . ."

But Robeson was shaking his head no again. This time the gesture was accompanied by a smile. "What we can do is get you on the stage," he said. "From behind the door at the right, you could watch the audience and the rear entrance. However, no one but cast and minimal crew are allowed backstage."

"Fire marshal," I guessed.

"Fire marshal," he acknowledged. "We could have paid him off, which is probably what he wanted, but I neither wanted to nor could I take a chance that a payoff could lead to a leak, which could lead to a scandal. This production is very important to me, Mr. Peters. Next week I will be forty-four years old. The opportunities for me to make aesthetic statements are limited."

"So," I said. "What's your plan?"

His smile was broad and I wasn't sure I liked it. I know Shelly, who was tugging at my arm, didn't like it. Someone knocked on the door and said, "Five minutes, Mr. Robeson."

"Gertrude," Robeson called out, "come in, please."

She was as thin as one of the tarnished instruments I had seen Shelly probe into the mouths of the unwary, somewhere in her thirties, washed-out red hair tied back in a ribbon. She wore a dull purple gown that dragged on the floor as she entered. Gertrude looked at Robeson and then at us.

"Gentlemen," Robeson said, "you are about to make your theatrical debuts in a masterpiece by William Shakespeare."

Gertrude looked at us in disbelief.

"There's only five minutes, Mr. Robeson," she began, "and . . ."

"Soldiers," Robeson cut in. "They can be soldiers for this night and this night only. It's important, Gertrude. Believe me."

It was evident from her face that Gertrude would believe whatever Paul Robeson said. She nodded at us to follow her.

"She'll take care of you," Robeson said, a hand on my shoulder to guide me out.

"Take care?" Shelly asked, hesitating.

"We'll see you after the show," I said, giving Shelly a shove.

"You will see me on stage," said Robeson, arms folded across his chest, gold lions growling at us.

In the hall Gertrude waited for us to clear the door, then closed it. "Come on," she said. "We've got about four minutes."

We came on, following her down the short corridor. She pushed a door open and we stepped into a large room cluttered with props and costumes. An old man in a soldier costume and a helmet rummaged around in the props looking for something, a cigarette dangling wetly and incongruously from his lip.

"Jake," Gertrude said, "two soldiers. Get them in uniform fast."

"I can't find the short sword," Jake groaned. "Some asshole took the short sword."

"Use a long one," Gertrude said, unfazed. "It's only a dress rehearsal."

"Only a . . ." Jake began, looking at us. "She says it's only. . . . What did you say?"

"I said Mr. Robeson wants these two soldiers ready for Act One in three minutes," she said, opening the door.

"Can't be done," cried Jake.

Gertrude left. Jake looked at us, smoke almost closing his eyes. "Shit," he said, turning and going quickly through uniforms on hangers on a wooden bar. He looked back at us, did some calculating in his head, and started throwing clothes at us.

"Show business is changing," Jake sighed. "Amateurs in the theater. Even the movies are going mad. You know who they just signed to direct Deanna Durbin in *Three Smart Girls Grow Up*? Jean Renoir. Renoir? He should be doing Shakespeare. Molière, Ibsen."

"What's going on?" Shelly said, catching a cloak in the face.

"Get dressed," I said. "We've only got two minutes."

"The short sword," Jake cackled. "Right here. If you two hadn't come, I'd never have found it behind that rack." He swung the sword a few times, spit on it three times for luck, and told us to hurry up.

"Don't worry. Just stick with me. I'll give you some pig-stickers to hold in your hand. And you," he said, pointing at Shelly and coughing, "those glasses come off when you go onstage. They didn't have glasses five hundred years ago in Venice. Even if they did, they didn't look like that and soldiers didn't have them. You don't look much like a soldier anyway."

I was undressing as fast as I could. Shelly stood there baffled.

"Get dressed, Shell," I said. "We're going to be in Shakespeare."

"No," shouted Shelly.

"Yes," I said. "Think of all the lies you can tell Mildred. I'll back you up on every one of them. Hurry up, Shell, we've got lives to save."

"I'm not forgiving you for this, Toby," Shelly said, unbuttoning his pants.

"Hurry up," said Jake.

We hurried. With Jake guiding us through and Shelly stuffing himself painfully in a pair of tights, we made it in about five minutes.

"We're late," I said.

"Naw," said Jake. "Dress rehearsal like this for backers always runs late, maybe ten, fifteen minutes. You look perfect."

There was a mirror in one corner with a huge cardboard box in front of it. I kicked the box away and looked at myself. I didn't look like a soldier. I looked like a fool in tights and a tin helmet. Shelly looked like a fugitive from a Wheeler and Woolsey movie. He was good for at least one prolonged laugh at Othello's expense.

"The glasses," said Jake, reaching out for them.

"Nooooo," moaned Shelly as I took off his glasses and handed them to Jake, who folded them neatly and put them on the stack of Shelly's clothes on the table. My clothes lay next to his, with holster on top. The .38 was tucked into my belt under my grey tunic. Jake led me and the blind dentist down the hall. We were ready for war.

Act I went fine. We followed Jake onto the small stage a couple of times and watched Robeson and the cast go along with no problems. No one laughed at me or Shelly. The stage is a wondrous place. I had trouble looking out into the audience, because of the overhead lights, but the audience was small and I thought I could see enough. Shelly couldn't see anything. When we looked at the entering messenger, Shelly squinted back in the general direction of the curtain.

Robeson was too busy between acts to talk to us, though he did give Shelly an approving pat on the shoulder as he eased past us.

"What was that?" asked the myopic dentist.

"Paul Robeson letting you know you were doing a great job," I said, looking through the curtain onto the audience.

"He did?" Shelly beamed, looking everywhere but the right direction.

"He did."

We got well into the second act before trouble came. Robeson had just announced, "Come, let us to the castle. News, friends! Our wars are done . . ." when I spotted a head of white hair in the audience. Povey was seated behind a smiling woman. He peeked out and our eyes met. I didn't like what I saw in his eyes.

"Povey's here," I whispered to Shelly.

Shelly panicked, turned, and tried to head for the exit, but he didn't know where it was. When Robeson said, "Once more well met at Cyprus," Jake led us out through the curtain.

I grabbed Robeson's sleeve in the small space offstage. "Povey's out there."

"I know," sighed Robeson. "I saw him. What now?"

"How long before you have to get back on stage?" I said.

Shelly squinted, strained toward us.

"Iago and Roderigo conspire for about four minutes. Then the Herald comes on. I'd say five minutes at most."

Holding Shelly's hand, I pushed past the actors hovering in the small corridor waiting for their return.

"What's going on?" Shelly cried.

I pushed into the prop room, grabbed Shelly's glasses, handed them to him and said, "No time to change."

Shelly put on his glasses and blinked.

"I thought we were still on stage," he said.

"All the world's a stage," I answered, throwing my tin helmet in the corner. "Let's go."

With Shelly crabbing and scrambling behind me in full uniform, I worked my way to a window in the corner. The only way to Povey through the theater would put us in view of the audience. I hoped for surprise and didn't have much time, not if he planned to kill Robeson the next time he came on stage. I had the feeling that he wanted not only Robeson but me too. Povey was not an easy man to discourage.

Using the prop pike, I got the window open. I crawled through and helped Shelly grunt after me.

"Our clothes," he moaned.

"We'll come back for them," I assured him.

We were on a fire escape, a fire escape that swayed with our weight and probably hadn't been used since it was built after the Civil War. I held the rusty railing and made my way down, not worrying about Shelly anymore but hearing him slip and slide, moan and groan behind me. I hit the alley, figured out where I was, and ran out to the street. The entrance to the theater was to my right. A cold breeze shot through my tight tights and I was afraid they were going to split. They didn't. I hurried to the door, opened it, and ran up the wooden steps. In the lobby, the young man who had led us to Robeson looked up at me from his folding chair near the theater entrance. I hurried past him, making a sign with my finger to my lips that he should be quiet. The .38 in my other hand helped to convince him. I could hear Shelly galumphing and panting up the stairs behind me. Povey was staring straight ahead at the stage, where the Herald was proclaiming, "Heaven bless the isle of Cyprus, and our noble general, Othello."

Robeson and most of the cast then came back on stage, Robeson's eyes finding Povey. I moved as quietly as I could behind the chairs, but even in the semi-darkness, with my gun behind my back, people looked up at the sight of one of Othello's guards in the audience. Somehow I managed to get behind Povey as Shelly burst through the entrance door. Almost everyone in the audience looked at him, everyone but Povey, whose eyes were fixed on the stage.

Povey was in the back row. I was right behind him, my gun out.

"Surprise," I whispered in his ear as I jammed the pistol into his back, but the surprise was mine. The touch of the barrel was enough to send Povey slumping forward. I reached out to grab him as his head hit the woman in the row in front of him.

"Sorry," I whispered. She turned back to the show.

The man to Povey's left tried to ignore us. Maybe he did. It was hard to ignore a man with a knife sticking out of his back.

13

I pulled Povey into a sitting position, his blank eyes aimed in the general direction of the stage, where Robeson was looking in *our* general direction and saying, "What is the matter here?"

I almost answered, "Someone just put a knife in Gurko Povey's back," when I realized the question was addressed to one of the characters on stage. I hurried to where Shelly stood, panting in his torn tights, and hustled him into the lobby.

"You left him there," Shelly cried.

I put my finger to my lips and pointed to the closed door to let him know there was a performance happening onstage almost as good as the one in the audience and the lobby. Shelly didn't care.

"He'll kill somebody," Shelly said. "Maybe me. Maybe he'll come out here and kill me. I don't want to die in a pair of tights and a silver jacket."

The lobby attendant who was standing next to us and looking back at the door said, "Please" and "They can hear you."

"Did someone go in there without a pass during the last act or just at the start of this one?" I asked the attendant.

"I've got a wooden pike," Shelly said to himself. "You can't defend yourself with a wooden pike."

"He's dead, Shell," I said. "Povey is dead. A knife this big in his back."

I spread my hands to show how big the knife was. Maybe I

exaggerated a little, but both Shelly and the attendant were impressed. Then the attendant remembered.

"A man in a coat and hat," he said, looking at the door as if he could see the man or his ghost coming or going through the door. "Said he had an urgent business message for Mr. St. Carle, would give it to him and be right out. Naturally . . ."

"What did he look like?" I asked.

"I don't know. Tallish, not too heavy. Raspy voice like he had a cold. Didn't get a good look at his face. He coughed, held a handkerchief to his mouth."

"And?" I prompted.

"Nothing," said the attendant. "He went in and came out about a minute later, maybe less. Came out and went down the stairs and out."

"The guy you said was following us," Shelly chirped. "I thought you said he . . . Toby, you lied to me."

"How long ago?" I asked.

"At dinner," Shelly said.

"No, *you*." I pointed at the attendant. "How long ago did the guy in the coat and hat leave?"

"Just before you came running in here," he said. "You probably passed him on the stairs."

I was tempted to check my father's watch, but that wouldn't have told me anything. We were three, maybe four minutes behind him. It was worth a look, though he was probably in a cab on his way to a warm bed by now. I started down the stairs, shouting at Shelly to follow me.

"Should I call the police?" the attendant horse-whispered behind us.

"No, we'll take care of it. I'm a detective. Don't stop the show. We'll be back," I called over the noise of our clomping feet.

"I'm not coming back here," Shelly shouted.

"Then you'll go through life as a colorful soldier of Venice," I reminded him. "Your pants are in that costume room upstairs."

We were outside the door now and I was looking both ways when I spotted him about half a block away, waiting at the corner. Shelly plowed into me and we made enough noise for the guy to look our way. A car pulled up in front of him as I recovered from the Shelly Minck attack and took off down the street.

"Hold it right there," I shouted, holding up my .38. He didn't stop, didn't look back. He opened the back door of the dark car and climbed in. The car took off as he was closing the door.

I looked up and down the street. Cars, not many, were driving both ways. I spotted a cab about a block down and ran for it with Shelly grunting behind me. "My tights are tearing," he moaned.

"The sky is falling," I called back. "Hold onto your pike and follow me."

The cabbie was in the front seat, reading a book. We jumped in and I said, "Hurry it up. Straight down the street and catch a black four-door. I'll let you know when I see it. I'm a detective."

Shelly collapsed next to me and the driver turned to us. I could see he had been reading *General Douglas MacArthur: Fighter for Freedom*. He could see two winded middle-aged men dressed for the wrong century.

"You missed Halloween by half a year," he said with a smile. He was a small guy, with a dark, lined face and a space between his two front teeth almost big enough for another tooth.

I showed him my gun and as mean a smile as I could muster. He turned around and started the hack.

"I told you I'm a detective," I explained as he shot past a Ford coupe.

"You got a gun and you're anything you want to be in my cab, pal," the cabbie said.

"You'll get paid," I assured him.

"Whatever you say, Sir Walter Raleigh," he said, eyes forward.

"We're . . . not. . . ," Shelly grunted as he slumped back in the corner, one hand on his chest to keep in his pounding heart, the other clinging to his wooden pike. "We're not crazy."

"There's the car," I shouted, poking the cabbie in the back.

He saw where my .38 was pointing and made for a space to catch up. We were on Twenty-fifth heading west. I strained to see into the car we were chasing. There were two figures, a driver and the guy with the hat, who looked back and spotted us.

"Can you make out his face, Shell?" I asked, but Shelly was still slumped back.

We headed uptown, zagging through traffic, keeping up with the killer's car. Neither of us was speeding. Speed might attract the police, and the guy who had knifed Povey didn't want that. I wouldn't have minded but I couldn't think of a way to get both him and us stopped at the same time. The killer's car made a sudden turn around Thirty-second Street. Our cabbie stayed right with him, but when we turned the car was gone. There hadn't been enough time for him to get to the end of the street. He was still here somewhere. The cabbie pulled over and we watched, waited. There were no cars on the street. No one was walking, and the stores were closed for the night. A few sheltered light bulbs glowed lonely over doorways and delivery docks.

"Where'd he go?" asked Shelly, squinting forward into darkness.

"One of those docks," said the cabbie. "Probably someone waiting to pull the door down behind them."

I opened the door, yanked at the tights, which were death-locked on my crotch, and got out.

"Come on, Shell," I said, my eyes on the empty street in front of us.

"Out?" Shelly said behind me. "Out there?"

"Come on," I insisted.

Leaving the cab, he tripped on the running board and did a neat waltz step, using his pike for balance. The cab door closed with a snap and the driver shot forward like Brick Bradford's space rocket.

"No," moaned Shelly.

"Yes," I said.

"Why?" Shelly cried.

"Look at us," I answered.

Shelly looked, first at me and then at himself. Even he couldn't avoid the logic of the cabbie's decision to forgo the fare and get back to a normal night of Manhattan madness.

"Let's go," I said and started down the street, keeping my hand on my .38 under my flapping black tunic, or whatever the hell it was called. I checked two docks before Shelly caught up with me, muttering, adjusting his glasses, holding up his pike to ward off sudden bullets that might spit out of the shadows. Halfway down the block I was ready to give up. We had lost them. Maybe they were in one of the dark windows above us, looking down and laughing. Then I did hear someone laughing. A door across the street from where we were standing opened, and four figures stepped out. They weren't quite boys but they weren't men yet either. What they were was big.

"Look at that," the one who came out first said, pointing at us in case the guys behind him had any thought of looking somewhere else.

"Pansies in the garden," said the second young man, who looked somewhat less human than Bushman, the gorilla back at the Lincoln Park Zoo in Chicago.

"I don't like this," whispered Shelly. "Let's get out of here."

"I'm having a great time myself, Shell," I said through my teeth, a ventriloquist's phony smile on my face as the quartet advanced on us. There was nowhere to run. Shelly was too fat and frightened, and my legs were about ten years past outrunning what was coming toward us. As they spread out in a line,

I got a better look at them. Only one was small. The others, including Bushman, were almost dark triplets. All four wore the same dark zipper jackets, with what looked like a hand-painted picture of a skull over the spot where the normal human heart should be. I guessed that three of them were named Bruno. The little one would be Sal. They spread out to block us from going up or down the street.

"You girls lost?" one of the Brunos asked.

The other three members of the iodine-bottle gang laughed.

"Or are we late for the ballet?" said the little guy.

They laughed even louder at this.

As they moved in on us, Shelly stepped forward, lifted his pike, and squealed, "Don't touch me—I've got this and I'll use it. I'm a dentist."

They started to laugh, and one of the Brunos reached into his pocket and magically produced a piece of metal I was sure would open into a knife about as long as Shelly's prop. Shadows from the dock light behind us shuffled on the street. Behind Shelly I opened my tunic and pulled out my .38. I held it up and aimed at the skull on Bushman's jacket. It was the biggest target around, and if he took one more step forward even I probably wouldn't miss. Movement stopped. Their eyes were on my gun, but Shelly in his myopic hysteria, and with his back turned to me, got the scene wrong. Convinced that his threat had turned the tide of battle, he took a step forward and brought his weapon up as if he were going to pole-vault over them.

I could see in their eyes that the group couldn't decide if the gun were real or not. Then they decided it might be. This was followed by a moment of truth in which they considered rushing us, even with a real gun. It might not be loaded. I might miss. The odds were better against two pansies in the street than against the Japs on some little island.

"I mean it," shouted Shelly with a sickly giggle.

They didn't even see Shelly.

"We think you boys should turn around, walk away, and live to piss another day," I said.

"Yeah," said Shelly, trembling.

"Shit," spat one of the Brunos. "They're not carrying any cash anyway. There's no place to carry it in those."

"They ain't worth taking apart," said Bushman. "Too easy."

"We catch you again," said the little one, "and you both get a spanking you won't forget."

The Brunos laughed, then they turned away and headed up the street, agreeing that they had milked all of the fun they could out of two night-loonies without risking a hole in the belly. I put the gun out of sight as Shelly turned around in triumph.

"God. It worked. Did you see that, Toby? Four of them." He held up his pike in one hand and hitched his sagging tights with the other.

"I'm proud of you, Shell," I said.

He beamed and adjusted his glasses, and we headed down the street in the opposite direction of the departing night raiders. When we got to a street busy enough to draw traffic, there were no cabs. We started back toward the theater, Shelly in a state of heroic bliss, me in sullen anger and sore feet. It isn't easy to walk on a city sidewalk in thin, flat-heeled shoes that curl up at the toe.

A few cabs passed. One had a pair of passengers, the other slowed down. The cabbie took a good look at us, shook his head, and pulled away. The streets weren't crowded but what pedestrians there were steered out of our way. We were either victims of a time warp who might attack them in confusion, a pair of drunks on the way home from a tasteless costume party, or something more frightening that they would prefer not to deal with. Like true New Yorkers, the people we encountered acted as if we weren't there and managed to maintain their conversations or straight-ahead concentration without letting us know that they saw us.

Twenty minutes later we slouched up the street in front of the theater, like last-place finishers in a marathon for the improperly clad.

Shelly had left his state of heroic bliss to join me in sullen silence after three blocks of walking. He limped about five paces behind me as I tried to open the door to the theater. It wouldn't open. Shelly groaned but I didn't look back as I headed for the alley. By standing on a garbage can, I managed to reach the fire-escape ladder and pull it down. We clanged our way up two flights to the window. It was open. I climbed into the darkness followed by the heavily breathing Shelly, who rolled on the floor with a thud. I was groping my way in search of a light switch, when the door of the room flew open and a man stepped in and snapped on the lights.

"What are you two doing?" Jake said in disgust, his cigarette bobbing in his mouth. He was no longer in uniform. A flannel shirt dangled almost to the knees of his worn grey pants.

"Coming back for our clothes," Shelly said.

"You walked out on the show," Jake said in disgust.

We stood before him, two sentries who had failed to protect the west gate of the castle.

"We were chasing the killers," Shelly explained.

"Killers?" said Jake. "Clothes are where you left them. Pile the uniforms neatly on the table. I'll put them away."

"The ones who killed the man in the audience," I said.

Jake took the pike away from Shelly, who looked as if he were going to protest but changed his mind.

"Man killed . . . ? Jake began and shook his head as he coughed.

"The guy with the knife in his back," I said. "You couldn't miss him. How many guys were out there with knives in their backs tonight? I mean, was it the usual count of corpses or are we behind on our quota?"

"You two don't belong in show business," Jake said, finally

removing what was left of the butt and pointing his finger at us. "At least not on the legit stage."

"There was no corpse?" I asked.

"No corpse," Jake said. "I helped clean up after the show, just like always. I've got the feeling I would have noticed a dead man."

Shelly wasn't even listening. He was frantically getting out of his costume and into his familiar oversize, not quite clean suit. I was changing, too, but not as quickly. Someone had simply come in after we left, quietly removed Povey's body, possibly smiling at the mildly curious who glanced away from the stage. But why the hell would they bother to remove the body, I thought as I changed and Jake hurried us along. The best answer I could come up with was that the killers had come back for Povey after they led us on a chase to that empty street. They didn't want him found, didn't want publicity, didn't want added protection for Robeson. They had something to do, and the corpse of Gurko Povey in the hands of the police would make it a little harder than they would like.

I didn't know why they had killed Povey, but he was dead. My job was to see to it that Einstein and Robeson didn't join him. Povey scared the hell out of me when he was alive, but at least I knew who he was. Now I was down to a name, Zeltz, without a face to go with it, and Walker, whom the FBI had told me to stay away from.

When we were finished changing, Jake followed us through the dressing-room corridor, into the empty theater, and out of the building. Back on the street we said good night to Jake, who grunted and coughed and faded into the night. Getting a cab with normal clothes on was no problem. Back at the hotel, I checked for roaming Carmichaels, predatory Pauline Santiagos, and unidentified assassins, but it was late and the lobby was empty, except for a man and a woman whispering earnestly on a sofa under a potted fern. Back home in California it would have been a palm, but the conversation would have been the same. Their heads were together. The man, who was thin and wearing a dark suit, was trying to convince the woman of something, probably to go up to his room. The woman was serious, head down, telling why she couldn't go but listening just the same.

Shelly dragged himself across the lobby. I told him I'd be right up and headed for the public phone booth near the lounge where I'd met Pauline the first time. I dropped a nickel in the slot and asked the operator to give me the number of the May house in Princeton. She made me drop most of my loose change in before putting the call through. I let it ring about fifteen times and then gave up. I scooped up the change, fished out my original nickel, and asked the operator to get me the FBI office. With a war going on, the FBI should be in business 24 hours a day. They were.

"Federal Bureau of Investigation," came a deep female voice.

"I want to leave a message for Craig and Parker," I said.

"Special Agents Craig and Parker are on assignment," she said. "Can someone else help you?"

"No, just get in touch with them or give them a message when they call in. Tell them to call Toby Peters. They know where to find me."

"I'll give them the message, sir," she said, and hung up.

I was tired when I stepped out of the phone booth, tired but not ready for bed. Another crisis stood in front of the phone booth. Her name was Pauline Santiago. She was dressed in serious black with a black sweater that looked good on her. What didn't look so good was the firmness of her jaws and the fact that her hands were folded tightly before her, as if she were next in line at Shelly's office.

"We've got to talk," she said as seriously as I had known she would.

"I've got to get some sleep," I said, letting my eyelids droop and trying to force a yawn.

"This is serious."

"A man was murdered tonight," I said, putting my hand on her clenched fists and whispering, "with a big knife in his back. That man tried to kill me. I've been chasing his killer through the night in a ballet costume. I'm tired."

"This is New York," Pauline said seriously, a quiver in the corner of her ample, red, and rather nice mouth. "People get killed and wear ballet costumes all the time. I'm pregnant."

I let go of her hand with sudden fear that even the slightest touch might impregnate her again.

"No," I said.

"Yes," she said, looking around to see if anyone had heard us.

My mind was busy shuffling the cards of death, destruction, pain in various parts of my body, and consideration of my next step in trying to protect Einstein, Robeson, myself, and Shelly while finding the killers. A bouncing baby boy or girl or both just wouldn't materialize.

"It can't be me," I said, pointing to myself to make clear to her who "me" was.

"There's no one else," she said, leaning forward, "no one. My mother said I should get this settled. My mother said we should decide as quickly as possible when we plan to get married, because she needs to give Nathanson's at least two weeks' notice to get the small banquet room. I don't know if you'll want any of your friends to come from California, but . . ."

"Let's sit down, Pauline," I said, gently taking her arm and leading her to the Tap Room, which in an era of patriotic good will was staying up all night to keep our boys in uniform and the millions who supported them drunk for a few hours so they didn't have to think about bombs, bullets, and blood. We stepped in and looked around for someplace we could have a little privacy. It was easy. There was no one in the bar except a bartender, who sat behind the bar reading a book called *Cross Creek*, and Charlie the piano player from two nights

ago, sitting alone at the bar playing with a slice of lemon, and
the two of us. We moved to a table as far from bar and piano
as possible. The bartender, a burly old guy with a thin mustache, put down his novel, sighed, straightened his little black
bow tie, and came around the bar toward us. He limped, not
much but enough to keep from looking jolly. Charlie looked
back at us over his shoulder, looked at his lemon as if asking
it for advice, decided with citric certainty that he had to go to
work, and shuffled off to the piano after dropping the last of
the lemon in an empty glass in front of him.

"What'll you have?" the bartender asked, as the piano
started playing behind us.

"Gin and ginger ale," said Pauline, on the point of tears.

"Ballantine ale," I said.

"Check," said the barkeep and limped away. I watched him
as Charlie began playing "After You've Gone," which I took
as a hint.

"Well," said Pauline.

"They're planning a second Louis–Conn fight," I said.
"Army emergency benefit relief. Conn almost won the first,
but I don't think . . ."

"Marriage," Pauline insisted.

"It's Sunday, right?" I asked.

"It's Sunday."

"Pee Wee Reese is getting married today," I said turning to
look at the bartender, who was bringing our order.

"No," she said as the drinks were placed in front of us.

"You said gin and ginger," said the bartender.

"Right," I told him. "The 'no' was for me."

"Good," said the bartender, turning his head to Charlie at
the piano, who was now playing "Ramona." "That song always gets to me, I don't know why. You wouldn't think songs
would get to a bartender, but they do."

"Are you married?" I asked, as the couple who had been
talking in the lobby came into the Tap Room, possibly lured
by Charlie's piano.

"Naw," said the bartender. "I've been a bartender all my life. I better go see what they want. Give me a wave if you want refills."

When I turned to Pauline this time, her eyes were fixed on me with burning accusation. Bette Davis and George Brent, that was us.

"Well?" she said as I took a gulp of cold Ballantine's.

"No, not too well," I admitted, putting down the glass. "How old are you, Pauline?"

"I . . . thirty-five," she said, lifting the glass defiantly to her lips.

I figured her for at least forty. It was a lie I could understand. I could even understand the lie about her name, about the husband at home. I could even understand the lie about being pregnant.

"It's too soon to know if you're pregnant, Pauline," I said. "If I'm the prospective dad."

"No it isn't," she said, her voice rising enough so that the semi-guilty couple at the table across the room turned to look. "My doctor said . . ."

"What's his name? I'll give him a call later."

"It's Sunday," she said, putting her red-painted but bitten fingernail in the drink and then pulling it out to taste it.

"I'll call him Monday, then. What's his name?"

"He doesn't have a phone," she said with an I-dare-you smile. "He doesn't believe in them. Against his religion. He's a . . . a . . ."

"Quaker?" I supplied.

"Yes," she said, "a Quaker."

"Okay, where's his office? I'll go there Monday morning if I'm still alive and walking."

"He's very busy."

"I'm sure he can work in a couple of seconds for a prospective pop."

"You don't believe me, do you?"

Charlie at the piano was playing "Tara's Theme" from

Gone With the Wind. The bartender was reading his book in the amber darkness, and the other couple was sitting silently. I wondered whose move it was at their table. Pauline thought it was mine at ours but I didn't answer. I went back to my Ballantine and almost finished it. Pauline had only tasted a fingernail of her drink.

"You don't believe me," she repeated.

"Pauline, I'm almost fifty," I said. "I've been a kid all my life. I have no sense of responsibility to anyone but my clients and a few friends. I had a wife once, a lot like you, a beauty, a good woman. She threw me out. How do you think it's going to work out for us when I find out in a week or two or ten that there isn't any baby? We get married and what do you get? A new last name, and that's it."

"Mary Louise Peters," she tried softly.

"Pevsner," I corrected. "Mary Louise Pevsner, that's my real last name."

She thought about that for a few seconds, while Charlie got carried away and started humming along with the piano. Then Pauline sighed, took a real drink, and looked up at me sadly. Her eyes were large, brown, and nice, but they sagged. She wasn't beautiful. I wasn't beautiful. The couple across the room wasn't beautiful.

"You wouldn't marry me even if I were pregnant, would you?" she asked, almost too quietly to hear.

"I don't know. I guess . . . I don't know."

Behind us the couple applauded, not for me but for Charlie, who had ended his song with a rippling flourish.

"So I just go back home to my mother and a bowl of Cheerios for breakfast?" she asked.

"No," I said. "Stick with Shredded Ralston or Wheaties. Cheerios are just a fad, like jazz and the war. They'll be gone in a year."

"And you?"

"I'll be gone in less than a week," I said, finishing off my glass of ale. Charlie was now belting out "Where Oh Where

Has My Little Dog Gone?" complete with "woof-woofs,"
which the two happy couples were supposed to help him with.
No one helped him. "Come on," he called, "let's all join in."

"You feel like woof-woofing?"

Pauline shook her head. I took that for no and got up to
pay the tab. The other couple got up too. They didn't look
much like woof-woofers. Where was Shelly when someone
really needed him? I paid the bill and took Pauline's hand as
we walked out of the Tap Room. The piano and Charlie's
voice went on serenading himself and the bartender.

"You want to stay with me tonight?" I asked. "I mean for
what's left of the night?"

Pauline shrugged. Righteousness had been replaced by total
defeat. She looked blowsy, flat-footed as a middleweight
who's gone through six or seven rounds with Henry Arm-
strong. "Sure," she said, finding a weak smile. "Beats going
home to Mom."

"That's the nicest thing anyone's said to me all week."

That got a small laugh out of her. We got in the waiting
elevator and roused the operator who took us up to twelve.
When we got to the room Shelly was snoring gently. We
didn't wake him.

We got undressed in the darkness and moved under the
cool blanket and sheet of my bed. We didn't even whisper as
we made love to Shelly's snoring. I thought of Anne, pushed
the thought out of my mind, and strained in the darkness to
see Pauline's face. Enough night light filtered through the
drapes to see her closed eyes. I wondered who or what she
was thinking about. Suddenly it was easy. I thought about
here and now and Pauline and it was good.

We slept for about three hours. I kept waking up with
Pauline's hair in my mouth and a variety of body aches. The
worst ache was the one in my head from my sea battle with
the now deceased Povey. I had a dream. At least I think it
was a dream. Maybe I just imagined it as I lay there waiting
for the sun.

In my dream, Povey was standing down a deep dark corridor, beckoning to me with his hand, beckoning for me to follow him. I didn't want to follow him. Koko the Clown leaped out of the door to my left, scaring hell out of me. He took my hand and tugged me in the direction of Povey, who kept motioning for me. Koko was marshmallow-soft, no strength, but I couldn't resist him because the floor was made of ice. I slid forward without moving my feet. Maybe the hall had tilted downward or maybe the slight pull of the clown was enough to get me moving. I slid closer and closer to Povey who, when I got close enough, turned to show me the stiletto in his back.

"They stabbed me in the back," he said, rubbing one hand through his bristly white hair. "And now I stab them." Povey pointed at a door in front of us in the darkness, with only a little light coming under it to betray its presence.

"Open it," said Povey.

Koko skated around me out of sight, and then appeared before me, his face huge as he stuck out his tongue and said, "Open it."

"Killers are there. Iago is in there. Betrayers are in there. Traitors are in there," Povey said. "The worst thing about having a knife in your back is that it itches and you can't reach it."

The hell with it. I opened the door. The sudden light was blinding. I was afraid that the killers could see me but I couldn't see them. Koko and Povey were gone. On my left was Einstein in a little sailor cap, on my right Paul Robeson, still dressed as Othello.

"Too much light," said Einstein.

"You can't see when there's too much light," said Robeson.

"You can't see when there's too much light or too much dark," said Einstein. "When there is too much of either in the spread of infinity, one imagines and tests the imagination. What do you see, Tobias Leo Pevsner?"

"Nothing," I said with a dry mouth. And then I saw, or

imagined I saw, two or three figures. I screwed up my face
and strained into the light but I couldn't make out the faces.
One of the figures was tall. It moved forward holding something out to me. It looked like a club.

"Take it," came the hollow voice of the figure.

I reached out to take it. Whatever it was I wanted it, even if
it came from a killer, but before I could touch the thing in his
hand, Koko shot in front of me, laughed, and said, "Back to
the inkwell."

"I know the ink well," said Robeson at my side.

"Hold it," I said, slipping backward away from the tall figure with the club. But they didn't hold it.

My eyes opened. Pauline was looking down at me. "Hold
what?" she whispered. "Are you having some kind of dream
or something?"

I sat up and looked around, hoping to hold onto something
from the dream, some piece of truth. My eyes hit the mirror,
the empty beer bottles, our clothes in a pile on the chair,
Shelly on his back, blanket drawn up to his chin, still snoring.
He looked strange without his glasses.

"I'm okay," I said. "What time is it?"

"I don't know, morning. I want to get out of here before he
wakes up."

The morning light didn't do good things for her. I was sure
it didn't for me either. I knew it did hell for Shelly. Pauline
wanted to escape and I wanted to let her. We both felt guilty.

"I'll get up and we'll get some breakfast," I said, starting to
follow her as she crouched over to the chair for her clothes.
She was not light but there was a nice softness about her
across the room. Shelly stirred, opened his eyes, looked
around, fixed on Pauline, blinked and fell back, lids dropping
to snore again.

Pauline shook her head no to my breakfast offer and put
her finger to her lips to indicate that I should be quiet. I was
quiet, trying to hold onto the truth of the dream. Something I
had seen in the room touched, worked, connected to the

dream, almost woke up a truth. I watched Pauline dress quickly. She pulled on the black sweater, messing her hair even more. "See you later maybe," she said.

"Later," I said.

Then the door clicked and she was gone. The click of the door shot through Shelly, who sat up suddenly, yelled "What, What" and scrambled for his glasses. He found them next to his cigars on the night table and hurried them onto his eyes to see what was going on.

"A naked woman," he said, looking around. "I saw . . ."

"What, Shelly?" I said with a yawn.

"I saw a . . . Forget it."

I forgot it and tried to think, to imagine, but it was gone. Shelly was out of bed, staggering in his two-piece blue flannel pajamas and making unholy sounds in his throat. He made it to the bathroom door, turned on the lights, saw himself in the mirror, groaned, and staggered back to the door to look at me.

"And you," he said, pointing a pudgy finger in my direction. "I'm not talking to you. I'm not forgiving you. Last night was . . ."

"Like a bad dream?"

"A nightmare," he returned.

"Like a naked woman running by your bed."

"Naked wo . . . I didn't dream about . . . I've got to get in the bathroom."

He closed the door behind him and turned on the water in the tub. Shelly would soak for an hour, maybe two, depending on what he had in there with him to read. I remembered the pile of dental pamphlets and looked around for them. They were gone, probably neatly stacked next to the tub. I got out of bed, examined black and grey hairs on my chest and the scars of half a century. The stomach looked reasonably flat, the legs reasonably strong. I got up, ready to meet the day and put on my underwear.

A church bell rang outside. I hadn't heard one before. It seemed strange to hear a church bell in Manhattan, and then I realized it was Easter Sunday.

14

Pants, clean shirt with all the buttons, socks and shoes. I was looking at my unshaven face and wild hair in the mirror when a knock came at the door. I kept looking in the mirror, finding new strands of stiff, wild grey in the jungle of brown, and called, "Who is it?"

"Carmichael," came the voice of the house detective, brogue back for Easter services.

"Who is it?" shouted Shelly.

"House detective," I shouted. "Something about a naked woman."

Shelly splashed wildly behind the bathroom door and I let Carmichael in. His suit was pressed, neat, dark. He wore a matching vest complete with watch fob, his tie silky with grey and brown stripes and his hair plastered back. He was also carrying a large white cardboard box.

"Natty," I said.

"It's a holiday," he answered, stepping past me and looking around the room for bodies or contraband. "You should shave, brush your furry teeth and hair. It's Easter Sunday." He put the white box on the bed.

"Carmichael, you don't need that Cheshire Cat of a brogue in here," I said. "You're among enemies."

"Can't help it. Gets in the blood. Package was delivered for you two this morning from Leone's Costume Rentals. You boys planning to dress up as bunnies, are you?"

The bathroom door burst open and Shelly staggered out,

soaked, a towel around his too-much waist. One hand held the towel in place. The other kept his glasses from sliding to the floor. He almost fell in a puddle of his own making. "There's no naked woman in here," he cried at Carmichael.

"No one said there was, you madman, you," sighed Carmichael.

"I'm a dentist," Shelly shot back.

"I hope not in this state or Kansas where my brother lives," said Carmichael.

"I resent that," cried Shelly.

"A healthy response," said Carmichael approvingly. "Now if you'll just slide back in the bathroom, I've got some business with your chum out here."

Shelly gurgled, retreated, and closed the door behind him.

"Not the most festive of sights on a holy day," whispered Carmichael.

"He fits in just fine on April Fools' Day," I said, finding a comb in my rotting suitcase and applying it to my reluctant hair. "Were you going to pass the morning insulting helpless dentists or is there something on your mind? If you're going to try to . . ."

"Two gentlemen want to see you in room nine-oh-nine," said Carmichael, watching my face for a reaction. "Room's registered to a Mr. Orville Potts. Mr. Potts seems to be among the missing and, according to the maid on the floor, our Mr. Potts looks a lot like the gentleman you say tried to put a bullet hole through you. You wouldn't know anything about where Mr. Orville Potts might be?"

"Have I got time to shave?" I said in answer.

"Make it fast. The gentlemen might get impatient."

I went through the bathroom door without knocking and Shelly, deep in the water, pamphlet in hand, looked up in fear and then sullen anger. I wiped off the bathroom mirror with a clean towel and lathered up.

"God," sighed Shelly. "A dentist right here in New York has a plan for replacing teeth. Pull out the bad ones, make a hole right in the bone under the gum, and stick in a permanent artificial one."

"That's sick," I said.

"No," Shelly said, splashing, "it works. It's a great idea."

"Might put you out of business," I said, finishing off my face. "If everyone has permanent artificial teeth, they won't need cavities filled. Chew on that one for a while, Shell."

I could see Shelly in the mirror, worrying about the future of his dental practice. "I'll be back in about an hour," I said and left him to ponder his fate. "Why don't you hang up the tuxedos?"

Carmichael was in a good mood as he led me into the elevator.

"Nice suit," I told him again.

"Wife says it's spiffy. Not as spiffy as a tux, though. You boys planning to crash a party?"

I didn't answer.

The female elevator operator, a ringer for Una Merkel, examined Carmichael and didn't seem to find him particularly spiffy. It didn't bother him at all. On the ninth floor, Carmichael led the way to Povey's room, knocked at the door, and waited till a familiar voice called, "Come in."

We went in, with me first. Spade, whose name was really Parker, stood at the window, looking out as if he had a piece of stringy meat caught in his dentures. He turned to be sure it was us, started to reach up to adjust his hairpiece, decided we weren't worth it and turned back to his view of the street. Archer, whose real name was Craig, paid more attention to us. He sat on the edge of the single bed, as if he had just been awakened from a nap, which he may have been. "Thanks, Mr. Carmichael," Craig said. "Your country appreciates your cooperation and your commitment to keep this business within your confidence."

"That I'll do," Carmichael said. Then the house detective stood watching, hands behind his back, as if he expected a tip.

"We'll give you a call if we need you," Parker said from the window.

"Oh, right," said Carmichael, losing his accent again. "I'll be in the lobby till eleven, then I'm going to church."

"A very good idea," said Craig, standing up and grimacing as he massaged his lower back. "My partner will show you to the door."

"I showed him to the door the first time," Parker grumbled.

"You can show yourself to the door then," the stork-shaped Craig said. Carmichael turned, walked to the door, looked back, hoping they had changed their minds but they hadn't. He adjusted his vest, checked his pocket watch, and left.

"We've got no Pepsi or tuna to offer," said Parker, turning to me slowly. "Just some information and advice."

"We've lost track of Povey," Craig said, still rubbing his back.

"That's why I called you," I said, leaning back against the desk at the foot of the bed. "He's dead. Someone, probably your archenemy Zeltz, or one of his crew."

"That's why you called us?" said Parker, looking up at Craig.

"Right. It happened at the theater last night. Dress rehearsal for *Othello* backers. Povey showed up with a gun. Before I could get to him, someone put a knife through him. I went after the guy who did it and lost him. When I got back to the theater, Povey's body was gone. No one even noticed he'd bought a one-way ticket to spy hell."

"That's when you called us at the Bureau," Craig said.

The conversation was getting boring but I said, "Right. You said you had some information."

"And advice," Craig reminded me. "Povey's being dead . . ."

". . . if he is dead," Parker picked up.

"He's dead," I said.

"Povey's being dead complicates things a little," said Craig, letting go of his back slowly, ready to grasp it again if it called for help. "Now we don't know what the guy looks like who'll try to kill Einstein and Robeson tonight."

"Tonight?" I said, to keep the conversation flowing.

"Tonight, just at the break in the charity concert," explained Parker. "He'll . . ."

"Maybe she'll . . ." Craig cut in.

"He, she, it, the Frankenstein monster, will blow them up or shoot them down when they're together in public. New game plan seems to be to show how vulnerable the U.S. is, to show we can't protect anyone they want to get rid of," said Parker.

"How did you . . . ?

"Wire tap," explained Parker. "Walker. They were talking in code, simple code. D'Amato in the Washington Bureau listened to the wire recording and broke it in about five minutes, seemed upset that we bothered to bring such an easy one to him. The break in the concert should be about nine tonight, give or take fifteen minutes."

"You stick with Einstein," said Craig. "We'll have men in the ballroom, outside the ballroom, serving drinks, drinking drinks, maybe even playing the piano."

"Why not just cancel the concert?" I asked.

Craig and Parker looked at each other in mutual sympathy. "Because," said Parker, "we're not sure when or where the next time might be. We got a little lucky . . ."

"There was some skill and a lot of money involved here, too," entered Craig.

"A lot of money, skill, people, machines, whatever," agreed Parker. "It's better to flush them out like . . ."

"Decayed pulp in a rotten tooth," I tried.

They both looked at me as if I were not to be trusted or treated as a sane human being.

"That's not the way I'd put it," said the birdlike Craig, cocking his head to one side. "But my partner's not a manic dentist."

"Just a manic-depressive," said Parker. For some reason the joke got them both. They smiled at each other and at me. I smiled back.

"You guys make a mistake and my client and Robeson get killed," I said, pushing away from the desk and removing the last of their smiles.

"We've got a pretty good record, remember," Craig said.

"These guys aren't Dillinger and Alvin Karpis," I reminded them.

"You just stay with Einstein and leave the rest to us. Maybe we'll send a couple of dozen cartons of Camels in your name to our boys overseas," said Parker.

This was even better than "manic-depressive." They both laughed and shook their heads, small laughs but definitely laughs.

"And . . ." I began.

"We've got one of our best men on Albanese," Craig said, correctly anticipating what I was going to say. "But after the try on Einstein and Robeson tonight, the Chief . . ."

"J. Edgar . . ." Parker began.

"I figured," I said, as Craig went on.

". . . believes that Albanese won't be of any interest to Zeltz. Zeltz won't care who or what he identifies if he lives. The assassins will be on their way home through Canada or Mexico or on a submarine, or they'll dig in so deep in a little town somewhere that his description won't help. Any more questions?"

"No."

"Then," said Parker, pointing to the door, "goodbye."

"And good luck. You've got time to take in the Easter Parade. We'll see you at the concert, but you probably won't see us."

I left and made my way back to Shelly, who was out of the bathtub and sitting in a purple robe on his bed, a stack of pamphlets in his lap. He started to say something when I came through the door, remembered that he wasn't talking to me, and held the pamphlet in his hands in front of his face. A belch of smoke from his cigar came over the top of the pamphlet. The empty tuxedo box was on the floor and I could see both tuxes on hangers in the open closet.

"I thought you wanted to meet Albert Einstein?" I asked Shelly.

The pamphlet came down slowly, suspiciously. "I met Paul Robeson last night," he said cautiously. "I didn't get a chance to talk to him. I didn't even get a good look at his teeth. What are Einstein's teeth like?"

"Not bad," I said, trying to remember the scientists's teeth.

"I've got some things I'd like to ask him," Shelly said to his cigar.

"Maybe we can arrange an impromptu interview," I said, sitting on the bed.

"One man of science to another," Shelly said, beginning to enjoy the idea. "I'd like that."

"But . . ." I said. "There is something I'd like you to do."

"Something you'd like me to do," laughed Shelly. "But . . . aha. I knew it. Who do I have to let shoot at me? Or throw me off a roof? Or saw off my legs? Or . . ."

"Shell, forget it. I have to stick with Einstein this afternoon and tonight, and I thought you'd like to be with me. You could help. Don't worry. I just met with the FBI and they know what time the Nazis are going to try to get to Einstein. You'll be long gone by then, back in the room or taking in a play on Broadway."

"Paul Muni's in something that just opened," Shelly said, getting out of bed. "Remember, in *Scarface,* he looked like a monkey? Tony, that was his name. I took Mildred to see that on our second date. I told her Muni looked like a monkey and she said he looked handsome. It was our first fight."

"Young love."

Now that Shelly and I were pals again, I called Einstein in Princeton. I wasn't worried about Pauline being on the other end. She was home in Queens with mom. A woman answered on the fourth ring, and when I asked for Einstein after identifying myself, he came on about a minute later. I told him about Povey's death and asked him how he planned to get to New York.

"A colleague will bring me in his car," Einstein said. "I don't drive. I plan to get to the Waldorf Hotel about six."

"I'll be waiting at the front entrance," I said. "One more thing. The FBI says that a group of Nazis is planning to kill you and Paul Robeson tonight at the break in your concert. If you want to call it off . . ." I didn't tell him that the FBI had got this information by tapping Walker's phone.

"So they can try again when the FBI is not ready for them?" he asked.

"They made the same point," I told him.

"It's nice to know that Mr. Hoover can be so logical," he said with amusement.

"Tell him about me," whispered Shelly behind me. I didn't look back, but I could smell his cigar breath over my shoulder.

"I have a friend with me, a Dr. Minck, who'd like to meet you when you get here," I said.

"Fine," replied Einstein and hung up.

I hung up and turned to Shelly.

"What'd he say?" Shelly asked. "About me?"

"That he had heard of you and was looking forward to hearing your ideas about space, time, infinity, and gum surgery."

Even Shelly wouldn't buy that, but I had him hooked so he didn't push or pull. I told him we had someplace to go before lunch, that it was safe. He wasn't sure whether to believe me but he had gone in for the ride now. He put on his clothes, selected some dental brochures to show Einstein, and plunged them into his jacket pocket in case we didn't get back to the room to change into our tuxedos.

"Ready," he said.

Shelly wanted to take a cab, but I was already thinking of

what my expense account for this case would look like. I asked the doorman how to get to Bellevue Hospital by subway. It sounded easy.

We were in the hospital lobby about a half hour later, at four o'clock according to my Dad's watch, eleven according to the clock over the reception desk.

"My name's Alfredo Albanese," I said with a fake Italian accent. "This is my brother Franco. We come to see his son Alex."

The woman behind the desk looked at us suspiciously. Her white hair was stylishly piled up to show nice white ears and pearl earrings. Her white blouse had a nice billow at the neck and a gold cross dangled from a thin chain around her neck. She looked from me to Shelly, who squirmed, fixed his glasses, and said, "That'sa right." If my attempt at Italian dialect was bad, his was early Chico Marx.

The FBI might have a no-visitors-of-any-kind notice on Albanese, or they might just let us up and grab us at the door, or maybe we could make it to the bedside if we were lucky. Part of me wished we didn't make it. Part of me wanted to believe the Bureau could do no wrong, but Craig and Parker did not inspire confidence.

"Room two-thirty-one," she said, putting down the phone and handing us a card. "Elevator at the end of the hall. He is no longer critical but the doctor in charge says you should stay for no more than five minutes."

"Thanks," I said with my least sincere smile.

"Blessa you, lady," Shelly said, clasping his hands together. I grabbed his arm and pulled him down the hall toward the elevator.

"Pretty good, huh?" he said, beaming and looking back at the receptionist, who had turned to another visitor.

"Best supporting actor," I agreed.

We got up to two with no trouble. At the nursing station we showed our pass and were escorted to Albanese's room by a burly blond guy with muscles, who was dressed in hospital whites. I figured him for FBI, figured that he would march us to the guy in charge, and I'd have to explain about Craig and Parker. They'd call Craig and Parker, find out I was all right, and then boot Shelly and me out of the hospital. But the orderly led us right to Albanese's room.

"Craig and Parker called, right?" I guessed.

"I wouldn't know," the blond said with a slight Southern accent. "You've got five minutes. I'll be right out here waiting'."

We went in and I closed the door behind us. Albanese was alone in the room, on his back, his eyes closed. The small Philco table-model radio next to the bed was turned on and a bass announcer's voice was saying, "against the Chinese and British lines. And that's the eleven A.M. news bulletin from the New York *Times*. Stay tuned every hour on the hour to WMCA, 570 on your dial for the latest news."

I turned off the radio and looked down at Albanese, Shelly at my side, breathing heavily. I think it was Shelly's breathing that woke Albanese. His eyes clicked open, focused on the ceiling, then turned in our direction, while his head kept pointing upward. Only when he saw us did he start to slowly crank his head toward us. Shelly was a puzzle to him. His eyes said I looked vaguely familiar. He looked even younger lying there than when I had first met him.

"How are you doing?" I said. I could see how he was doing.

"I was shot," he said softly, so that I had to lean toward him to catch the words. "I believe it was you who shot me."

"What did he say?" asked Shelly.

"He thinks I shot him," I explained. Then to Albanese I said, "I didn't shoot you. It was a guy named Povey, the one you thought was a movie director."

Albanese looked around anxiously. I put a hand on his shoulder.

"Don't worry," said Shelly with a smile. "Povey's dead. Knife this big right through him." Shelly's hands were spread far enough apart to hold a baseball bat. Albanese looked even worse.

"Can you answer a few questions?"

Albanese nodded, closed his eyes, and opened them again. "Yes, I believe I can. The doctor said I'd be laid up rather a long time. I'll probably lose my part in *Othello*. I would have made a most convincing soldier."

Since he didn't know he had been on the verge of a pink slip when Povey shot him, I nodded in sad support.

"We were in it last night," Shelly said proudly. "Soldiers. I think Toby played your part. We weren't professional enough. Robeson said he really could have used you on that stage. I had one of those pike things. Like this." Shelly spread his hands the same distance apart as he had for the knife that had killed Povey.

"Shell, go ask the orderly if we can get a cup of water for Alex."

"Sure," said Shelly, fixing his glasses. And then to Alex, "you'll be fine, fella. I've seen them in worse shape than you." With these words of comfort, Shelly left the room.

"He's a doctor?" Albanese ask in confusion.

"A dentist," I said. "But some of his patients are in worse shape than you are."

"I've mucked things up, I'm afraid," he said, closing his eyes and starting to drift off. "No role, no moving picture."

"You saved my life," I said. "And you helped catch a Nazi assassin. You can do more, too. You can give me information to catch the rest of the gang or spy ring, or whatever it is. Just slowly, carefully tell me whatever you can about the other people who worked with Povey on the movie you were in . . ."

"*Axes to the Axis*," he recalled with a smile. "I really did have several fine scenes in the film. Pity they're gone."

"Pity," I agreed, leaning even closer as the lids of his closed eyes began to flutter. "Tell me what you can about the people who made the movie."

He talked. I missed some of it. He repeated some. Some
didn't make much sense. I didn't interrupt, even when he
gave me the plot of the movie he didn't make. When he was
finished, I asked a few questions. He answered. The last word
he said before he drifted into sleep was "hair."

The door behind me opened and the blond orderly stepped
in. "Time's up," he said.

Shelly tried to move past him into the room, but the orderly
filled the door and kept him out.

"I try to tella him I gotta get in, buta no," said Shelly.

"Drop it, Shell," I said. "Let's go."

The orderly stepped back and moved to check on Albanese. "Hold it," he called.

Shelly looked like he was going to run. I grabbed his jacket
and held on tight. The orderly checked Albanese and, satisfied, turned to us. "Okay. You can go."

I didn't have much to say on the way back to the subway,
and even less on the train. I let Shelly talk. He didn't seem to
notice my silence. He pondered on the possibility of a joint
career, dentist and actor. "The acting dentist," he tried, trip-
pingly on the tongue. "The first acting dentist."

"Edgar Buchanan," I muttered. "He's a dentist."

"Nothing wrong with being second," mused Shelly as we
rocked uptown. In spite of Easter, the subway wasn't very
crowded. The few passengers were better dressed than we
were, but neither of us seemed to mind. We got off the subway two stops early and ate hot dogs and Pepsis at a corner
stand. Shelly breathed in three koshers with the works. I
looked at the clouds.

"Let's get back and brush our teeth," Shelly said, after
gulping down his second king-size Pepsi.

"I just rinsed my mouth with cola," I said.

"Not the same thing," he said.

"I've got other things on my mind," I said, starting up
Broadway toward the hotel.

"More important than your teeth? More important than your body? Your teeth go and then . . ."

". . . your mouth, your gums, your whole body. And then where are you?"

"Right," he said, "where?"

"In New York trying to figure out how to outsmart a killer."

"That's changing the subject," said Shelly, with the superior smile he usually reserved for helpless patients reclining awkwardly in his dental chair back in the Farraday Building.

People of various sizes and ilks passed us. We walked through Times Square and Shelly suggested that we stop off for dessert at Streifer's, which was about a half block away. He still had memories of our seven-course dinner for seventy-five cents. I had memories of the person with the hat who had followed us there, tailed us to the theater, and killed Povey. "No dessert," I said. "I'll watch you."

"It's not the same when you do it alone," he said, looking longingly down Forty-fourth as we kept walking.

"True of a lot of things, Shell."

"Don't worry about Einstein and Robeson," he said reassuringly. "The FBI will take care of them. Enjoy the city, the sea air, the good food. Hey, it'd take an Einstein to figure out who killed Povey."

"Maybe that's who we should ask."

"We'll just go brush our teeth and have a nice walk down Fifth Avenue. Maybe I'll give Mildred a call," Shelly went on. "That's it. I'll give Mildred a call. What did you say about Einstein?"

"Nothing important," I said. "Let's go brush our teeth and call Mildred."

15

When we got back to the Taft after lunch, Shelly tried to call his wife in Los Angeles. Mildred wasn't home or wasn't answering.

"At her sister's," Shelly said, hanging up. He called the sister, who said she hadn't talked to Mildred in a week.

"A friend's," Shelly said, putting down the phone with a shrug. "I wanted to tell her about the convention."

"You can surprise her with it all at once when we get back," I suggested. "Meanwhile, let's get into those tuxedos and over to the Waldorf."

Lady Macbeth from Leone's Costume Shop had been right. The tuxes fit us perfectly. Shelly looked like a waiter, and I looked like a hood at the testimonial dinner for Little Caesar. It felt like the cardboard backing was still in the shirt, and a few stray pins were waiting to get me, just when I thought I had them all out and neatly stowed in the hotel ash tray.

"Shell, I can't guarantee that this is going to be a quiet afternoon and evening with a string quartet," I said, trying to stretch the stiff white collar so I could breathe.

Shelly was busy admiring himself in the mirror over the dresser as he replied, "Hey, it won't kill me, but if it does, I can live with it. How do you think I look?"

"Like Eugene Pallette in *The Male Animal*," I said.

"I know that name," said Shelly, looking at me.

"A movie star," I said, looking at my reflection but not admiring it. "Let's go."

The phone rang as we were about to leave and Shelly waddled back, his tails flapping in the hope that it might be Mildred or a mad dentist with a scheme for making false teeth out of synthetic rubber. It was neither.

"For you," Shelly said, disappointed, glancing one more time at his rotund reflection in the mirror and holding out the phone for me. I took the phone and a look in the mirror, seeing nothing there that would account for the pleased smile on his face as he adjusted his shiny black collar. Did he see Robert Taylor where I saw Eugene Pallette?

"Toby?" It was Pauline's voice. I feared another assault on my bachelorhood.

"Pauline, we're on the way out. We've got to get to the Waldorf."

"Carmichael is looking for you," she said. "He called in about twenty minutes ago and said he was on the way, that it was important and I should tell you to wait for him."

"We've got to go, Pauline," I said, examining myself in the mirror over Shelly's shoulder to see if and how much my gun showed under the jacket. It showed. I unbuttoned the jacket. It was better but not perfect. "Carmichael can find us at the Waldorf. I'll talk to you later." I hung up before she could tell me more. I prodded the Narcissus of the Taft Hotel and he reluctantly parted from his reflection and went to the door.

Tuxedos bring you respect. They also earn you some snickers and odd stares if you look like stand-ins for Abbott and Costello. We were the comic relief of Easter Sunday. We were a few light-moments away from the war news. We were nothing special in the Manhattan Easter light show. The doorman got us a cab and held the door open. The only other person who had ever held a car door open for me was a hood from Chicago who, along with his partner, had taken me for a ride and a talk about my rude behavior. The partner had stood behind us with his hand in his pocket, holding on to a pistol of European origin. But the doorman, ah, the doorman at the Taft recognized gentry, even comic gentry. As we got in the cab, I felt like Herbert Marshall.

"You guys doin' some kind of practical joke or something?" the jowly cabbie said, looking over his shoulder at us. The doorman closed the door and backed away.

"We're going to the Waldorf for a private concert," said Shelly.

The cabbie shrugged and looked into his rearview mirror so he could pull out onto Seventh. "No skin off my nose," he said.

The ride was short and the cab fare about what I expected. I entered it in my notebook as Shelly got out of the cab. The doorman at the Waldorf hurried to open the door for us. "Good afternoon," he said, big-chested and blue-uniformed with braid.

"Good afternoon," Shelly said, adjusting his cuffs. "We're here for the concert, the charity concert."

"Certainly, sir," the doorman said. "Which charity do you represent?"

"We don't represent any charity," Shelly said, grabbing for his glasses as they slipped down his nose. "We . . ."

"Excuse me," the doorman said, moving past us to open another cab door.

"Let's go, Shell," I said, taking his sleeve.

Shelly glared back at the doorman who had forgotten us and mumbled, "Charity, charity. Do we look like charity cases?"

"We don't look like patrons of the arts," I said, and pushed through the door into the lobby. The lobby looked like an MGM set. People were crowded together, talking like extras. You couldn't make out what they were saying but you could hear the busy hum. A waiter in a red jacket danced gracefully past carrying a tray covered by a starched white cloth in one hand. Signs indicated that there were restaurants all over the place. I moved from under a fancy chandelier hanging from the ceiling and toward the busy desk. No one backed away from us, but I felt a few glances.

The guy behind the desk looked as if he had just stepped out of a barber shop. His dark hair had one wave, not a strand out of place. He wasn't young. He wasn't old. He wasn't skinny. He was elegantly slim. "Yes, sir?" he queried with a small professional smile and both hands resting gently on the desktop, ready to spring into action and meet any request we might have.

"We're here for the relief concert," I said, "the Einstein–Robeson concert."

"Yes," he said. "The extra waiters aren't scheduled to arrive till three."

"We're not waiters," Shelly said. "Look at us. We're guests, guests. Do you know whose guests we are?"

The clerk's mouth moved. It was too good a straight line to pass up but he was too good a clerk to take it. He was a class act. "I'm sorry, sir, I don't know."

"Albert Einstein," Shelly said, looking around triumphantly to see if anyone was listening to us. No one was.

"Your names?" the clerk said.

"Peters," I said. "Toby Peters. You can check with either Professor Einstein or Mr. Robeson about us."

"Certainly, sir, I'll do so. Meanwhile, if you'd like to wait in one of the lounges or the lobby till the parties arrive . . ."

Shelly put on his pouty bulldog face. A trickle of sweat rolled over his white collar as he prepared to growl. I pulled him away and told the clerk we would have a drink and be back.

"I'm not accustomed to that kind of treatment," Shelly grumbled as I dragged him away. He kept his eyes fixed on the clerk, who was on to other problems.

"You are accustomed to that kind of treatment and worse, Shell," I said, nodding at a tall woman in black with a small white dog in her arms. "We're both accustomed to it. Let's get a couple of beers and complain while we wait."

We were in the middle of the lobby, people bubbling around us, when I heard my name called from behind. I let go of Shelly, turned, and didn't see anyone I knew. Then the voice called, "Peters, Mr. Toby Peters."

I grabbed the caller by the arm as he moved past me into the lobby. "Hey," I said. "I'm Peters."

The kid, a blond who looked as if he should be a lifeguard, examined me from floor to head and said, "A Mr. Carmichael would like you to join him in room three-two-four-one as soon as possible."

"Okay," I said, "thanks."

The kid held his hand out. He didn't want me to shake it. I fished into my pocket, where I'd thrown my loose change. The pocket was stiff and the fit too snug. I struggled for change doing a little dance while people moved around us. I managed a couple of quarters with lint and handed them to the blond kid.

"Thank you, sir," he said politely, pocketing the change.

"You like this work?"

"Sure," he said, "but this is my last week. I'm taking next week off and then I'm going into the army."

"Good luck," I said.

"I hope the fighting's not over before I can get into it," he said. "I want a crack at the Nazis."

I felt like coming up with an extra few quarters, but they wouldn't change his mind, save his life, or make me feel any better. I wished him good luck again and turned back to find Shelly. He was doing something with his face when I found him standing in front of a mirror near a bank of phones.

"What are you doing with your face, Shell?" I asked.

"Ecmo-plasmics," he explained, looking up. "Variation on dynamic tension. You know, the thing Charles Atlas does on the backs of comic books? I've got the literature back at the hotel. Dentist named White in Mississippi thought it up.

Tightens teeth, strengthens gums, and you can do it anywhere."

"If you don't care about people thinking you've lost your mind," I said. "Let's go. Carmichael, the house dick from the Taft, wants to see us."

Shelly got up, still making faces, and almost bumped into a woman in a frilly white blouse, who backed away from him in fear. We found the elevators and made it up to the thirty-second floor. The room was around to our left. We padded down the carpeted corridor, and I kept trying to find some space in my collar, which was cutting into my neck.

There was no answer at the door of 3241.

"Shelly, cut out the exercises," I said, knocking again. "It looks . . ."

"Grotesque," he said. "It's supposed to. It means I'm doing it right." He looked like a bloated gargoyle.

Something moved behind the door. A shuffle. A sound.

"Tightens everything," Shelly explained. "You see here?" He pointed a stumpy finger at his jaw. "It puts tension on the muscle here. Now if . . ."

The door to 3241 opened, but narrowly, maybe enough to stick a finger or two through, if someone were dumb enough to risk losing a few fingers. I wasn't. I waited. Nothing happened.

". . . you massage with the fingers like this, you can build jaws and teeth that can bite through wood."

I pushed the door with my left hand and reached under my jacket with my right. Carmichael should have thrown the door open. He should have been standing there in front of us, barking out orders and information with a touch of the Old Sod in his voice. Shelly noticed nothing.

"I know what you're going to say," chuckled Shelly at my side as I pushed the door open wide. "You're going to say, 'Why would anyone want to bite through wood?' They *woodn't*." Shelly giggled, poked me to be sure I got his joke. He laughed louder so I knew it was a joke, but I didn't turn. I stood staring at Carmichael across the room. It was a nice room. Much larger than the one I was sharing with Shelly at the Taft. No one seemed to be staying in it, not even Carmichael. He was still wearing his best Easter suit, still looked spiffy, but his face was pale and his mouth was open. He swayed back and forth like an Orthodox Jew in prayer. But he wasn't praying. The trail of blood on the floor showed what he was doing. He was dying. Shelly didn't notice.

"Well?" Shelly said to Carmichael, adjusting his tuxedo jacket. "How do we look?"

I jumped forward to grab Carmichael's arm. Shelly just stood there watching. Carmichael was trying to say something. I eased him onto the bed, careful not to touch the knife, not to let him slide on his stomach. He half-curled like a baby, but he winced and coughed when he tried to raise his knees toward his chest.

He whispered something and I leaned forward to catch the odor of blood and fried onions, and the last few words he was saying: ". . . a good day for a Catholic to die," he whispered, his Irish accent in full bloom.

"Good day," I said, watching his eyes dart around the room, his thoughts wandering, and I wondered where they had been, where they were going.

"Too late for a priest. . . . Get one when I go."

"I'll get one." Behind us Shelly moaned.

"The FBI," Carmichael said, turning his head to me as if he had remembered the very thing he wanted to tell me.

"I'll get the FBI," I said.

There was no strength left for him to speak. He shook his head "no" once, his eyelids fluttered, and he went limp. I stood up.

"He's dead," Shelly said behind me. "One second I'm telling you about, about gum exercises, and the next I'm looking at a dead man with a knife in his back. This has got to stop, Toby. There's a history of heart attack in the Minck family."

"I'll bear that in mind, Shell," I said. "Let's get out of

here." I checked Carmichael's pockets and found the room key.

"Okay, let's go," said Shelly, pulling at my sleeve. "Let's go, get a cab, pack a bag and go home."

I stood, looking down at Carmichael's body and trying to make sense of this. He had learned something, figured out something, noticed something important, something he had to talk to me about. It had to involve the Einstein case, to be something the killer knew he knew, something worth murdering Carmichael for. It beat the hell out of me what it might be.

"We've got to find Einstein before the killer does," I said.

"Before the . . . What if this guy with the knife factory finds us?" Shelly cried. "Huh? You thought about that?"

"Let's go," I said and hurried past him into the hall. I locked the door behind us.

"Okay," said Shelly, hurrying to keep up with me as I ran for the elevator. "Then we tell the police. They ask us questions. All right. It'll be a little uncomfortable, but I'm a dentist. I have professional respect. And they can take over."

I didn't answer him, I didn't even look at him while we waited for the elevator to come. I tried to think, couldn't, gave up and thought about Carmichael. He hadn't looked natty or spiffy on the bed in that room. He'd looked pale, rumpled, and dead.

The elevator came and we stepped in. There were other people already on. Shelly gave a guilty smile to all assembled and slunk back in the corner behind me.

When we hit the lobby I strode to the entrance. Carmichael had probably gotten the room for our meeting from a fellow house detective at the Waldorf. Eventually, that fellow detective would come looking for the room key when the desk clerk told him it hadn't been returned. I didn't want the police now. Police would mean Shelly and me tied up answering questions about Carmichael, gum exercises, and Einstein.

While we were being entertained by the New York police, Einstein and Robeson might be fielding cutlery.

We waited about thirty minutes, Shelly looking as if he desperately needed a bathroom. He threatened to leave, to call the police on his own, to denounce me to the government, to bar me from conversation with him for a decade, to tell Mildred all of my known indiscretions and the comments I had made about her. None of it worked. I looked at Shelly, whose tux, soggy and loose, had begun to give up the battle for respectability. Maybe it was a wise old tux that realized it was no match for Minck. A car pulled up and this time, following a man in a tuxedo that fit him better than ours fits us, Einstein stepped out and looked around. His tux looked even worse than ours. The knees were baggy, the collar too large, the jacket sleeves too long. His hair was pushed back but not brushed. With a battered violin case under his right arm, he looked around and his large nose twitched as if he smelled something unpleasant.

Einstein was quickly surrounded by people leading, talking, smiling as he entered the hotel. I moved forward and was intercepted by the first guy who had come out of the car. "No, no," said Einstein, putting a hand on the guy's arm. "I know Mr. Peters."

"We've got to talk," I said.

Einstein looked at me and at Shelly, who looked like a great horned owl. "Who . . ." Einstein began, nodding at Shelly.

"Dr. Minck," I explained. "A friend and colleague."

"He appears to be undergoing some kind of seizure," said Einstein, examining Shelly with curiosity.

"He'll be fine," I said. "Let's talk."

Two of Einstein's escorts tried to talk him out of the detour, but the scientist insisted, telling the oldest of the men, "I prefer not to create a lobby show."

A non-tuxed man with glasses, who looked like a hotel manager, turned out to be one and ushered us to an office to the right of the desk. He opened the door and asked us if we'd like anything. Shelly was about to come up with a room-service order but I declined for all three of us and stepped into the room. Einstein's escort waited outside. I pushed the door of the small room shut. Desk, a couple of chairs, no window, a painting on the wall of people in a park near a lagoon. The people were sprawled around in shirtsleeves having lunch.

Einstein looked at the painting. "Renoir, I think," he said, putting his violin down. "It would be nice to have a cigar."

Instead of a cigar, Einstein got a story. I told him everything. The time passed. A knock came at the door. One of the white-haired escorts said we should get upstairs. Einstein waved him away after cadging a cigar. I went on with my tale, leaving out nothing as Einstein got behind the desk, smoked slowly, patted his violin case, and listened. He asked a few questions when I mentioned what Parker and Craig of the FBI had said about Walker. He asked a few more when I got to Carmichael, and then he sat, quietly puffing. Shelly started to speak. Einstein's hand went up to silence him. Shelly shut up. I looked at the picnickers in the painting, the wheezing Shelly, and the calm Einstein. Einstein fished a pad of paper out of his jacket pocket and took some notes, scratched them out, scribbled some others, and looked up at us.

"I believe I know who killed these two men, why they killed them, and when they plan to kill me and perhaps Mr. Paul Robeson," the scientist said. "Of course, we will need evidence to convince others but that evidence might be . . ."

This time the door opened and it wasn't an escort, but Paul Robeson. He didn't look crumpled or uncomfortable in his tuxedo, but like a man who wore the damn thing every day and could probably play tennis in one. "Dr. Einstein," he said, leaving the door open. "Good to see you again."

Einstein smiled, stood up, moved the cigar to the side, and

shook hands with the dark man before him. "You know Mr. Peters and his friend, I understand?"

"Yes," said Robeson, glancing at us.

"It seems there is a slight problem in our concert plans," Einstein said, looking at the three men standing behind Robeson. "I'd rather it be kept in confidence, however."

Robeson said something to Einstein in a language I didn't understand.

"I speak no Russian," said Einstein with a smile.

Robeson tried another language.

"And no Hebrew," Einstein said with a smile.

Robeson tried something that sounded like French. Einstein answered and the rest of the room waited. When they were finished, Robeson turned to the rest of us and said, "We need a safe room somewhere in the hotel for an hour before the concert."

The hotel manager looked at the escorts, didn't hesitate, and said, "Certainly, please follow me."

There was no point in trying to hide as we crossed the lobby, not this group. I knew who I was looking for now and that gave me some kind of edge, but I wasn't comfortable with it. Einstein whispered something to Robeson, who nodded as the two walked ahead of us. I left my jacket loose and followed. Shelly mumbled and complained at my side. At the elevator Robeson suggested to the confused escorts that they make arrangements for the concert, that he and Einstein would be doing some rehearsal, and that they would be done in time for the festivities. We left them in the lobby and the five of us got on the elevator.

We stopped on the twenty-eighth floor and I checked the corridor. The hotel manager led the way to a room, opened the door with a smile, asked if there was anything we wanted, and departed. The room turned out to be a suite with a large room in the middle and a couple of bedrooms to the side. Einstein put down his violin case and Robeson looked at me. It was time for me to act.

"You'll be okay here," I said. "Shelly and I will take care of things and come back when it's safe."

Robeson's smile had no humor in it. "Maybe I can be some help," he said, as Einstein removed his violin from the case and stood tuning it. "My grandfather was a resourceful man who worked the underground railroad during the Civil War, helped smuggle slaves into free territory. My mother was part Indian. Aside from football and an occasional bigot, I've done little to test the possibility of my inherited resourcefulness."

Shelly had drifted over to Einstein and was saying something to him while Robeson spoke to me. I thanked Robeson, told him that I thought things were under control and that I'd get back to him if it seemed we needed help. "Shelly and I have enough experience to see us through," I explained.

Robeson looked at me and at Shelly. He was a good enough actor to hide his reaction but he wanted a little of his skepticism to show. After all, I was dealing with his and Einstein's life.

"Trust me," I said.

"I've heard that from too many people who've betrayed me," he said with a sad smile.

"White people."

"Mostly," he agreed, "but not all. And all the white ones didn't betray me either. I'll give you some cautious trust."

"I'll take it," I said, and walked over to rescue Einstein from Shelly the Minck.

". . . be just your name," Shelly was saying earnestly. "'Rainbow teeth are the way of the future,' signed Albert Einstein. It would be worth a hundred thousand in publicity."

Einstein raised one eyebrow at Shelly, adjusted a string on his violin, and looked at me. I grabbed Shelly's arm. "A minute more, Toby," he whispered over his shoulder. "The professor and I are working out a professional arrangement here, between two men of science. You wouldn't understand."

"I understand, Shell. Let's go." He was dragged away, protesting in a whisper Robeson and Einstein would have heard even if they hadn't been listening.

"I've almost got him convinced," Shelly said. "Just a few more minutes, half a minute."

"You weren't convincing him, Shell."

"Good luck," said Robeson.

"Throw the bolt behind us," I answered.

"I wasn't con . . ." began Shelly. "Now you're a scientist." We were out in the hall by now, the door closed behind us. I paused till I heard the lock click, then hurried down the hall.

After cursing me down in the elevator to the lobby, Shelly went into a silent sulk as he followed me through crowds and clusters. It took me about five minutes to find the kid who looked like a lifeguard. I called him over, tipped him a buck, and gave him a name to call and a message to go along with that name.

"Stay with it," I said. "It might be a few minutes, might be an hour. If nothing happens the first fifteen minutes, give it a rest and try again."

"What'd you tell him?" Shelly asked, following me back to the elevators. "I've got a right to know."

"The same message Carmichael had for me," I said. "Let's go."

We went up to the thirty-second floor. I used the key and went in. Nothing much had changed, only the blood was a little drier, Carmichael a little paler.

"Has to be in here," Shelly moaned, looking at the corpse.

"Has to be," I agreed, sitting on the edge of the bed.

"And I have to be here?" he said, pointing at himself in case I might not know who he was identifying as potential victim.

"No," I said, smiling, "you can go."

"I'm opening the window," he answered. "It's starting to smell like. . . . I'm opening the window. Then I'm getting out. I'm your friend, Toby, you know that. But I think I'll just go back down and talk to Einstein and . . ."

He had the window open when a knock came at the door.

"Fast," I said.

Shelly looked around in anguish for another exit. There wasn't one. "No, no, no," he mumbled.

"Come in," I said.

Shelly moved behind me as far from the door as he could, which brought him next to the open window. I had my .38 out now, aiming at the opening door. Standing in the doorway with another person behind him, the killer looked at us and at Carmichael, without trying to fake shock or surprise. "You want to see me?"

"I want to nail you," I said behind my most lopsided grin, watching for a sudden move, a long knife.

"Do we have to stand in the doorway?" the killer said. "We might upset some of the guests."

"Just stand there," I said. "And answer a question or two."

"Ask."

"Toby," Shelly groaned behind me. "I need the toilet."

"Why did you kill Povey?"

"He would have ruined the concert, sent Einstein for cover. Even if he got Robeson and Einstein, it would have been the wrong time, the wrong place. Today, with the press here, that's the time. That's what we're getting paid for. This has to be big. It's got to strike terror into the Allies, make every American feel that they aren't safe. It's something new. Povey got a little too angry with you, made it too personal. And he was a professional."

"Carmichael?" I asked, holding my gun level and aimed at the killer's chest.

"Made a call and discovered . . ." the killer began.

"That you're not FBI agents," I concluded, as Shelly moaned massively behind me.

16

"You know what had me fooled?" I asked, wishing I could see more of Parker, who was partly covered by Craig.

"Everything," said Craig. "We told you we were FBI. You believed it."

"Enough already," Parker said behind him. "We got a job. We're not getting paid to explain mysteries."

"How's it going to hurt us?" Craig said, without turning his head to look down at his partner.

"Someone comes by in the hall and sees this, that's how it's going to hurt us," said Parker. Parker adjusted his toupé in case someone did wander by.

"I called the FBI," I said. "I left a message. You got the message."

Craig was smiling, the phony smile of people with false teeth they're afraid will come out. "There are two agents named Craig and Parker," he explained, "both on assignment in South America. The FBI always answers the same way when their agents are on assignment. They won't tell the caller where they are and just take messages. What could it hurt for you to call and leave a message? They won't be back to get it for months. And when they did it wouldn't make any sense to them. We didn't know you called. You just figured we knew when you saw us, and we went along with you. Carmichael, however, did a little checking. And we went back to check on Carmichael, who acted a little too nervous, a little too Irish."

"Come on," Parker nagged behind him.

"You begrudge me a few moments of simple exposition?" Craig asked.

"Let the man expose if he wants to, for God's sake," whined Shelly behind me, clutching my sleeve.

"We followed Carmichael here," said Craig.

"You weren't as efficient this time," I said. "He was still alive when we got to the room. He tried to tell us to call the FBI to check on you, but he couldn't get it together."

"But you figured it out," said Craig with admiration. "I didn't think you had it in you, Peters."

"I don't," I said. "It took an Einstein."

"No jokes, Toby, please, no jokes. Just shoot them or something and let's get out of here."

"Two more questions," I said, "okay?"

"Shoot," said Craig with a smile. "I'm not talking literally, of course."

It wasn't the first time I'd heard that joke. The last time it had been me saying "shoot." That was in Chicago and I still had the little white scar where the bullet went in.

"Zeltz," I said.

"There is no Zeltz," said Craig. "That was my arithmetic teacher's name in grade school."

"Walker?" I asked.

"He doesn't know from anything," Craig said. "We threw his name to you to keep you running in circles."

"That'll do it, then," I said with a sigh. "We'll work out the details with the real FBI."

"Enough," said Parker in exasperation.

"Enough," agreed Craig, who suddenly stepped to one side like a gangly bird that couldn't fly. What did fly was a bullet from the gun in Parker's hand. Shelly yelped and let go of my arm. I fired as Parker's bullet tore into my arm. I dropped my

.38 as Craig or whoever the hell he was backed out of the doorway to give his partner more room. The second shot from Parker hit the wall and jarred his hairpiece. Shelly screamed behind me as if he were a block away but I didn't have time to figure it out. I lunged forward—gun in one hand, pain in the other—and threw myself against the partly closed door. Craig tumbled backward over his partner. I slammed the door shut and threw the bolt as a fourth bullet came through the door over my head.

I had the vague idea that I should look for my gun, but my eyes took in something else as I stood there. There was Carmichael on the bed, there was my .38 on the floor, but where the hell was Shelly?

Behind me, Craig and Parker hurled themselves at the door. Over the sill of the open window, a bald head rose and then Shelly's red face. His glasses were clinging, ready to fall from his right ear. I dived for the open window and grabbed at his sleeve. His feet scrambled for a foothold that wasn't there, which made it even harder to hold him, but he wasn't in the mood to listen to reason and I wasn't in the mood to speak it. Then Shelly became dead weight and sagged, almost pulling me over the sill.

"Help," he whispered, so quietly that I could only read his lips and then he started to sink out of sight below the level of the window ledge like a punctured beach ball in a calm pool. The door splintered behind me. It had done its damnedest. So had we all. I should have thought of something, but all I could find in my memory as I clung to Shelly's dead weight by his sweating wrists was that once as a kid I had bitten off a fingernail. The fingernail had gotten stuck in my gum behind a tooth. I couldn't get it out. I had tugged, brushed, worked at it with the stub of dirty fingernail remaining. I think I had even cried, but finally I had to tell my father and face the blast of laughter from my brother Phil. My father, after cleaning his hands, had located the lodged fingernail with the use of a small mirror and a flashlight. It had come out with a tweezer and with it a moment of relief I have never forgotten. Where was my dad now? Where was that tweezer? All I could conjure was my brother's laughter as the door gave up and shot open.

I couldn't hold Shelly. I couldn't hold the blood that was pulsing from the bullet hole in my arm and trickling through my fingers, staining my hand and Shelly's a deep red. I couldn't even look back to face Parker and Craig, who would be standing there like ancient imitations of George Raft, guns drawn and ready to shoot me once, again, and for the final time.

"I don't want to fall," Shelly screamed, feeling my grip slip.

Now I had a plan. I'd let go of Shelly, dive for my gun, hope I got it before I died, and start shooting in the general direction of the door. I probably wouldn't make it, but no one was there with a better plan. The problem was that I couldn't bring myself to let go of Sheldon Minck, in spite of the act of charity I would be performing for his future patients. I clung, sweated, bled, and waited.

Behind me people grunted, feet shuffled. There was a shot and a groan, but it wasn't me groaning and I was fairly sure I hadn't taken another bullet.

"Sorry, Shell," I whispered, feeling the stinging sweat in my eyes and knowing I was about to let go.

"Pull, pull, pull!" Shelly screeched the words he usually reserved for the moment of joyous extraction of the molar, but I had no pull left.

A hand shot past me and grabbed Shelly's sleeve. Then an arm reached out the window, as I let go and slumped on the floor, looking up at the ceiling and smiling at a curl of white paint that looked exactly like Africa. I was pleased, honored to think that I was probably the first to notice this phenomenon, that I had to remember to call Robert Ripley and tell him, so he could get someone to do a picture for his column.

Shelly came up over the windowsill, a limp penguin, eyes dazed and in need of the glasses that dangled by one ear down

to his right shoulder. Whoever had pulled him in was big and
dark-suited. The face was blurry and unfamiliar. From my
position on the floor I looked back over my head and saw an
upside-down Parker, hands against the wall, hairpiece askew.
Even upside down he looked suddenly very old. I didn't feel
sorry for him.

"Who?" I croaked, feeling myself lose consciousness.

"Federal Bureau of Investigation," came a voice from
somewhere.

"No, no, they're not," I said, trying to sit up.

"We know," came the voice. "*We're* the FBI."

I think I said something about the rented tuxedos before I
passed out, maybe not. Koko was waiting for me impatiently
at the top of a snow-covered hill, sitting on a sled, a Flexible
Flyer just like the one my brother Phil and I had when we
were kids—or was it like the one I had given Phil's sons Nate
and Dave? Koko waved to me to hurry. I hurried and got on
behind him. I clung to his billowing costume, felt the fuzzy
buttons on his chest, smelled the makeup, and was about to
say something when he pushed off and we went over the rim
and into a white void of snow. There was no difference between hill and horizon. We shot forward. I wasn't sure
whether it was down or up, but it was forward. Koko laughed,
a high hysterical scream of a laugh, and I joined him. What
the hell? I joined him, not worrying about the snow that was
ruining the rented tux, not worrying about a damn thing.

Koko's laughter was loud, too loud. It woke me up. I
opened my eyes and searched for the outline of Africa in the
ceiling of the room at the Waldorf, but this ceiling was a different shade of white and the patterns weren't there. Koko
was still laughing. I looked around for him. He wasn't there.

"Where's Koko?" I asked.

"I don't know," said Shelly, following my eyes as I
searched the hospital room. There was no cartoon clown, but
someone was standing behind Shelly.

"Who's laughing?" I asked, trying to sit up and point at the man. "Him?"

"Jeanette MacDonald," said Shelly. "On the radio. Charlie McCarthy just made a Nelson Eddy joke. He said . . ."

"Forget it." The tux was gone. He was wearing his brown suit. "Is this a hospital?"

Shelly looked around as if he were seriously considering the question, and then confirmed that it was.

"And it's still Sunday. That's Charlie McCarthy, it's Sunday."

"It's Sunday," he agreed.

"Unoriginal or not, I have to ask it—what the hell happened?"

The guy behind Shelly stepped forward past the dentist. There was something familiar about him. I tried to place him from high school, Warner Brothers, the ring announcer at the Garden in Los Angeles, and then I remembered that he was the guy who had pulled Shelly through the window. He was about six-something, dark, built like Lou Gehrig, some age over thirty-five, and wearing a haircut that looked as if it had just come out of the barber's chair.

"You're the FBI," I said.

"Right," he answered. "Special Agent Kaiser." He pulled out his wallet and showed me a card with his picture on it.

"Suchart is dead," he said. "We've got Lambert in custody."

"Who?"

"Craig and Parker," Shelly explained. "Spade and Archer. They were German spies."

"No, sir," Kaiser explained, "they were hired by a Nazi organization. They're Americans. We hoped that they would lead us to the people who hired them and we could break the Fifth Column."

"But . . . ? I put in, trying to focus as I listened to him talk and Jeanette sing "The Bell Song."

"But," Kaiser said, looking down at me with his hands folded in front of him, "you came along. We were watching those two and Povey, had been for some time. We were well aware of their surveillance of Professor Einstein."

"You were . . ." I started and then changed direction. "You knew about Povey? Were you guys there when . . ."

". . . Povey was killed," Kaiser said. "And when the attempt was made on your life at the lake. We've been on the job all the time."

"You guys could have gotten me killed," I said, trying to sit up despite the pain in my tightly bandaged arm. "You could have gotten Einstein killed. You could have gotten Paul Robeson killed."

"Toby," Shelly said, "they saved our lives."

"We were on top of the situation, Mr. Peters," Kaiser said confidently.

"The hell you were," I said, trying to look dignified on one elbow wearing a hospital gown.

"We're at war," Kaiser said patiently, as if I were a stupid six-year-old. "it was vital that we do whatever was necessary to find and destroy the Nazi cycle. And besides, we were not at all certain whether Professor Einstein and Mr. Robeson were not somehow involved or if this might be a subversive situation involving radical causes, even the communists. Both Einstein and Robeson have been under surveillance for some time."

"Do you hear that?" I asked Shelly, who was listening to Jeanette's final trill. "That's the same sewage Craig and . . . the other two handed me."

"I prefer Lily Pons," he said.

"I'm not talking about that," I wailed. "I'm talking about this man, this . . . man who thinks Einstein and Robeson are enemy agents, maybe that you and I are enemy agents."

"I'm not an enemy agent," Shelly said suddenly. "I buy defense stamps."

"Take it easy," Kaiser said. "This entire operation was set

up directly by Mr. Hoover. Povey is dead. Suchart is dead. I think Mr. Hoover will consider this a successful operation, even though we didn't achieve our goal."

"I've got another question," I said, reaching over to turn off a Chase and Sanborn commercial on the radio. "Why didn't you just stop me, catch me when I first crossed the street in front of Einstein's house or when Povey took those shots at me?"

Kaiser looked at me and Shelly and then back at me before answering, "We determined that you would be a catalyst, accelerate the situation, and bring it to a more expeditious conclusion. We determined that your presence would not cause Suchart and Lambert to abort their operation."

"Because I was no threat to them?"

"Because they would conclude that while you were a minimal threat they could handle you," Kaiser explained.

"Carmichael?"

"Thousands of men in the armed services are giving their lives for their country," said Kaiser. "We didn't anticipate that."

Shelly reached for the radio. I slapped his hand away. "But they . . . forget it. Forget Carmichael. Forget Albanese," I ranted, turning my back and dragging my aching arm with me.

"They won't be forgotten," Kaiser said. "A personal letter from the director will go to Mr. Carmichael's widow."

"I'm sure that will be a great comfort."

"Toby," Shelly warned.

"Your country appreciates what you've done, Mr. Peters," Kaiser said.

"How do you know?" I asked over my shoulder.

Before he could tell me, the door to the room opened and Einstein stepped in, wearing his baggy tuxedo and a worried smile. He glanced at me, then at Kaiser and Shelly.

"I'll have to be going now," Kaiser said, not acknowledging that he even recognized the scientist. "We would appreciate it if the events that transpired over the past few days were forgotten."

"They're forgotten," said Shelly immediately.

I didn't answer. Kaiser excused himself and eased out of the door. I didn't hear his feet touch the hard linoleum floor.

"How was the concert?" I asked, shifting my body back to face a weary Einstein.

"Passable," he said. "Paul Robeson sang perfectly, I played adequately, and the rich people paid dutifully to see the trained seals. Your arm . . . ?"

". . . will be fine in a few days," I said, not knowing the condition of my arm or the world.

"Doctor says about five days," Shelly added. "Bullet went through, didn't hit bone."

"I am pleased to hear that and grateful for your efforts," Einstein said, stepping close to the bed. "I am sure I owe you more than gratitude, however."

"I'll send you an itemized account," I said. "But I know what you owe me. One dollar payable by check, not cash."

"By check?" Einstein said.

"I don't plan to cash it, just put it on the wall of my office," I explained. "Might impress the clients, even if my office doesn't."

Einstein smiled, shrugged, and pulled a checkbook from his pocket. It was worn at the edges, but the checks were clean and white. Using the table on which the radio sat, he made out the check and handed it to me.

"Thanks," I said.

"No, I thank you for your professional service," said Einstein. "If you'd like to spend a few days recovering at my home . . ."

"No thanks," I said, putting the check back on the table. "Shelly and I have to get back to Los Angeles. Give my best to Walker."

"Goodbye then," he said, and then to Shelly, "Goodbye to you also."

"Goodbye," Shelly said solemnly, adjusting his glasses. "Can I ask you one question before you leave?"

"Certainly," said Einstein, plunging his hands in the pockets of his baggy trousers.

"Did you know that miraculous things can be done with modern science to take care of an overbite, even a small one like yours?"

"Shelly," I warned, and Shelly clenched his teeth and backed off.

When Einstein was gone, I put my head back and closed my eyes. The radio snapped on and Ella Logan sang me a song I'd never heard before. I woke up hours later, with Shelly dozing on the chair near the bed, the radio still on, and my leg aching. I checked Einstein's check and next to it found an envelope with my name on it. I opened it and read the neatly inked message:

> Keep up your bright swords, for the dew will
> rust 'em;
> Good signior, you shall more command with years
> Than with your weapons.

It was signed, "With thanks, The Moor."

The next morning I got up and told Shelly to return the tuxedos, pay whatever the woman at the costume shop demanded for the damage, pack our things, get our plane tickets, and meet me at the airport. He reminded me that I wasn't supposed to leave the hospital for four days. I told him that I wasn't staying in the hospital for one more hour.

A doctor, a nurse, and a woman whose job I never figured out tried to talk me out of leaving, but they were amateurs at the game. It took me about half an hour to dress with one arm in a sling, but I was out the front door of the hospital before lunchtime. The bill was thirty bucks, but it was worth it. I hobbled into a cab and made it to the airport, ignoring the cabbie who cursed the other drivers, the Japanese, his wife, the gas ration board, and someone named Oscar. I gave him a small tip. I had considered stopping to say goodbye to Pauline, to visit Albanese once more in the hospital, maybe even to look up Carmichael's widow, then told myself I was too sick, that I had things waiting for me in L.A., that Shelly was waiting. All of it was true and all of it was a lie. I didn't look out the window when we took off. Airplanes scare me. I closed my eyes and slept, while Shelly read eternal truths from the dental brochures he had taken as trophies.

I remember changing planes once or twice, I don't remember where. I remember landing in Los Angeles but I don't remember taking a cab. I remember my landlady, Mrs. Plaut, tapping gently at my door and entering to say in her precise high voice, "Mr. Peelers, it is the telephone for you. Dr. Minck says that his wife has run off with Peter Lorre. What shall I tell him?"

"Tell him," I said, sitting up and testing my arm, "that I'll be there in half an hour."